I0582305

DEMON HUNTER ACADEMY BOOK 1

CINDY CARROLL

To my husband, always.

<u>Chapter One</u>

Y ou know that voice in the back of your head that whispers words of caution any time things have the possibility of going to shit? Mine pestered me all day and well past the witching hour, reminding me how shit things were and how they could always get worse. As I speed-walked along Yonge Street, the voice screamed at me, blocking out the rumbling sounds of the cars and the high shriek of horns Toronto drivers in rush hour traffic liked to rely on.

Winded, I paused for a moment, checking my watch to make sure I wasn't late. Maybe that was why the nagging feeling in the pit of my stomach refused to subside. If I hurried for the last leg of the journey, I'd make it with a minute to spare. Possibly even two. City transit would have dropped me off closer, making the trip fifteen minutes shorter, but right now every penny I earned went into savings. For that thing that could go to shit once I walked through the door of the Child Protection Society.

Options existed, but my caseworker might not be on my page when it came to me getting the hell out of the foster home that currently "looked after" me. Sometimes it wasn't better to have any roof over your head. Don't get me wrong, the family that took me in, that took all six of us in, did okay. If okay was modeled after how Cinderella's stepmother treated her. At almost eighteen, I should have my own fucking room. My own things. Everything I owned could fit into a small carry-on bag. That included the stuff my foster "sisters" decided belonged to them.

I quickened my pace when I reached Gloucester Street. The August sun beat down on me, but a breeze stirred up the dirt in the road, moving the humid air enough to give me a slight respite.

Pedestrians glanced at me as I pushed through the crowd on the sidewalk. Everyone wanted to get somewhere, but everyone refused to move out of the way to let others through.

Finally, I jogged across the road just after I passed Isabella Street and stopped in front of the concrete building. As a kid going into foster care, the cold gray building intimidated me. Now, I tolerated the visits with my caseworker with a little more enthusiasm. About as much as a night owl could muster before their first cup of coffee in the morning. But hey, it was something.

Cold air slammed into me when I stepped inside before I could cool the whole street as my foster father liked to complain. Areas of exposed skin chilled. My arms, hands, nose, knees. Holes in your jeans being fashionable made the lack of new clothes somewhat bearable. All two pairs of my jeans had the "worn-out" look. My co-worker at the coffee shop boasted about paying over 150 dollars for the last pair she bought. All I had to do for the same fashion statement was wear mine for two years.

A cacophony of sounds—phones ringing, the low hum of conversations, printers spitting out documents—greeted me. I nodded to the receptionist, who covered the mouthpiece of the phone she was holding.

"She's waiting for you." The woman frowned at something the caller said. That was never good.

Calls came in daily reporting children in need of protection, in need of placement. In a few weeks, I was finally not going to be one of them anymore.

Bonnie Reed sat in a tiny cubicle at the back of the open office. An in tray piled with at least a dozen folders, each one for a child in need, dominated the corner of the chipped brown desk. Faux wood was giving it too much credit. She smiled at me as I sat, the twinkle in her eye throwing my stomach into a nervous mess.

Despite her happy demeanor, I had no idea if the conversation would go my way. The smile, the cheerful countenance she always showed the world, helped calm most of the kids who passed through the Society's doors. But for me, it just meant she was good at wearing a mask. I never knew what she was feeling until she revealed whatever news she had to impart, good or bad.

"Right on time." She pulled out a file from her desk and opened it, a piece of paper curling with the force of her gesture. "We have a few things to talk about."

"We do," I agreed. So many things about me getting the hell out of the house on Grace Street. Getting a place of my own.

Her eyes darted to someone behind me, and a look of mischief crossed her face so quickly I almost missed it. With a nod, she pulled something else out of her desk. A large chocolate cupcake with fluffy white frosting. A single candle adorned the center of the cake.

"Happy birthday to you!"

I jerked in my chair, my heart racing. My vision blurred

and I drowned out the chorus of voices behind me singing the catchy song.

"It's not my birthday for two more weeks," I protested.

She lit the candle and pushed the small plate with the confection across the desk toward me. "I know, but I won't be seeing you on your birthday. Vacation, remember? And it's an important milestone."

"Only if I get to take the next step." I sighed and blew out the candle because it was clear she wouldn't discuss business until we got the "fun" over with.

She clapped her hands and handed me a napkin.

My stomach grumbled. I'd eaten breakfast but skipped lunch because I hadn't wanted to go "home" in case the other girls were there. Summer break meant everyone crammed into that small house. And I'd rather not fight with them if there was an alternative. I was the last to arrive there. The girls had already bonded over similar backgrounds and had no room left in their foster kid clique for the new girl. Suited me just fine. I didn't want to get too attached to anyone anyway. As soon as I was able, I was blowing this pop stand and heading to Vegas. It was where my parents died, and I knew I needed to go there.

She nodded at the cupcake. I rolled my eyes and picked it up, ripping the paper off and shoving the sugary treat into my mouth for a huge bite.

"Are you sure you don't want to stay with the Brennan family for another few years? We don't kick you out of care at eighteen."

I swallowed the cake and wished for a cold glass of milk to wash it down. Unless dreams suddenly came true, I'd have to make do with nothing. Like usual. I took a smaller bite of the cake and shook my head.

"I want my own space." Maybe if my parents hadn't been killed when I was five, I would've grown up with real siblings. But I was an only child and I wanted to live in a place where I didn't have to wonder what would befall my stuff when I wasn't there. Even if the place turned out to be so small I'd need to go outside to change my mind.

Bonnie pulled out a few sheets of paper from the file and turned them toward me to read. "These are the forms you need to fill out to get continuing care. The province will provide a stipend monthly, but it won't be enough on its own for you to get a place unless you want a group home."

I cringed at the idea. Jumping from one group home to another, even one with all independent residents, wasn't my idea of moving up. "I'll pass on that idea. I want something I can call my own."

"Where you are now there's so much support. Won't you be lonely all by yourself?"

I finished the cupcake and swallowed what I really wanted to say. "I'll be fine."

She handed me a pen emblazoned with the Child Protection Society logo. I filled out all the spaces with an X, signed and dated it, and returned it to her.

"Once we file this and it's approved, you'll get the monthly allowance. You'll need money from your part-time job to augment that if you want to afford a place. You'll most likely have to explore outside the Greater Toronto Area."

"Not a problem. The GTA hasn't been that great for me. I'd like to try something a little more west of the city."

I didn't bother telling her that eventually I'd be in Vegas. As a caseworker, she was more than decent. She actually cared about all of her charges. All the caseworkers did. The system was frustrating at times, and some people slipped through the cracks. But mostly my dealings with the Society had been good. It wasn't their fault Mr. and

Mrs. Brennan could have won acting awards for their portrayal of a loving, caring family.

"Your foster sisters will miss you." She peered at me with bushy eyebrows drawn together.

"They'll miss my stuff that they won't be able to steal anymore."

"Steal is a harsh word. They might have just been borrowing it."

"Sure. Borrowing it permanently."

She sighed and picked up the forms, tapping them on the desk to make sure all the sides were even. Then she stapled them together and flipped to the last page to add her signature.

Spirits lifted above zero, I took a deep breath before pushing open the door to the coffee shop. In a few weeks, I would have my own place. First and last month's rent collected a minuscule amount of interest in a bank account no one in the world knew about except for me. I wouldn't put it past my "sisters" to forge my signature or somehow wheedle their way into having the debit card reissued with a new PIN.

With high school over, I planned on asking my boss for full-time hours. The more I made, the better the apartment I could afford. And get furniture, like a bed that wasn't so lumpy it felt like I was sleeping on rocks.

Lacey, behind the counter, looked up at the jingle of the bell and I nodded to her. A small smile touched her lips and she gave me a nod back. We were not friends or anything, but I didn't mind her company when we worked together. She knew about the orphan thing, but I couldn't bring myself to take people to the house. My "sisters" were unpredictable, hateful. There was no telling what they would say about me, lies or not.

Soft music filtered through the air. The coffee shop's few patrons chatted in groups at a sprinkling of tables. The clink of spoons stirring coffee soothed my nerves.

Mr. Archer looked up from his desk in the back office and frowned at me.

"I'll be ready in a minute," I said. Might be better to wait until after the bank deposit to ask him for more hours.

In the locker room, I yanked off my jeans. A belt loop ripped off in my hand. With a sigh, I plopped down onto the bench. I had enough thread to fix it before I left for the night. I took off my T-shirt and shoved both garments into my locker, then pulled out the polyester brown uniform, the scrape of the new material itching my skin.

Freshly dressed, I hurried out to take my place behind the counter.

"Mr. Archer wondered where you were." Lacey grinned at me.

"I was on time."

"Exactly on time. He thought something was wrong when you didn't waltz in thirty minutes early."

The time before my shift was the only respite I had most days. If I could hang out for hours before I started work I would, just to be out of the house.

"It won't happen again." I grinned back.

"Do you mind putting on a fresh pot of coffee?"

Lacey liked serving the customers. I preferred to do anything else if at all possible.

"No problem."

Mr. Archer raced by, holding up the bank deposit bag. "I'll be back in fifteen minutes."

The bell jingled when he opened the door. He held it and stepped aside as a customer entered. The man swaggered in, dark eyes surveying the coffee shop. Muscles too thick for a normal man bunched when his gaze turned to me.

Cold seeped down my left arm when the man's eyes bored into me as he strode closer. The spot where I was vaccinated as a child tingled and a mark glowed around that scarred area. A symbol, too precise to be a birthmark, grew brighter the closer the man got.

What the fuck? When the hell did I get an invisible tattoo?

His gaze focused on my arm. His eyes lit up—if dark pupils could light up. Now that he was nearer, I noticed they weren't just dark. The irises were red, and the rest was black. It could be a trick of the light. Or contact lenses. It was a little early for Halloween, but strange things happened all the time in the city.

Another jingle of the bell barely registered in the back of my mind. My entire focus fell on the stranger. Intense fear skittered up my spine with every footfall that closed the distance between us.

Despite my trepidation, I flashed him a smile when he reached the counter, like any good food service worker.

"What can I get for you?" The shrillness of my voice made me cringe.

Thin lips pulled back, revealing abnormally sharp, yellowish teeth. Chills raced down my spine. That symbol on my arm I'd never seen before glowed again. How the hell had it gotten there?

The man zeroed in on the symbol. His smile widened. "I knew you were the one."

The mark brightened, so cold it burned. I sucked in a breath. Behind me, the coffee I'd made froze and the glass pot cracked and broke, sending chunks of coffee tumbling to the floor.

"What the hell is that?" Lacey asked.

Was she talking about the tattoo or the man? Because every instinct in my body told me he wasn't a man.

"The one?" I asked.

He cracked his knuckles in front of his chest, claws growing from his fingers. "The one I was sent to kill."

Chapter Two

S waying slightly, I took a step back as if his words had a physical impact. I couldn't have heard him right. "I'm sorry, what now?"

The guy—maybe he was a demon, but I didn't want to go there yet—tilted his head back. I couldn't tell if he was rolling his eyes. He looked like the type to threaten someone and then roll his eyes when they questioned him, though.

Fear skipped up my spine. A soft glow from my arm pulled the demon's grin even wider, and I squinted at it, still not believing the thing was even there. Behind me, the other coffee pot cracked with a quick freeze.

A soft yelp from Lacey pulled my attention away. "What the hell is going on?"

Taking another look at the guy, Lacey might be spot-on with the hell comment. The demon hissed at her. She jumped back.

The guy reached over the counter and instinctively I threw my hands out as if to push him away. He flew through the air and landed on a table with shattering force. Customers screamed and scrambled to get out of the way.

The glass coffee pot shattered. So much for the customers looking for decaf.

Gasping, I looked at my hands like I'd never seen them before. What the hell was that? All the times I'd been bullied and pulled into fights at school, that had never happened.

"I'm not paying for that!" Lacey said.

The asininity of her comment made me smile. One of those polite smiles that you don't really mean, but what else are you going to do.

The demon shook himself off and pushed up from the table, springing to a standing position like a gymnast. A tall, black-eyed gymnast with razor-sharp claws capable of embedding themselves into wood. Bet that would be a violation during a balance beam routine.

The guy dashed forward, reaching the counter almost before I could blink my eyes. I wanted to keep them closed and wish all of this away. Part of me thought it was a dream. A very screwed-up, scary dream that would disappear as soon as I reopened my eyes and cleared my head. But all the stuff leading up to this told me it was very real. Unless I got hit in the head somehow on my way to work from the Child Protection Society, a demon wanted to kill me. And I didn't even know why.

It's not like I lent him money. As if I had any spare money lying around. If that were the case, I would've fucked off from my foster home ages ago. The absurdity of my train of thought hit me like a double espresso on no sleep. I was entertaining the notion that demons existed. And that they needed money for some reason.

He jumped over the counter, not careful where his legs landed. All the cups and the glass domes protecting sugary treats hurtled to the floor. The domes crashed, glass scattering all over the place.

Lacey screamed.

The determination in his eyes sent a shiver of fear through my limbs. How could someone who had just met me hate me so much? Enough to want me dead. If you asked my foster sisters, I bet they'd have a witty response to that. For some reason, they hated me on sight too. Maybe it was because resources were already spread thin and I was another mouth to feed. The demon had no such reason. He looked pretty well-fed already, and I didn't want to be his next meal. Did demons eat people? I shoved the demon angle out of my head. They were a myth. They didn't exist. There had to be another explanation for how the guy looked, how quickly he moved. How strong he was.

I crouched down on all fours and half crawled, half ran around the edge of the counter, to the front of the coffee shop. There was more room to maneuver out there and I wanted to draw him away from Lacey. There was no reason her day had to end up as shitty as mine.

The constant jingle of the bell above the door heralded the mass exodus of the customers. Even the curious opted for safety and left the coffee shop. Lacey stayed behind the counter, eyeing the demon guy as he stood there. His ears perked up and his head turned in my direction when I bumped into an overturned table. The wooden leg hit me in the shoulder and I grunted as pain exploded through me. No time to worry about the massive bruise I'd have later. I needed to get away from the crazed beast.

One customer remained. He sat near the entrance, away from most of the action. He regarded me with a smug grin and a tilt of the head, nodding to something behind me. I spun around to see my attacker jump over the counter again. What he missed the first time went flying off the counter. More takeaway cups, mugs, and another tray of goodies spread across the floor.

"Help me!" I yelled at the customer.

Before I could plead with the man, the demon thing charged. He swiped out a huge hand, the razor-sharp claws barely missing my face as I jumped back. My leg hit the overturned table and I almost went down. I righted myself and managed to block the next blow with my left arm. The impact caused my legs to buckle. I had clearly underestimated his strength.

I punched back. His eyes widening, the guy's arm didn't come up in time to block me. I landed a right hook straight into his jaw. For all the damage I did, it might as well have been a light flick. I raised my arm again, a snake of fear slithering down my back. My tattoo glowed. My punch landed, heavier this time. He stumbled backward. I let out a whoop of relief, then ran around to the other side of the table.

The dude's arms were longer than I thought. He reached out and grabbed me, lifting me before throwing me into some tables and chairs that had managed, up until that point, to remain in their proper position.

Wood splintered as the table broke my fall. With the wind knocked out of me, I struggled to drag in a few breaths. Aches in my hips, arms, and legs protested as I pushed myself up from the floor.

Laser-focused, the guy bored down into me again, not missing a beat. There were no real weapons in the place, not out front anyway, where the customers could get them and cause damage. I wouldn't be able to make it past him to get to the kitchen. At least there I would find big knives.

I kicked the leg off one of the tables and brandished it like a bat. Every time the guy got closer, I swung it. He jumped back, his grin revealing those yellow teeth that looked too pointed to be natural. A gleam in his eyes brought on a tornado of acid swirling in my stomach.

With lightning speed, he yanked the makeshift bat away and tossed it aside. The place was a shambles.

Was that determination flashing in those black orbs?

"I guess talking about it is out of the question?" I asked, hoping to catch him off guard.

He smiled this time. "No need to talk."

He lashed out with his hand, the claws protruding from his fingers lengthening like shadows across the pavement. I jumped back, my gaze traveling over the shop. A few spoons littered the ground. A stray fork peeked out from under an overturned table. Nothing sharp enough to do any damage.

That customer still sat at the front, watching the fight, a neutral expression on his face. What the hell happened in his everyday life that a teenage girl fighting a demon didn't even raise an eyebrow?

"But talking can help work through these anger issues you seem to have," I said.

The guy growled. It was a deep, low rumbling sound that raised goose bumps on my arms.

"I'm finished playing. It's been fun and the attempts to stop me have been cute, but I'm done now."

He lunged forward and I raised my hands to block his attack. He was so close, the smell of sulfur teased my nose. I gagged, and that made him angrier. His lips curled, nostrils flaring. I dove behind a table. A chair lay on its side. I picked it up and used it as a shield. Anything to keep the demon at arm's length.

I lost track of Lacey. I hoped she left through the back door or was at least hiding somewhere. Just because the demon said he'd come for me didn't mean he'd stop once he accomplished his goal. Maybe he would go on a spree. The customers had been smart to flee in terror.

Except for the one who still sat there now looking half amused, half disappointed.

Disappointed that he wasn't witnessing a blood bath yet?

Demon guy flipped the table out of his way. Exposed, I stared up at him. Movement from the front door caught my attention. The customer stood and tossed me a small dagger.

"What the fuck am I supposed to do with this?" It would be like sticking an elephant with a pin.

"Stab him." The customer had the nerve to sigh heavily. "In the heart. He'll be more pissed if you miss and it doesn't kill him."

"Great, no pressure."

The dagger was so short, I'd have to let the demon get way too close for my comfort. But I didn't see any other choice. It was the only pointy object within reach unless the customer could whittle one of the table legs into a stake.

The demon lunged again. I think I actually saw smoke coming out of his ears. Or maybe that was my imagination because the situation was too impossible for me to believe. I wanted to pinch myself, but I was afraid this wasn't a dream.

I rolled away, dagger up. He came forward, blind fury guiding him. His mouth frothed, reminding me of a rabid animal going after its prey.

"The prestige I get for killing you will not go to waste."

He pounced.

I dodged, careful not to poke myself with the tiny dagger. I guess it wasn't tiny, but it wasn't big enough to do much damage to the fiend.

"Why? I'm just me. Nothing special. Ask anyone."

What kind of drugs was he on? Though I kept calling him a demon, I knew they didn't exist. There had to be all kinds of other explanations. Maybe I was the one who had been drugged. Something somehow must have gotten into a drink. Did I brush against anything on my way here? I racked my brain for anything that would prove this was all a hallucination. Though that wasn't ideal, it was better than some demon wanting me dead for no reason. Well, I was sure he had a reason, just not a good enough one for me.

Instinct kicked in when he lunged at me again. I leaned to the side so he barreled past me, then lifted a foot to kick him in the face. His body propelled backward, but the kick didn't slow him down. He landed in a heap, only to get up and barrel toward me again. It didn't look like he was even getting tired.

I dragged in another breath. Too bad there wasn't a time-out or something so I could get a second wind.

My hand clutched the handle of the silver dagger tighter as I held the small weapon in front of me when the demon charged forward. I swiped through the air, nicking his arm. A line of red bloomed on his skin. He hissed, black eyes staring into my soul. I shivered under the intense glare.

"I told you not to do that," the customer said.

"Instead of critiquing my technique, how about some help."

I ran around the strewn tables, tossing chairs at the demon as I went until I was behind the counter again. I rummaged through the drawers and along the back counter for a weapon. Anything bigger than the dagger but just as pointy.

"Sorry, not my fight. He's after you."

Crashing behind me pulled my attention away from my frantic search. The demon threw more tables out of the way, lifting them as if they weighed no more than a feather.

Lacey peered around the corner from the back room that was for employees only. Eyes wide, she followed his progress and ducked into the room, slamming the door when he reached the counter.

From out of nowhere, the customer stood at my side. Attention focused on my attacker, I hadn't seen the man's approach. He held up a hand and mumbled something in a foreign language.

The demon froze. Yellow teeth bared, he screamed as if in pain, doubled over. Intense hatred filled his eyes, and he put one large foot in front of the other against an invisible wall that was repelling him. Finally, in a burst of light and a cloud of smoke, the demon vanished.

I sagged against the counter and sucked in breaths of air. "Good riddance."

The bell above the door jingled. My muscles tensed until I heard the gasp.

"What the hell happened?"

A muscle in Mr. Arthur's jaw twitched. Red splotches dotted his face as he took in the destruction. Nothing I said would make any of it better, but I had to try. I saw my dreams puffing out like the smoke that took the demon away if I couldn't get my boss to calm down.

"I'm so sorry. We had a bit of an incident, but I'll clean all this up."

He stalked toward me, stiff-limbed, head swiveling to take in the mess. A cartoon of someone with steam coming out of their ears and fire burning from their head flashed through my mind.

"Don't bother cleaning it up. You're fired."

With ten people in the small craftsman house, the place was never quiet. Most times it was party-level noise from the five other foster kids and Debra and Geoff's two girls. The two biological kids could do no wrong in their parents' eyes. We, on the other hand, could do no right most of the time.

Tonight was no different. I trudged up the stairs, music blaring from Ramona's room matching my footfalls. The parents argued in the kitchen over who had to take Megan to soccer practice this week. It was a good thing I never wanted to be a joiner. The six of us foster kids got bare necessities only. Extra stuff, forget about it. Unless we wanted to pay for it ourselves.

Shuffling in the room I shared with the other girls spurred me up the stairs faster. The back of my neck tingled. I threw open the door. Caught with her hand under my mattress on the top bunk, Ramona glared at me. Pink rose up her neck and settled on her cheeks. How many times had she done this while I was at work?

"What are you doing?" I rushed over and shoved her out of the way.

"I was looking for something." Chin held high, she glared at me. "This is my house."

There it was. The reminder that me and the rest of the foster girls were as welcome as unwanted guests who had overstayed.

"You won't find it there." I yanked up the mattress to make sure everything I'd stashed was still there. I'd need to find a different hiding place for anything important. Not that it would help. The sisters were tenacious when it came to tossing the place to find things that didn't belong to them.

I turned to Evie, who sat on her bunk filing her nails. "Why didn't you stop her?"

Evie shrugged. "Not my stuff. Don't care."

Brooklyn jumped down from her bunk. "Why are you home so early?"

Evie looked up. "Did you do something different to your face?"

All five foster sisters laughed, Ramona joining in.

Ramona moved closer, and with a finger on my chin, moved my head from side to side. "That's not a good look for you. I'm sure someone here could teach you how to properly apply makeup."

Laughter erupted again, the foster sisters cackling as they held their sides.

I pinned each one of them with a stare. Claire shoved something behind her back when my gaze reached her. Anger boiled up in my veins. I pulled her arm from behind her. She clutched a pack of my favorite cookies, the ones I splurged on a week ago when my boss gave me a raise. They'd have to last now that I didn't have a job.

"Found it!" Ramona said.

I grabbed my cookies and spun around to see what the first princess of the house held. My quilt, the patchwork one my mother made for me, the only thing I had that reminded me of her, was tucked under the girl's arm.

"That's mine." Heat rushed to my cheeks.

I didn't have much, so it mattered what they did to my things. When you don't feel welcome, you don't put down a lot of roots. But that quilt had been with me since I was five. I still remembered the Christmas my mother gave it to me. The few memories I had of her lived in that quilt.

I grabbed a corner, but Ramona's grip tightened and she pulled back. I yanked, jerking her forward. Eyes bulging, she stood with her legs wide and tugged again.

Grinding my teeth, my pulse raced. The sudden glow of my tattoo distracted me for a second and surprise flashed across Ramona's face. From behind me, Evie snorted with laughter.

"What the fuck is that?" Megan stepped away from the scene like I carried the plague.

"Freak," Brooklyn chimed in.

I clenched my jaw, gripped the quilt tighter, and simultaneously pulled the blanket and glared at Ramona.

She flew backward, stopping just before hitting the bunk beds set against the wall.

A gasp from the doorway made my stomach sink.

I turned, wishing, not for the first time that day, for the floor to open up and swallow me. Better that than face the foster mother.

Her usual pale complexion was pink. Nostrils flared, eyes wide, the scene would be comical if she hadn't witnessed her oldest daughter almost hit her head against the bed.

"What is going on here?" Hands on hips, legs spread apart, she eyed each of the girls, who all shook their heads. All except Ramona.

She stomped forward, an exaggerated pout protruding her bottom lip. "All I wanted to do was borrow Alex's quilt."

"You mean steal." The words flew out of my mouth before I could stop them.

The foster sisters chuckled.

Debra Brennan scowled at me. "You best behave, Alexandra. I don't need to keep you here once you're eighteen." A perfectly painted pink nail jabbed the air to punctuate each sentence.

If I had a nickel for every time she threatened to throw

me out, I'd have enough to rent a place for a year. And pay the utilities.

"I don't want your smelly quilt anyway." Like a five-year-old who couldn't get her way, Ramona threw the quilt on the ground and stalked out of the room.

Debra glared at me again before turning on her heel in a huff. Her footsteps echoed down the hall. I waited until I heard the creak of the stairs before rushing to the closet to get my small suitcase.

I shoved everything I owned in the small case and my oversized backpack. The quilt, my other pair of jeans, five tops, bras, underwear, nightgowns, socks. The few toiletries I had followed the clothes. On top of it all, I threw in my cookies.

Backpack slung over my shoulder, I stormed out of the room, dragging the suitcase along behind me. My foster sisters stood at the top of the stairs, watching me struggle with the case. None offered to help. No surprise there. Over the three years I'd been there, not one gesture of help popped into my head. With me gone, the room would feel a little bigger. With three sets of bunk beds squeezed into a room meant for two beds at most, they'd be able to use my top bunk for storage. Or just spreading out.

"You have nowhere to go," Claire reminded me when I hit the bottom stair.

Nowhere was better than here. For a few days, there was always the shelter until I figured things out.

On the front porch, I waited until I heard the soft click of the door behind me before digging into my suitcase for my cookies. The deadbolt slid into place. They'd probably change the locks before I got back. If I came back.

In reality, I would let everyone cool off, swallow what little pride I had left, and beg to be let back into the house. I shuddered at the thought. But what were my alternatives?

I took a bite of the cookie and glanced up. The sun had sunk lower in the sky, plunging my surroundings into shadows. Across the street, the customer from the coffee shop smiled at me and gave a quick wave. After looking both ways, he darted over to my side.

"Need a hand?" He took my suitcase and effortlessly carried it down the few steps.

"Now you offer to help." I stopped when I hit the sidewalk. "Wait, did you follow me?"

"Of course. It's not the only way to find out where you live, but it is the easiest."

I glanced over my shoulder at the closed door. They had even turned out the porch light. I didn't get a weird vibe from the guy, though. Nothing like the chill I had when the demon walked into the coffee shop. If this guy was trying to kill me, he could have left me to the black-eyed demon.

"What do you want?"

"How about a meal? You look hungry." He nodded at the cookie. "I'm Damien."

"I'm guessing you already know my name."

He smiled and tilted his head down.

I shoved the rest of the cookie into my mouth. Every lecture on talking to strangers I ever heard ran through my mind. I should have screamed no. But my stomach grumbled. As much as I loved sugar and ginger in a sweet confection of chewy cookie, it wasn't enough. I needed real food.

I eyed him up and down. Crisp, clean dress shirt. Black dress pants. Black shoes that still shone in places dirt hadn't reached yet today. Firm jaw, inquisitive eyes. Graying around the temples with a full head of dark hair. Put some glasses on him and he looked like a teacher. A somewhat fitter one than any at my high school, but a teacher nonetheless.

"A meal? That's all you want?"

He gave a sheepish grin and alarm bells rang in my head.

"There are things I need to talk to you about. Things you need to know."

"Like why that freak was trying to kill me?"

He pulled my suitcase behind him, walking off in the direction of College. I jogged to catch up.

"Among other things. Any suggestions on where we can eat?"

Anywhere would be better than the soup kitchen. Not that their food was bad, but it was eat what you could get there, and lately all they'd had was vegetable soup and dry chicken breasts. Still better than the leftovers the foster family gave me. They assumed I ate at work, even though I told them I couldn't afford to buy food there. Even though we got a discount at the coffee shop, we still had to buy our meals.

"There's a place that serves simply delicious Italian food not far from here."

"Italian it is."

We walked in silence to the restaurant, a million questions swirling in my mind. I snuck a side glance at the guy, his face looking more familiar the more I watched him.

In front of the restaurant, I stopped him at the door. "I've seen you before."

He yanked the door and stepped aside with a wave of his hand. "Have you?"

"I'm sure of it."

He held up two fingers at the hostess, who nodded and grabbed menus. "Follow me."

As we passed other diners, the pungent aroma of garlic and fresh bread wafted through the room. My stomach protested again.

We slid into the booth the hostess indicated. She dropped the menus on the table and hurried away to attend to the next customers.

"Know what you want yet?" He nodded at the menu.

I didn't need to look at what the place offered to know what I wanted. Even if it wasn't on the menu, I was sure they would have it. What self-respecting Italian restaurant wouldn't?

"Chicken parmigiana. Don't change the subject."

"We're at a restaurant. Food is the subject."

I rolled my eyes. "You know what I mean. You've been at the coffee shop before. More than once."

Now that I said it out loud, other instances of him being there flashed through my mind. He usually sat at the table near the front.

"Guilty."

My mouth fell open. "Just like that?"

"We don't have a lot of time to get you up to speed. And you do need to get caught up."

He reached into his back pocket, dug out an envelope, and pushed it across the table. My name, written in perfect calligraphy, adorned the middle of it. What looked like a crest of some sort took up the left corner. Upon closer inspection, the crest resembled the disappearing symbol on my arm.

From out of nowhere, butterflies took flight in my stomach.

"Open it."

Trembling hands reached out to pick up the envelope. I

turned it over a few times before ripping the end off and pulling out the sheet of paper inside. I scanned the letter, confusion filling me.

I shoved it back across the table. "This says I need to report to Hell's Watch Academy by next week. I didn't apply for university. I can't afford to go away to school. Or even stay home for school."

Secretly, I envied my school acquaintances who would be off to higher education when the new school year rolled around. I didn't want to be a coffee shop worker forever. Guess that wish came true. I'd worry about finding another job later. But this ruse was cruel, especially from a stranger. I expected something like this from Ramona and Megan. Even the foster sisters.

"You don't apply. They know who to send the letters to. They know who needs help with magic. And you definitely need help."

"Magic? Magic isn't real."

The waitress came to our table and asked about our orders.

"She wants the chicken parmigiana with penne and rosé sauce. I'll have the lasagna."

He rattled off drink orders too as he handed the menus back to her. Pop for both of us. Based on how often he came into my work, I expected him to order coffee. My mind searched back again. On every visit, he sat at the same table, watching the place, keeping track of the people who entered. Not once did he have a cup of coffee.

"How did you know what I wanted with the chicken?"

"Magic." He regarded me with a serious expression.

I expected him to grin at any moment, but his face remained impassive. "I don't believe in magic. I'm a little surprised a man your age does."

He leaned back in the booth, arms wide, an eyebrow raised. "Even after what you've seen?"

"Smoke and mirrors. Illusionists have been pulling stuff like that disappearing act for decades."

Cold eyes assessed me. "That was the real deal. And that demon wasn't make-believe either." He shoved the letter back at me.

Despite the absurdity of it all, a part of me believed him. Why go through all that to trick a stranger? If it was a scam, it was the worst one ever. The joke would be on him because I had nothing worth stealing that had more than sentimental value.

"I still can't go." I pushed the letter back. "Even if magic is real and I need training, I can't pay for tuition."

The look of satisfaction that spread across his face loosened a sliver of hope in the depths of my mind. "Tuition has been taken care of."

Forget for the moment that I didn't have a magical bone in my body. The thought of sleeping somewhere nicer than the shelter and cooler than the streets on a humid August night in the city tempted me to accept.

"Nothing is free. Especially not some fancy school." I didn't believe that someone who hadn't even met me forked over money for me to attend some school I'd never heard of before.

The thought that this was a scam bubbled to the surface again. What would he gain by conning me? There were far more likely candidates on the street. He had no way of knowing my foster family wouldn't give two shits if they never saw me again.

"True, but this is a sort of scholarship."

"I didn't apply for one of those either."

I hadn't even considered I could go to university. Higher education was always something other people got to do. Even if I got a scholarship, it would only go so far, pay for so much. What about the rest of it? Books, clothes, stationery supplies.

"You didn't have to. Magic, remember?" He glanced at my suitcase. "You'd live on campus during the school year with only one roommate. We can get you settled in tomorrow after a supply run."

"What happens after the school year is finished?" I asked. Sharing a room with only one person seemed like paradise. Anything would be better than living with my foster sisters.

He grinned. "We'll figure something out."

Chapter Three

The familiar sounds of phones ringing, the hum of conversations, and the printer churning out paper accosted me as I walked down the corridor of the Child Protection Society. Not my usual check-in day, Bonnie did a double take when she looked up.

"I wasn't expecting to see you until after my vacation." She gestured to the seat in front of her desk.

I settled into the chair, resting my arms on the thin metal sides, trying to read upside down as she shoved folders from the top of her desk into a drawer.

"I know. But something has come up and I wanted to let you know so you wouldn't worry if you couldn't get a hold of me." Not that I thought she'd worry. She had too many younger charges to fuss over, who were more important.

Her head snapped up. "Why wouldn't I be able to contact you?"

She leaned forward, eyebrows drawn together, hands clasped on top of her desk.

I quickly filled her in on the school, leaving out the

magic part. I barely believed it myself. If she knew, she would throw up alerts all over the place. And then somehow block me from going. It would be with the best intentions, of course, but the more I thought about it, the more I wanted to go. Hiding the fact that I didn't have any magical ability paled in comparison to getting out of my foster home.

A chill settled over me at the thought she would push for more details.

"Are you sure it's legitimate? There are predators out there, eager to take advantage of a pretty girl like you. Can I see the letter?"

Nausea churned in my stomach and I looked away. Funny she should mention predators. The look on the demon's face as it attacked me resurfaced. I shivered. From the corner of my eye, I noticed the mark on my arm glow.

"I left it with the school recruiter. It's legit, I promise. This will be good for me."

Especially after the fight with Ramona. Storming out of the house wasn't something I did on a regular basis. The cost of getting back in was too great. They wouldn't even notice that I wasn't back.

She pursed her lips, tilting her head to look at me with her sometimes omniscient gaze. Finally, she sighed and nodded. "Okay, but you have all of my numbers. There has to be some sort of signal wherever the school is located."

"Niagara Falls," I supplied. Damien had filled me in on the school in depth before dropping me off at Lacey's place to crash last night.

After a barrage of questions from my former co-worker that I didn't have answers to, I'd slept dreaming about the school. I had no idea what it looked like, so the details in my dream were vague. Just me walking along dark corridors with red, yellow, electric green eyes peering at me from the shadows. I hoped that wasn't some sort of omen.

"I could be there in"—she sat up straighter, doing math in her head about distances and time—"under two hours if I pushed it."

Satisfied, at least for the moment, that I wasn't going to be a victim of some underground sex trade, she smiled. "I'll sign off on it."

Relief flooded me, chasing the slight chill away. We said our goodbyes with an awkward hug that was somehow comforting. With a final gentle squeeze, she pulled away and it struck me that she really did care. I mean, I knew she did, but not this much. The worry was real.

"I'll be fine, promise."

Her shoulders sagged and a small smile turned her lips up. "I know you can take care of yourself. You'll do great in school."

If it was just math, science, English, geography, sure. I'd kill in those classes. Nothing like not wanting to go home to help get your grades up by spending all your time in the school library or at your part-time job. But at this school, I was going to have subjects I'd never heard of. How could I fake my way through those?

I pushed through the front door, the heat of late August glomming onto me to chase any cool air away. Damien leaned against a black muscle car in the parking lot. If that was his ride, why the hell did we walk to the restaurant and Lacey's place yesterday?

As I approached, he pulled open the passenger side door. "We have shopping to do. I was just about to go in and give her a magical whammy."

"This is your car?" I folded myself into the seat and settled into the worn leather.

He slipped into the driver's seat. "Yep. Been with me

through everything." He caressed the steering wheel lovingly.

"Where was it yesterday?" My legs still protested the walk. I'm not out of shape, well, not that out of shape, but the forty-five-minute walk to Lacey's after a big meal hadn't been the best idea.

"We needed the exercise. You'll need to stay in top shape for your defense and weapons class."

That sounded a lot like gym. Which I hated. "As long as I don't have to climb some stupid rope."

He pulled the car into traffic and turned onto Church Street. Despite downtown congestion, we made it to Cottage Lane in under five minutes.

Cars squeezed together without so much as a centimeter between them. Along both sides of the road, every available space was occupied. I groaned. More walking from wherever he could find a parking spot.

As we approached a bookstore with two grotesques standing guard on either side of the door, Damien mumbled something under his breath. He flicked his hand at the red car in front of the door. In a blink of an eye, the car was gone and he pulled into the vacated spot.

"What just happened? Where's that car?"

"The driver will find it. If we're out before they get back, I'll return it to its spot."

I shook my head, the notion that it was all an illusion fading from my mind as quickly as a puff of smoke on a windy day. There was no denying that his car sat in the spot where the other car had been. How did you fake something like that? Unless the red car hadn't been there to begin with. Smoke and mirrors.

He shook his head as he held the intricately carved wooden door of Leinster Books. "You still don't believe in magic?"

"If magic existed, wouldn't people know about it?"

The smell of old books, candle wax, and pine soothed my nerves. Tall wooden bookcases lined every wall, the shelves bowed with the weight of the tomes. A warm yellow glow covered every inch of the space, leaving no shadows, just cozy nooks perfect for reading. I could spend a lifetime in the place and not get through all of them.

He walked past all the shelves, not even glancing at the occult or history sections, stopping at the back wall of the place. He looked over his shoulder, drew a symbol on the wall, and knocked three times.

I jumped back with a gasp as the outline of a door glowed bright orange for a split second, then vanished. He grinned, pushing the door inward.

"Welcome to Laigin Books."

I followed him through and watched the door disappear behind me when it closed. A tendril of panic slithered down my back, but if magic got us into the place, it would get us out.

Before me was an even larger bookstore than the one we'd just left. Dozens more bookcases, older, taller, held thousands of more books. Books I would wager couldn't be found in the front of this place.

"But how? The bookstore shares a back door with the sub shop."

"In the human world, sure. There's a veil that separates the ordinary world from the magical world. Sometimes we need to take up the same space. The ordspops, ordinary population, have no idea any of this is here."

The thought that someone in the sub place could be walking right through me didn't sit well. He grabbed my arm and pulled me in the direction of a bookcase near the back. Was it the actual back of the store? Or would there be another magical entryway?

He pulled out a list from his jeans pocket. "This is what you'll need for textbooks for your first year. You should be able to find them all on this bookcase."

"Wait. Where are you going?"

He nodded to his right. I glanced in that direction to see various other items of a magical bent. Cauldrons, candles, a variety of plants and herbs I'd never seen before.

"Besides those items, you'll also need a suitcase."

"I have a suitcase." I pulled one of the books from the list off the shelf. I turned it over and flipped through the pages, unable to find a price.

"You'll need more than that. You'll have belongings now. When you get to the school, you'll also have a few changes for your uniform. You need a place to put them."

"I can't afford it." I handed him the book. "What is the price of this?"

"Don't worry about the price."

I scoffed. "Spoken by someone who never had to worry about money."

I eyed him again, paying more attention to the tailored shirt. His shoes, polished now, screamed expensive. Even the belt he wore exuded wealth.

"The scholarship will cover all of this. It was designed to take care of all the student's needs, including incidentals. So if you have favorite snacks you want to bring, let me know and we can pick those up too."

I hurried through the book list, piling my arms with tomes that weighed me down so much I could barely move. Before I could complain, a large basket appeared beside my feet. I could get used to this magic thing.

A few minutes later, he returned to my side, dragging a trunk the size of a large-screen television.

"That's not going to be big enough." I looked at the pile of books at my feet, calculating the space needed for my other things in my head. Not to mention the cauldron, candles, and plants Damien had picked up for me. The depth wouldn't hold even half the stuff I was buying.

He pulled the lid open. Inside, the trunk was huge, with shelves of its own. The items Damien fetched while I worked on the books were already inside. With a shrug, I added the textbooks.

"You'll soon learn that nothing is as it appears."

"I'm getting that." Made me rethink my whole childhood. How many times had magic been all around me and I never noticed? "But you know I'm not magical, right? I can't pull a rabbit out of a hat to save my life."

I followed him to the cash register. A matronly woman of indeterminate age attended it. Tortoiseshell glasses framed her sparkling blue eyes. Light golden hair flowed over her shoulders. She rang up the sale with long, ethereal fingers.

"Have a good year, dear," she said and handed me a receipt.

Scholarship stamped in red across the items obscured the prices. I had a feeling I didn't want to know how much any of this cost.

"Thanks."

I shoved the bill in my pocket and pulled the trunk, which was surprisingly maneuverable, behind me. At the car, Damien opened the trunk, shoved aside a pile of tools, my suitcase, and backpack, and we tossed my stuff inside. Well, he tossed. I watched, waiting for him to throw his back out.

Once seated in the vehicle again, he turned, eyebrows drawn together, his face serious. "Based on observation and your comments, it seems your magic is bound for some reason."

"Who would do that?"

"I suspect it was your parents. To protect you. Dean Garrick can unbind it when you get to school. Until then, keep your head down and try to fit in on the bus ride. It won't take long, maybe three hours, but other students from the academy will be on the bus too."

My heart somersaulted in time to the lurch of the car shooting out into traffic. They would have magic. If they decided to use it against me for some reason, I would have no way of fighting back. Based on past experience, there would be at least one who wanted to make a name for themselves by bullying the new kid. If they were all first-year students, though, maybe I didn't have to worry.

I'd never fit in. Not in any school I got shuffled to. It was my norm to keep my head down, do the work, get out. Mostly, I avoided the bullies, the well-meaning, and the plain nosy.

Too soon, he pulled the car into a parking garage on York Street.

* * *

A headache teased my temples. The mark on my arm glowed slightly as I stood waiting for him to retrieve my belongings. He hefted out the things we'd bought at the bookstore, then pulled out my suitcase and backpack. He placed both of those inside the bigger trunk. If I didn't have a place to stay after school was over, would a mattress fit in there?

"Come on." He grabbed the handle of my luggage. "It's a short walk to Union Station."

The bustle of the train station added to my anxiety. People walking in all directions, heads down looking at their phones so they didn't have to make eye contact with anyone. I was right there with them. Avoiding confrontation was at the top of my to-do list. The scent of freshly made bagels teased my nose and hunger struck. Too bad. I didn't think anything would stay down at the moment, even if I could afford to buy one.

"There will be food on the bus." He increased his pace until we reached the bus platforms.

Embarrassed, I trailed after him, head down. "I'm not hungry."

I don't know why I lied. Hunger wasn't something to be embarrassed about. Neither were the clothes I wore, but there it was. I was almost 100 percent sure no one else on the bus was going to be a foster kid.

He stopped at a platform that appeared deserted. Walls dark and dusty. Broken lights flickered, while other lights remained dark. "Follow me."

"But there's nothing there." My protest fell on deaf ears. He'd already disappeared into the darkness.

Taking a deep breath, I trudged after him, wondering what I was getting myself into. On the other side of the magical barrier, the platform was pristine. Freshly washed walls sparkled. Bright lights illuminated all corners of the platform.

A large bus idled, the gentle purr of its motor filling the quiet inside the magical bubble. Splashed with red and blue, with a school crest on the side, its doors opened.

Damien nodded. "You get on board and I'll put your trunk in the luggage compartment." As he said the words, the door to the storage opened.

"Did you do that?"

He shrugged. "You'll get used to the magic." Then he pulled out a remote and grinned. "The magic of technology."

I pierced him with an exasperated look at his dad joke and climbed the steps. The bus driver wore a dark blue suit with a cap to match. He smiled as I approached.

"Welcome to Hell's Watch. Take any seat available and enjoy the ride."

I peered down the aisle, my gaze stopping at the dark-haired girl in the third row. With her light brown skin and blue-green eyes, she was stunning. Probably one of the cool kids. Internal alarms went off. Avoid at all costs. But she smiled up at me, shifted over one seat, and patted the vacated space beside her.

Damien had embarked, but he was talking to the driver like they were old friends. He took a spot in the first row and jerked his head back, indicating the rest of the bus.

The aisles were wide, making travel down them easy. I shuffled along, taking as much time as possible, wanting to stave off the inevitable. Beyond the girl in the third row, there was a handsome guy. Same dark hair, brown eyes, with a bit of scruff covering his brown face.

At the back of the bus, two girls who could have easily fit into my high school giggled as I walked down the aisle. Both blond, both perfect, one with long hair past her shoulders, the other with a pixie cut that showed off her fairy-like face, their blue eyes pierced me with looks of hatred so intense I shivered. Their friend, a black girl with flawless skin and long black hair, yawned, indifferent to what was going on. Maybe that was my superpower. Making total strangers hate me.

"Nice clothes, red," the one with the long hair said.

"Don't mind them," the girl who offered to share her row advised. "They don't like anyone. They're new magic."

"New magic?" I slipped in beside her.

"Yes, not one of the original magic families. They got

their magic by marrying into it." She held out her delicate hand. "I'm Priti."

"Alex."

"Nice to meet you." She turned to the guy behind us. "That's Saad. And those two are Tess and Hailey. Tess is the one with the long hair. Their friend is Nia. She's okay. I don't know why she hangs out with the twins."

Before I could get settled, the seats merged, creating a booth. The booth pivoted to face Saad and the girls at the back. Saad's row also transformed. A wooden board came out of the wall to form a table large enough for four lunches.

"Lunch! I'm starving," Saad said.

Tess and Hailey sauntered down the aisle and squeezed in beside Saad, both girls giving him the most flirtatious smiles I'd ever seen. They could teach classes on it.

"Red, what's up with the air-conditioned jeans?" When Tess's gaze turned from Saad to me, her face transformed into one resembling an ogre from the sneer she leveled at me.

"They're comfortable." I shifted in the booth, wishing to sit somewhere else, but there were no other people on the bus. It's not like I could get lost in the crowd here.

"Whatever," Hailey said. "How do you know the teacher you came with?" She nodded at Damien.

"He's a teacher? Not well. We just bumped into each other on the platform."

"One of their best from what I've heard," Priti said. "You didn't get the school newsletter?"

I shook my head. So many things I was learning today made my stomach flip.

"How long have you been doing magic?" Tess asked.

"Not long." It wasn't a total lie. Okay, maybe it was, because the answer was not at all. But there was no way I was going to let them know that. They would pounce faster than a hyena on a wildebeest.

Tess held out her left hand and waved her right hand over it. Barely audible mumblings tumbled from her lips. With a flash and a soft poof, an apple appeared.

"I've been practicing for ages." She bit into the fruit. A hint of disgust crossed her face, but she covered it.

"How about you two?" I looked at Priti, then at Saad.

"They teach us a little, enough to get by until we can attend school." Priti tapped the table and a hologram of a sandwich floated above the surface. "*Solidus*." The sandwich, real now, landed on a small plate that had automatically appeared when she spoke the word.

If that's how lunch happened, I'd be going hungry until we got there. "That's not how all meals happen at school, is it?" I hated the hint of fear that crept into my voice. I couldn't do any magic, let alone turn a holographic sandwich into something edible.

Saad laughed. "No, it's just a time saver here. They don't have a lot of selections and it helps us practice the basics."

"You're not going to have anything?" Tess asked.

"Not hungry." I was getting good at telling that lie.

When they all had sandwiches, except for me, Tess pulled off a small piece and popped it into her mouth. She wiggled slightly in her seat as she chewed. Excitement flowed off her in waves.

"I can't wait for classes to start!"

Her apparent studious nature surprised me. Maybe she thought she could flirt her way into good grades with those smiles of hers.

"I heard we have to fight a demon for our final," Priti said.

My stomach churned. Fighting a demon hadn't gone

well for me the first time. True, I'd had no notice, no train-ing, and hadn't even known magic existed then. But somehow I didn't think it was going to be different in May when I had to fight another one.

The bus sailed along Whirlpool Road, slowing at a small service road just before the canal. A forest of green lay ahead, with the canal running parallel. When the bus turned down the road, a soft hiss sounded, followed by a gentle glow that surrounded the bus. Once through the magical barrier, a large building came into view.

"Is the school a castle?" I couldn't help the awe in my voice. Going from a three-bedroom home with ten people to a castle was the height of luxury. Even if there were a lot of students, I would have plenty of room.

The bus paused at a huge wrought iron gate with gold trim. The gate swung open and the bus trundled inside. A forest behind the school loomed, tree branches stretching to touch the three tall towers. At the foot of a horseshoe staircase that led to a heavy wooden door flanked by two large windows, an older gentleman stood tall in front of double French doors that were adorned with a windowed arch. Dark brown hair peppered with silver gave him an air of sophistication. Expecting someone from a magic school to wear robes, I was surprised at his crisp black suit. The emblem of the school was emblazoned above the right breast pocket.

When the bus came to a stop, the doors opened and Damien stood.

"Welcome to Hell's Watch. Before going inside, the dean will give you a small introduction. Your luggage will be sent to your rooms while you go on a short tour of the place."

I jumped out of my seat and followed Damien out of the bus. The August air was still thick with humidity. The rest of the students piled out behind me. This couldn't be it for first-year students. I'd be devastated if it were. A smaller student population meant more chances of being singled out. While more student to teacher time, I'd rather be a small fish in a really large pond.

We lined up in front of the dean. His smile made his eyes twinkle. "Welcome. The rest of the first-year students are already here. You're the last to arrive. I'm Dean Garrick. Mr. O'Connor will give you a quick tour and then get you settled."

"Before we get started, the dean will let you know some of the ground rules." Damien waved his hand at the dean.

A sober expression settled on the older man's face. "We don't have a lot of rules here, but the biggest one is no using magic outside of school. First years aren't allowed to leave campus unescorted by a teacher. And no one is permitted near the dungeon."

"Thanks, Dean. If you'll all follow me, we'll do a quick tour of the grounds, then I'll show you to your rooms."

We walked away from the horseshoe staircase and I found myself wondering where the door on the first floor led to. We stopped at a flat-roofed building attached to the main building.

"This is where Miss Carmina will get the plants and herbs for spells and potions class. If you look up, you'll see a greenhouse on the roof."

From where we stood, there was no discernible entrance to the greenhouse, but like everything so far, I figured the door was magically hidden somehow. For what reason, I had no idea. Maybe class wouldn't be held there, and she would just get the ingredients she needed.

At the edge of the forest behind the school, Damien waved his hand, indicating the vast expanse of trees. "This is also a forbidden zone unless accompanied by a teacher. During Ostara, the celebration of the spring equinox, you'll be allowed to venture into the area, but only so far."

Of course, now I wanted to explore the area. Tell me I can't do a thing and I want to do the thing. But I also didn't want to get kicked out of school. I would have nowhere else to stay, and the thought of going back to my foster family made my skin crawl.

After a quick tour through the courtyard at the back and the gardens, Damien guided us up the horseshoe staircase. The steps appeared old, and I expected them to crumble as we walked, but they remained solid.

At the top of the stairs, the wooden door swung open and I gasped as I crossed the threshold. Behind me, Tess murmured something I couldn't make out, but I was sure it was a derogatory comment.

A huge lobby, with a sweeping spiral staircase on either side, welcomed us. A chandelier adjusted its brightness as the door closed behind us. At the top of the staircase, long corridors branched off from the expansive landing. Heavy wooden doors lined the halls.

He trudged up the stairs and we followed him. I wondered how much more grand the place would be.

At a door right at the top, he pushed, revealing a brightly lit room with two rows of hospital-like beds.

A short black woman with dark curly hair, on the far side of the room, smiled and hustled over.

"This is Dr. Leigheis Dotair, the school's doctor."

"Try not to end up here too often," she said with a sparkle in her brown eyes.

The rest of the tour was what you would expect from a school that looked like a castle. The library had shelves that seemed to go on forever into the air. On the main floor, there was the dining hall, the gym, the pool. I loved swimming. Too bad I didn't have a suit. There'd been no need over the years. It was just one more thing to pack that I'd never use as I moved from one house to another.

Damien dropped Saad and the evil twins off at their rooms. On the third floor, Priti and I followed Damien down the hall until he stopped at a room that faced the forest.

My mind focused on the last time I'd shared a room with a bunch of girls. My muscles tensed. My heart raced. The tattoo on my arm, on its best behavior the whole time we'd been on the tour, chose that moment to glow slightly. My heartbeat quickened. I crossed my arms over my chest to cover it.

"You must be really old magic." The awe in her voice set my alarm bells off again.

"Why do you say that?"

She nodded at my arm. "No one is allowed that mark anymore. And it was reserved for old families."

I had no idea what that was going to mean for me while I was at school. But the butterflies took flight in my stomach again.

Chapter Four

"I'm excited that we're roommates." The smile on Priti's face looked genuine, but that didn't mean anything. My foster sisters could put on a smile to get their way like others might put on shoes. At least rooming with Priti was better than getting Tess or Hailey to bunk with.

When we stepped into the room, Priti slightly behind me, the first thing I noticed was how big it was. Two double beds, tons of space, two desks flush against the wall where the door was, one on either side, and a small fridge tucked into the left corner of the room where the desks were. The next thing I noticed was the demon charging toward us. I threw my hands up, cold rising through me, and from somewhere in the large room the sound of cracking glass and a freeing of liquid reached my ears.

Didn't the place have some sort of protection? A way to keep the evil out and protect the students?

Priti stepped in front of me and the demon vanished. "Are you okay? You know that was just a glamour, right?"

"Sure."

The next thing I noticed was that the room was already

decorated. Despite my trunk sitting in front of one of the beds, a pile of clothes lay on top that definitely wasn't mine. Motivational posters already adorned half the wall space.

"Sorry, my parents thought I'd have a double room to myself. You must have been a late enrollment."

"That's okay. Which side do you want?"

Priti pointed to the bed without my trunk in front. The bed I was left with was closer to the window on the side of the room. But the beds were in front of a huge window that let us see out into the forest.

"Let's fix the warding on the room so he doesn't scare the pants off of us again."

When I scanned the room, I noticed the cause of the cracking sound. A broken vase spilled ice chunks on flowers piled on the floor.

"Sorry about that."

"That's okay. You're pretty new to the whole magic thing, huh?"

"Is it that obvious?"

Just what I needed. To be the only one in the school who had no idea how to control this power they said I had. I still wasn't convinced. Anything could have caused the vase to break. Maybe the demon's glamour.

"A little but don't worry. I'll help you out."

"I've never done a warding before."

How much I should reveal to Priti about my lack of magic rolled around in my head until an ache started between my eyes.

"That's okay, copy what I do."

She rummaged through the suitcase at the foot of her bed and pulled out a cauldron similar to the one I'd bought. She put it in the center of the floor and sat down with her legs crossed. Next, she reached into her pockets and pulled out a penknife.

I sat opposite her, waiting for what came next. She chanted and I followed along with her, stumbling over most of the words because they were in a foreign language. Damien hadn't said anything about learning to speak another language. From the sound of it, I was guessing Latin.

When Priti put her room key into the cauldron, I followed suit. When she pricked the end of her finger, I pulled out my dagger and did the same.

She finished her chant and a puff of smoke erupted from the cauldron. She reached in and took out both keys, handing me one.

"This warding should allow each of us to invite visitors inside without the alarm going off."

Great. Not that I thought I'd be inviting anyone into the room. Keep my head down, do the work, and then what? I had four years of this and I had no idea what I was going to do at the end of the school year or the end of school, period. It's not like I could put attendance at the school on my résumé.

She said a few words again and the cauldron sparkled like new. She put everything away and dropped onto her bed. "This is going to be so much fun. I've been waiting to attend Hell's Watch forever."

Before I could do a similar flop onto the bed, notes appeared out of thin air and drifted down to each mattress. I snatched mine up and scanned it. "Time to visit the school quartermaster. We have uniforms?"

The school was so large, with so many twists and turns, it was easy to get lost just walking down a corridor. This was another place that appeared to be bigger on the inside, though the outside was huge enough.

Though our times to report for our uniform were different by twenty minutes, Priti insisted on coming with me just in case I got lost on the way to the school quartermaster. For never having been to the school, she knew her way around pretty well.

"How do you know your way around here?" I asked when we reached our destination.

"Parents. They went here ages ago. We have all the maps showing the various changes."

"Changes?"

"Sure. Each year they move things around a little. To keep us on our toes. You never know when the unexpected might happen. Four years ago, the pool was in the courtyard."

Before I could knock on the door, it swung open and a large man with tree trunks for arms smiled at me. Seriously, his arms were the biggest I've ever seen. One swat with his hands would send a pro wrestler flying.

"Alexandra?" He looked down at a list.

"Yes."

"You may enter."

I stepped through the door and saw rows and rows of clothes. All red, blue, and silver. The school colors, no doubt. The rows went on forever, seemingly housing an endless supply of clothes.

He pressed a button and the hangers moved until the right one had reached him. He pulled out a pair of cargo pants with two pockets in the front. And a cotton, collared shirt.

"No skirt?" Not that I was complaining. I hated wearing anything that showed off my legs.

"You think you can high kick a demon in a skirt?" He laughed, the sound booming through the room.

"I guess not."

"No, you can't. We aren't going to set you up for failure." He shoved the clothes at me, holding them up to make sure they were the right size. He pointed to a room to my right. "You get five uniforms, one for each day of the school week. There's a laundry hamper in your room. Put the clothes in there at night and they'll be fresh as a daisy in the morning. Try them on and we'll make adjustments as needed."

I did as instructed, dressing faster than I ever had in my life. With my regular clothes bundled at my side, I stepped out of the change room.

"Anything else I should know?"

He pointed a finger and muttered a phrase I didn't recognize. Suddenly, the cargo pants and shirt hugged my body like they'd been made especially for me. My everyday clothes disappeared. Unaccustomed to the slim fit, I smoothed my hand over the clothes. It had been so long since I'd worn one layer of clothing. And everything I owned was baggy, swimming on me most of the time.

"Your clothes are on your bed."

"Thanks."

"You also need a weapon. Mr. O'Connor said you already had one. That true?"

A weight in one of the front pockets prompted me to reach my hand inside. My fingers circled the handle of the dagger Damien had thrown at me at the coffee shop. I pulled it out.

"Will this do?"

"That'll work."

I dropped the weapon back in my pocket and realized it actually went into a pocket I hadn't seen at first. Hidden pockets now? How many pockets did the cargo pants have? They were deep, and possibly plentiful. I'd have to check later on when I changed out of my uniform.

"Check the other pocket," he instructed.

I reached my hand into the other pocket and pulled out a note. It was time to meet the rest of the class and have something to eat in the dining hall.

Chapter Five

I stood with Priti on the other side of the courtyard, outside the quartermaster's, waiting for a break in the sudden downpour. The rain would help with the humidity, but I didn't want to get soaked right before dinner. If there was a way to the dining hall from here that didn't require a dash across the grounds, I hadn't found it. Priti shrugged.

Saad joined us.

Other students walked through the courtyard, an invisible barrier protecting them from the rain. If I knew how to do magic, that would be a nice trick. Maybe a magical umbrella wouldn't turn inside out with a gust of wind.

"This is a good time to practice," Priti said. She uttered some words in Latin and stepped into the downpour. The rain bounced off the invisible barrier.

"I'm not at that point yet," I said.

Saad shrugged out of his jacket. "Use this." He held it above both our heads and we stepped into the onslaught. We hurried across the courtyard. When we got to the other side, he snapped the jacket out, flinging the water droplets from the fabric. "Good as new."

The dining hall was just as impressive as the rest of the place. Wood-paneled walls were home to portraits of previous students. Big tables, set up cafeteria-style, left large aisles for people to walk down. Judging by the number of chairs at every table, I calculated at least two hundred students attended the school. How many were first year? Could people flunk out of magic school? My stomach churned and my gaze darted to all the exits. The door we came through from the main hallway, one on the left side of the room at the back, and another one directly opposite on the right.

Priti already had a table picked out. She caught my attention, and Saad and I strolled over. The sudden feeling of belonging as I sat sent warmth spreading through me. I tamped it down as best as I could. Never get your hopes up and you can't be disappointed. I didn't know if I could trust anyone here. Not even Damien. Though I trusted him the most at this point.

Tess and Hailey sat two rows over with more perfect people. As soon as Tess saw me, she leaned in and whispered something to the group. Laughter erupted and I wanted to curl up into a ball. I guess it was possible they weren't talking about me, since I looked like any other student now. But I knew they were.

Once everyone was seated, servers weaved their way through the rows of tables, placing empty platters in the middle. With a flick of their wrist and an utterance of Latin, chicken, pasta, and steamed vegetables filled the platters. Empty plates popped up in front of everyone.

While everyone piled their plates with food, the dean stood at the front behind a podium, calling for attention.

"Welcome back, continuing students. And welcome, new students. Life at Hell's Watch won't be easy, but it will be rewarding. You will be charged with protecting the innocent once you graduate, so what you learn here is vital."

"My mother said she loved this part," Priti said. "They read off the names of the new students."

"As is tradition, I will announce the new students. Please stand so your classmates can get to know you."

I cringed. My stomach churned. So much for laying low.

He went down the list and when he said, "Saad of the family Hashim," Saad stood and flashed the room a grin.

"Alexandra, a Kavanagh."

I stood. All eyes turned toward me. Whispering filtered across the room. Tess and Hailey sat up straighter, eyeing me with a mixture of awe and hatred that didn't bode well for me. Nia rolled her eyes and turned her attention back to her plate of food. Before the dean got to the next name on the list, I sat again, wishing magic could make me invisible. Priti shot me an awe-filled look.

"Priti of the family Shah." Priti stood.

"Nathan adopted by the family Ward."

A boy one table over stood. He was tall, with dark hair, a Mediterranean complexion, and green eyes that took in the entire room as he waved like some sort of actor at a premiere. I couldn't shake the feeling that I knew him somehow. But that was impossible. I hadn't met anyone from the school before I got here, except Damien.

Priti grabbed my arm and squeezed. "You're not just a legacy. You're a founding family."

"Founding family? Of the school?"

Saad shook his head. "Of magic."

"Great. No pressure." That cold, tingly feeling around my vaccination scar flooded back. The water in glasses on the table froze. Three glasses cracked, throwing ice all over our plates. I sucked in a deep breath, concentrating on slowing down my racing heart. My family fucking founded magic and I couldn't even pull a rabbit out of a hat. How was that possible?

I gazed around the room as people murmured my name and shot curious glances my way. My mother's name floated through the air. My father's name whispered in the same breath. Everyone knew who they were, but what if the school got it wrong? How could I be a member of a founding family and not be able to do anything magical? What if they thought I was a fraud or an impostor? *Will the real Alex Kavanagh please stand up?*

"You'll do fine," Priti said. "When we get back to the room, we can go over our schedules. They're pretty much predefined for first years, but I can give you pointers on where to sit. And give you insight into some of the teachers. Plus, we have an elective."

"Where to sit is strategic?"

"If you don't want to draw attention, sure," Priti said. "Don't sit at the front or very back of the class. Sit in the middle, slightly left."

A headache joined the heart palpitations. Suddenly, I didn't want classes to start.

She clasped my hand. "You'll be fine."

"But what does this original family stuff mean?"

"You'll learn all about it in Arcane Knowledge," Saad said. "But basically your family is a pretty big deal."

Except I didn't have a family. Mom, dad, grandmother, all gone. If there had been aunts or uncles I wouldn't have ended up in foster care. So all the magic in the world hadn't protected my family. What made me think it could protect me?

When the reading of the list was over, everyone went back to eating, except a few extra curious students who put their forks down and marched over to our table. A pretty

Japanese girl flashed a dazzling smile. She thrust out a delicate hand. Startled, I took it.

"Aya, student council president. If you need anything, you let me know."

"Sure," I said.

A line-up had formed behind her. In a whirl of activity, people introduced themselves to me. From the highest ranks of the student council to first-year students who were almost as poor as I was. Their names and faces were a blur in my mind. Then Nathan sauntered over. He smiled, revealing even white teeth. A sparkle in his green eyes made me wonder if the twinkle was real or magic.

"Never thought I'd meet a founder."

I took his proffered hand. It was warm and soft and somewhat calming in the chaos. "It's nice to meet you too."

"Didn't say it was nice to meet you, just never thought I would." He smiled again to take the sting off his words, but it didn't help.

I snatched my hand back, suddenly wishing everyone would go away and leave us in peace. The line-up to meet me was never-ending.

From the front of the dining hall, the dean stood at the podium and cleared his throat. "Quiet, everyone! Go back to your seats and finish dinner. There is a whole school year ahead of you."

The people waiting to meet me grumbled and shook their heads but shuffled off back to the tables. I breathed a sigh of relief and slumped back into my chair. The food had gotten cold. I was sure there was a magical way to heat it up again, but I didn't have the ability, nor the desire, to ask someone else to do it for me.

We finished dinner, the whispers and the stares eventually dying down.

"I'm going back to the room to get ready for the party," Priti said.

Great, another thing I didn't know. "Party?"

"There's always an informal party for the students put on by third years," she said.

"I'm not sure. I wanted to check out the library some more. That tour didn't last long enough for me."

"I'll wait for you. Saad, see you there."

She hurried off before I could say anything.

The crowd began to disperse. Tables once bowing under the weight of the food were now picked bare, only crumbs left behind. Surely not everyone would be at the party. The dining hall and auditorium appeared to be the only rooms in the school capable of accommodating all students and staff at once.

"I'll see you at the party," Saad said.

Absently, I nodded. I tracked back in my mind to figure out where I had to go from here to get to the library. If I got lost it would be a good excuse to not attend the festivities, but I didn't want to get lost on my first day. Been there. Done that. Got thrown in a locker.

After getting turned around a few times, I finally approached the library. With everyone preparing for the party, I was sure I would have the books to myself. I pushed the heavy oak door. It gave way with a creak. Inside the library, I breathed deeply, savoring the scent of paper, polished wood, and old leather.

On my right, just inside the door, was the check-out desk. A sign, covered in dust, propped up against a jar of candies, said the librarian would be back in ten minutes. Behind the desk was a card catalog that reached the ceiling. In front of me, past the desk, was the first of many reading nooks. Each nook had four high-backed chairs with plush cushions surrounding a small table.

Straight ahead were columns of bookcases, at least twelve feet high, crammed with tomes both thick and thin. They stretched back as far as my eyes could see, and I suspected if I walked into the rows, the bookcases would never end. Like a nightmare of running down a hallway but standing still. Except this made my heart leap. Books had never steered me wrong. Never wanted anything from me. Never let me down.

To my left were more bookcases, but shorter than the main set. Their numbers were finite. I could distinctly see five rows, with a dark wooden door behind the last of the shelves. And to the right of those shelves, more reading nooks lined the wall. Not knowing where to start, I waited for something to speak to me. Nothing happened.

I shrugged and went right, directly to the card catalog. An endless stretch of bookcases would take more time to investigate than I had at the moment. And I needed to know who I could trust in this place. From the mob at dinner, I doubted I could trust anyone remotely impressed with who my family was. It would help if I knew for sure who my friends truly were.

A niggling thought in the back of my mind questioned Priti's loyalty, but she'd had no idea she would even have a roommate. Let alone a founder. Her initial offer of friendship on the bus had to be genuine. An image of Nathan flashed into my mind. He would be an enigma. And that was something I didn't need.

I pulled out the drawer for F. I found a card that looked promising.

Friend or Foe, spell, level 1
　Cross-reference Spells, first year, Kavanagh, Julie
　Section 100

I gasped at seeing my grandmother's name. I guess being a founding family, I should expect the library would have some books that mentioned us. But it was still a shock. I racked my brain and couldn't remember once witnessing magic, either from my parents or my grandmother, after my parents died.

The shelves on the left started with section 000. I walked down the aisles, looking for the section I needed, but 000 didn't end. I turned to the shelves in the center of the room and started with the one closest to the door, opposite the check-out desk. Section 100. Now all I needed to do was find the book. I pulled out book after book, flipping through pages. Finally, I found one that looked familiar, though I couldn't explain why. Bound in black leather, the title emblazoned in silver on the front, the book was thin. Not even a hundred pages. In the tiniest writing I'd ever seen, my grandmother's name was written on the spine.

Before I could read any of the pages, someone called my name. I turned to see Damien approaching. I shoved the book into one of my pockets, hoping he hadn't seen me with it.

"We need you in the dean's office. We thought it would be a good idea to unbind your powers before classes started."

Bummed at missing out on escaping into a book, I was relieved they were going to do something about my missing magic. I still wasn't convinced I had any, though things had been tending to shatter around me a lot lately.

<hr>

At the back of the school, in a room that blended almost seamlessly with the forest save for the definite corners indicating walls, the dean sat behind a large oak desk. Beside him, Mrs. Sapienti, the teacher for Deception and Wisdom, a fourth-year class, stood with her wrinkled hands clutched in front of her. Wisdom shone in her brown eyes. A lightly wrinkled face revealed deep laugh lines when she smiled.

Sitting on the other side of the desk, I shifted in the seat I'd been given. A cozy armchair that would have looked out of place in a classroom, but I was glad for the comfort. Damien stood behind the dean, and the longer the three of them looked at me, the more I wanted to flee. Three members of staff staring you down with sympathy written all over their faces was never a good sign.

"Before we unbind your power, there are things you should know," the dean said. "Things Damien wasn't at liberty to discuss until you arrived on campus."

I sat up straighter. "What things?" The first thing that occurred to me was they knew I didn't have power.

The dean nodded at Mrs. Sapienti. A quick flush of color rose on the woman's pale wrinkled face, but it disappeared almost as quickly. Didn't take a genius to figure out I wasn't going to like what she was about to say.

"It was in part my decision to bind your power, although others were involved as well." The woman took a deep breath. "And to put you into care to better hide you from the demons we knew would come for you."

My stomach lurched. "Where would I have gone otherwise?"

She stared at me briefly, straightened her back, and pursed her lips. She broke eye contact and looked down at her small hands.

"In the care of a school guardian."

"You threw me into the ordpops foster system on purpose?"

Body tense, heat rushed through me. Liquid from a mug on the desk bubbled, steam rising. The top of the mug cracked. Did they have any idea what their decision did to me? How it affected everything I did? I took a deep breath.

"It took you out of the magical community, which was safer for all." Mrs. Sapienti's sad eyes held my gaze for a beat, then she directed her attention to the dean.

"Safer why?"

The dean cleared his throat. "We'll get into that later."

"I think I have a right to know now."

Mrs. Sapienti sighed, wringing her delicate hands. "Placing you with another magical family might have been better for your emotional and magical upbringing, but this way saved lives."

"What the hell does that mean?"

It was the dean's turn to look sad. "The first family you were placed with was magical. They died. The parents died. Their son survived and he was put into magical foster care."

The hair on the back of my neck rose. *First family?* I didn't remember anything magical about any part of my life.

Mrs. Sapienti took up the story again. "We decided non-magical care and binding your powers was the safest course of action."

A flash of playing with Nathan entered my mind.

"When you were with Nathan's family, you saved him somehow when a demon attacked. It arrived to take you. But you couldn't save his parents. You accessed magic you shouldn't have been able to at that age." The dean leaned back in his chair, rubbing the back of his neck, the anguish of the memories written all over his face.

"So his real parents died because of me?"

"It wasn't your fault, Alex. You were seven. After that,

we thought it best if we kept you away from magic so the demons couldn't find you," the dean said. "Obviously, that isn't working so well now."

So not just one demon wanted me dead, there would be others. Great. The spell book in my pocket would come in handy if it had the spell I needed. Knowing who I could trust here would help a lot with fitting in and staying on guard when I needed to. For now, while at school, the demons shouldn't be able to find me. But that didn't mean humans would leave me alone. An image of Tess flashed in my mind.

"We can undo some of the past. It's time to let you have access to your powers." Mrs. Sapienti stepped out from behind the desk and stood in front of me. She took my hand and pulled me off the chair. With a low but strong voice, she uttered a few Latin phrases. The air in the room moved, lifting my hair from my shoulders. Lights flickered. Her hands squeezed mine harder until my knuckles turned white. She continued to recite the spell, her voice growing louder with each word. A grimace crossed her face, but she didn't let go of my hands. A rush of power surged through me.

Mrs. Sapienti sagged into the chair beside me as if all of her energy had been drained. "That should do it."

"If you have any troubles, come and see me," the dean said. "Now go have fun at the party."

The ominous order to have fun at the party still rang in my ears when I opened the door to my room. I tensed as I pushed it inward, half expecting another glamour of a demon to charge at me even though we'd fixed the warding. Nothing happened, and I let out a soft sigh. My shoulders relaxed. That is, until my gaze landed on Priti sitting in front of a mirror putting the final touches on her makeup.

She beamed at me, her eyes sparkling with excitement. A leaden weight rolled in my stomach at the thought of mingling with all those people. I still wasn't sure if the spell Mrs. Sapienti had performed worked. Did I have magic now? Not that it mattered. I still didn't know how to use it. And now I was paranoid that an innocent utterance of anything in a foreign language would set something on fire. Or make someone disappear. Strike abracadabra from my vocabulary.

"You're back!" She vacated her seat and, with a flour-ish, indicated I should sit. "We have enough time to do something with your hair before we leave."

About to protest, I stood my ground. "What's wrong with my hair?"

"Nothing. It's long and gorgeous and the flaming red sets off your eyes." She took my hand and pulled me to the chair, then gently pushed me to sit. "It's been a long day and it needs a quick taming." Priti picked up a brush and started on my tangles.

"I think I'll stay here tonight. It's been a crazy few days for me and I think I need the rest." I yawned loudly, raising my arms over my head. I wanted to read through the book from the library.

Priti's reflection frowned at me, but she kept working on my hair. "In the history of the school, I don't think a freshman has ever missed the party."

"There's always a first time."

I didn't know if I could trust Priti yet. She didn't give off a vibe that said "run away", but I didn't know what feelings to trust anymore. The enormity of what my life would be like now weighed down on me and I wished, for the millionth time, that my mother were there to talk to. Not only had she gone here, but she was somehow involved in founding magic. How the fuck did that work? Too many questions swirled through my head to be able to focus on having fun at some party.

"Voila!" Priti stepped back, arms in the air like a magician.

Distracted by my thoughts, I hadn't been paying attention to Priti's attempts to make my hair presentable. The long, tangle-free tresses framed my face, floating to my shoulders. I looked like a shampoo commercial.

"Thanks. Did you use magic? I can never get my hair to behave that way."

Priti smiled. "Maybe just a dash."

Despite my sour mood, I smiled back. If nothing else, I would at least have perfect hair. If the demons didn't kill me. Would the magic still be active if I was dead or would the tresses go back into their tangled mess? Relatively sure there would be no demons at the party, except maybe Tess, I shoved thoughts of evil to a back closet in my mind. A legitimate excuse to stay in the room and catch up on all the magic I didn't know existed until recently, remained elusive.

The excitement flowed off of Priti in waves. If she were a drink, she would bubble out of the top of a bottle with an explosion of fizz.

"It looks great, but..."

"No buts. You cannot be the only freshman to miss the party. How will people know who you are if you don't go?"

"Exactly."

She frowned, some of the sparkle fading from her eyes. "You don't want to get to know your classmates?"

My mission to stay under the radar, coast by on the

magic, assuming I had some now, was going to be thwarted by my over-enthusiastic roommate.

I shot her an accusatory look. "You liked school, didn't you? Not the learning part, but the social part."

"Of course! Classes were great, but lunch, that was the best. Sitting and catching up with friends."

"Thought so."

Realization washed over Priti's face and she sank onto the bed, staring at me with big brown eyes filled with sympathy. "You had friends at school, right?"

I remembered some of the girls' attempts, especially those new to the school, to befriend me, but once they learned everyone steered clear of Ginger Snapped, they made other friends. Not that I cared. I was there to learn, not socialize. I blamed it on my foster sisters. They went out of their way to make me unwelcome everywhere. But they didn't go here.

"Not really, but it was fine. I didn't need them."

"I am not letting you sit here by yourself on one of the only nights the teachers don't care if we party." Priti bounced off the bed, landing with her feet hip width apart, arms bent, hands fisted at her sides. "It's time to mingle!"

Too bad this magic thing didn't give me a crystal ball. I'd like to see what I was getting myself into before agreeing to go. But I knew she wouldn't leave without me and I didn't want to spoil her night. No sense in both of us being miserable. If it was crowded enough, maybe no one would notice me huddled in a corner, waiting for the minutes to tick by.

"Fine, I'll go. But I don't want to stay long."

Priti clapped her hands. "You say that now, but wait until you're having an amazing time. I'll have to drag you away."

At the end of a long corridor in the east wing of the castle, there was a set of stairs that Priti bounded up in time to the faint beat of the bass coming from the party room. I had no idea who was throwing the party, but I didn't want to tread up there and make a fool of myself this early in the school year. Juniors always held the party and it was a chance to get into their inner circle if you were interesting enough. Unfortunately, I was interesting enough when it came to magic. But would they like me for me, or because my family founded magic? How the hell did that work anyway?

Priti stopped at a landing. "Come on!"

Her enthusiasm made me smile. How long would that energy last once classes started and we had to study every day? A chill went through me at the thought of attempting magic. In front of people. I felt a little more powerful after the unbinding spell Mrs. Sapienti did, but I still doubted my ability to do anything magical except make an assistant disappear from a trick box.

I hurried up the stairs. Priti was already at the top of a second set of stairs. She spotted me and dashed down the hall. I raced to catch up, stopping at the top to suck in breaths of air.

Of course the party was at the end of that long hallway. I stalked toward the people milling about outside the room. Hopefully, that wasn't because the place was packed, but because they were leaving and just saying their goodbyes.

Loud music pumped, causing my heart to match the beat. Clusters of students dotted the room, with a narrow path between them to get to a refreshments table at the back of the room. The dorm was larger than ours. A bed on the far left was being used as seating. Cluttered with books, papers, and magic tools including jars of ingredients, a large desk was pushed up against the wall beside the refreshments table.

All the sounds stopped when I entered. All eyes turned toward me. Would anyone notice if I sat in that leather chair in front of the desk and willed myself to be invisible? The whispers followed me as I walked to the center of the room.

Somehow, the entire school was in the room. At least it felt that way with the crush of people, the rising heat from all those dancing bodies, the sheer volume of the chatter. Every nerve I had was on edge and I wanted to get back to the quiet of our room. I had more important things to do than hang out here.

Priti handed me a drink. I hadn't even noticed she went to the table where they were offered in varying sizes and flavors.

"Try to have fun," she said. Pink liquid sloshed in her glass as she took a sip.

I sniffed my drink and took a tentative sip. The deep purple beverage tasted like the sweetest grapes I'd ever had. If the sugar rush didn't keep me awake, the butterflies in my stomach would.

"This is good." I took another drink and sighed. I'd been thirstier than I thought. Or maybe the distraction was helping me forget I was surrounded by strangers who all appeared to be talking about me.

Finally, everyone went back to their conversations, and I was forgotten, at least temporarily. My congratulations for surviving the dreaded late to the party status was quickly quashed when I spotted Tess at the back of the room. She stared right at me, a tight smile on her lips. She nodded to her friends. Nia and Hailey nodded back, straightening their backs. They moved as one, like fashion models walking down a runway. Intense. Focused. My skin crawled. From the right, Nathan joined them. I hadn't even seen him during my quick scan of the room.

Instead of stopping in front of me, Tess walked by, bumping my arm. My drink sloshed onto my shirt, the wet material clinging to my skin. A chill crawled down my spine. My heart beat faster. Rising heat chased the chill away. From the corner of my eye, I watched the mark on my arm glow. It was an odd trinity framed by crescent moons. I slapped my hand over it, but not before Saad noticed it too. Where the hell had he come from? If all the rooms in the school were like this, I'd never know who was there with me.

Tess spun around on her heel, affixing a surprised look on her face. "Didn't see you there. You might want to get that cleaned before it stains." She pointed to the large purple splotch on my top.

The rage on Priti's face made my heart dance a little. I didn't have a lot of clothes, and having one of my tops ruined during the first day there didn't bode well for the rest of the year. Clenching my fist at my side, I took a deep breath, willing the rising panic to subside.

"Ignore her," Saad said. He put a gentle hand on my shoulder, urging me to turn slightly so I couldn't see her anymore.

Nathan's gaze moved from my arm to my face. Had he seen the mark too? "Yeah, she's just trying to rattle you."

Mission accomplished.

Tess made a soft humph sound, a frown turning her lips downward. Even ticked she was pretty. She stomped off to the snacks table by the door. Her friends trailed behind her. None of them looked back and I breathed a sigh of relief.

Saad nodded to the hand covering my mark. "I've never seen a black light tattoo before."

I removed my hand slowly, making sure the mark was no longer visible before I put my arm down. "Me neither. I didn't know I had it until a few days ago."

Nathan's eyebrows rose. "How does that work?"

Priti shot daggers at him and I liked her even more. There was real promise there for a lasting friendship if I didn't screw things up.

The skepticism in his question rankled. "It works because it didn't show itself until a few days ago."

The warmth from Saad's hand seeped into me as he squeezed my shoulder.

"Ignore him too." Saad nodded to a nook at the back of the room. Four chairs surrounded a small table. "Let's sit and chat for a while."

Every instinct told me to retreat. Rush back to my room, get some sleep, and start my academic career fresh in the morning. But hiding from the bullies would only make them dig in more. I sighed and followed Saad and Priti to the relative safety of the nook. I'd be counting down the minutes until I could make my safe retreat.

Chapter Six

Warmed by a late summer breeze wafting into the room, I emerged from sleep slightly disoriented. The usual noises of the past six years were absent. Used to Evie's snoring and Claire's sleepy mumblings, I savored the quiet. Priti made almost no noise as she slept except for the occasional shifting as she turned over. It had been so long since I'd woken to relative quiet, I lay there for several moments, able to concentrate on what I wanted to do that day.

First, I quietly flung my legs over the side of the bed and stretched. Then I got out of bed, longing even as my feet hit the ground, to snuggle back under the soft covers. The mattress was firm. No lumps kept me awake. I felt well-rested for the first time in years.

I thought about waking Priti, but she looked peaceful and I didn't want to ruin whatever dream she might be having. Besides, I didn't know if my roommate was a morning person or not. Brooklyn's temper if she'd been woken too early cautioned me from making the same mistake. There would be plenty of time to learn what Priti was like in the mornings. Today wasn't one of those times.

I wanted to take the opportunity to explore the school in peace. I was used to being up early. It was necessary to get out of the house before all the foster sisters woke up if I wanted to avoid their bullying. Since classes didn't start until Tuesday, I figured most people would still be asleep on a Friday morning.

I moved about the room as quietly as possible, donning my jeans and a clean top. Before leaving the room, I grabbed a snack from the mini-fridge. They served breakfast here, but I didn't want to risk running into anyone who might want to tag along while I explored.

I pulled the door closed, holding my breath at the small click it made. Pressing my ear against the smooth wood, I listened for any noises indicating Priti was awake. Nothing. Sighing with relief, I took a small bite out of a granola bar and traipsed down the hallway.

Eerily quiet at 6:00 a.m., the castle had an even more magical quality to it. There were so many places I wanted to explore, so many nooks and crannies to investigate, but I didn't have a lot of time. Students and teachers would be waking up soon.

I wanted to find a place I could call my own little hiding spot. If things got to be too much and I didn't want to burden Priti with my problems, I wanted a place I could go to think. A place that no one else knew or cared about.

I stopped in front of the library, tempted to check it out again, but any reading spots in there would get crowded, fast. Especially during the semi-finals and finals. The times I would most likely need solitude the most.

Back on the second floor, I stopped in the common area past the landing. A large spot filled with tables and big, comfy chairs, sofas, lamps that provided enough glow to read well into the night. The coziest spot was under the stairs that led to the third floor and the junior and senior dorms. The common area would probably be one of the most popular spots for students to congregate. No solitude likely there.

The third floor, as ornate as the second, provided the same options, except it didn't have an infirmary. I guess the school thought first and second-year students were more likely to need the services of a doctor.

The common area, also extending under the stairs, sported the same chairs, sofas, and tables, but in a different configuration as the second-floor space. I doubted I'd be welcome up there anyway until I was actually a junior.

I trudged up the spiral staircase to another landing. This one was smaller, with no corridors on either side like the other three floors. A door on my right, coated in dust, looked promising, but I trudged up another flight of stairs to see how far up they went. The steps stopped at a landing with barely enough room for one person to stand. And a door. Intrigued, I reached out, grabbed the wrought iron knob, and turned.

Tried to turn. The knob refused to budge. Would magic open it? Once I actually learned some magic, that is. I didn't have a lot of time to try. Even from the top floor, I heard the stirrings of people as students and staff roused from sleep, starting their day.

I trudged down the stairs, vowing to return later, and stopped at the door on the small landing. I turned that knob and grinned as it complied. With a soft click and a low creak, the door opened.

The room inside wasn't much to speak of. A tall window let in the morning light, bathing the floor in bright yellow. A chair by the window would be perfect for reading. On the far right wall near the window, an old bookcase stood empty and forgotten. A little dusty, but a quick cleaning would get rid of the cobwebs and particles clinging to every surface.

Did no one come up this far? The room looked like it hadn't had a visitor in years. Surely I couldn't be the only one to explore this far. Neither Damien nor the dean had said anything about parts of the castle being off-limits except for the dungeon. I didn't even know where that was, but I was pretty sure it wasn't up near the attic. Dungeons were usually in the basement.

Satisfied with my escape nook, I hurried down the stairs until I reached the lobby. I wanted to take a quick gander at the forest again.

I stood on the edge of the property, on the swath of grass before the forest. Even with the sun up, the darkness of the forest made my arm tingle. The mark on my arm glowed. Shivering, I stepped back. It was time to see if Priti was up anyway.

By the time I returned to the room, it was almost lunchtime. The room was empty, but Priti's energy still lingered. I pictured her bouncing out of bed and hurrying through her morning ritual to get to the dining hall.

When I closed the door I spotted a note from her on the chalkboard.

You were up early! :) I'll meet you in the dining hall at lunch for electives!

P

Electives? What the hell was that? I thought our schedules were already set. I had no idea what class I should *want* to take. My stomach flipped at the thought. I just found out magic was real a few days ago and now I was supposed to know what optional class was a good idea? At least it couldn't be worse than the introductions of the new students yesterday.

After doing a quick check to make sure I was presentable, I eyed my uniform. Last night after coming back to the room, I had flung it over the chair next to my bed. Did picking electives require the school attire? It was part of a school "event". I wished Priti were still in the room so I could ask her. How embarrassing would it be to show up wearing civilian clothes if everyone else was wearing their uniform? But what if I put on the uniform and everyone was wearing their everyday clothes? Indecision stalled me for a full minute. The uniform had way more pockets, deep pockets, so I could take more things with me.

Once I had the uniform on, I dropped my dagger in one front pocket and the spell book in the other. At this school, I figured I'd never know when I needed them both.

***

Sophomores ran past me into the dining hall. Wearing their school uniforms, I happily noted. At least that was one faux pas I didn't commit. No doubt there would be plenty of others while I attended the school.

I pulled out the spell book and flipped to the spell I wanted. School would be hard enough with learning magic and self-defense. It would be so much easier if I knew who I could trust and who I couldn't. In Toronto, I had to rely on my wits and experience with the bullies in the school. Sometimes rumors helped me weed out the possible friends from the definite enemies.

I spotted Priti and Saad at what I was beginning to think of as our spot. The smile on my face died when I saw

Tess, Hailey, and Nia approaching me. They were a striking trio. Before I could change my mind, I uttered the incantation in the book. Three different colors rippled around them. Metallic red, grey, and indigo. With them so close together, it was difficult to see which glow went with each of them.

I scanned the meanings of the colors listed under the spell. It wasn't hard to determine that Tess was likely the metallic red. I hadn't been witness to her temper yet, but I was sure it would be short. And she was definitely a bully. But the other two, I had no idea. While the grey wasn't horrible, it wasn't great. And the indigo could end up being someone I could be friends with. I should have waited until they were farther apart, or alone, before attempting the spell.

Tess stopped in front of me, a sneer marring her pretty features. "It doesn't matter if you're a legacy. You're still a loser. I haven't seen you use magic once since you got here."

Though anger boiled in my stomach, I took a deep breath. "Jealous much?"

Leaving her with a stunned look on her face, I walked away before she had time to recover.

I hurried over to Priti and Saad, watching out of the corner of my eye as the trio did an about-face and walked toward the front of the hall again to take their seats.

Chatter in the hall drowned out most conversations unless they were in the immediate vicinity. Excitement was palpable. Based on the snatches of conversation I could make out, everyone looked forward to selecting their electives. In some cases, the elective you ended up with determined what kind of year you would have.

Priti smiled at me when I sat. "Where did you go this

morning?" Though her smile was bright, hurt clouded her eyes.

"Sorry. I didn't want to wake you. I thought you would find it boring going around the school. It's all new to me and I wanted to orient myself more before classes start. I have nightmares about getting lost on my way to class."

"That's okay. I would love to go next time, though. I've only been to the school before on family day to see my siblings."

"Over the weekend then, let's explore." I turned to Saad. "You want to come too?"

Saad grinned. "Of course."

"What did the mean girls want?" Priti nodded in the direction of Tess and her followers.

"The usual. To make fun of me."

The frown on Priti's face made me smile. It was nice to know someone had my back.

"Don't even pay attention to her. You could kick her ass even without magic."

"Thanks." I wasn't sure she was right because I had a feeling Tess wouldn't play fair and would use magic anyway.

From the front of the hall, on the raised stage, teachers and the dean paraded across the platform and took their seats. The dean stopped behind the podium and raised his hands.

"Quiet down."

When the noise in the hall grew as more students filed in, the dean flicked his hand at the ceiling. He mumbled words I didn't hear. Why couldn't he have said them into the microphone? How was I going to remember all these little incantations?

The lights in the room flashed on and off. Bright like

the sun, then dark like the midnight sky for a few seconds. The chatter died down. Everyone took their seats.

"Thank you. As most of you know, it is time for the first-year students to pick their first electives. It's a hard but important choice. What you pick as your elective will dictate where your magical academic career takes you."

"Great, no pressure," I mumbled.

Priti laughed.

"It is my pleasure to call up Alexandra Kavanagh to select her first elective."

A roar of dissent rolled through the room. Tess sprang out of her chair. "Why does she get to pick first? She doesn't deserve it. She can't even do magic!"

"Everyone here can do magic, Miss Monroe."

"Have you seen her do any since she's been here?"

Murmurs of agreement rippled across the floor. I hated to agree with her, but she was right. Even with my powers now unbound, I hadn't done any magic except for the friend or foe spell, and that hadn't worked so great the first time.

Beside Tess, Hailey nodded. Nia looked bored. Her inability to choose first didn't seem to bother her at all.

"I assure you, Miss Kavanagh can do magic quite well. Now, if we may continue."

Tess crossed her arms over her chest. "Old magic always gets to pick first. There will be hardly anything left for us. Shouldn't new magic get a chance at some of those classes? We can't be better witches if you hold us back."

The words were out of her mouth so quickly they seemed to have a mind of their own. Then her eyes widened, and her mouth formed a perfect "O", her cheeks turning a sickly shade of pink. At the front of the class, the dean's face grew red. With his gaze piercing Tess, she crumpled back into her seat.

"It is tradition that old magic pick first. Remain silent and wait your turn." He stared at her for a heartbeat more, then turned his gaze to the rest of the hall.

Tess nodded meekly, but she shot daggers at me.

"Alexandra, please come forward to review your options and select your first elective."

With all eyes on me, I walked to the front of the hall. Why did they put people on the spot for so many things here? How the hell was I going to blend in and not cause waves when they kept having these ceremonies?

The dean pressed a few buttons on a tablet that sat on the podium and a display appeared in the air above the stage. A list of classes, none of them familiar, waited for me to choose. I turned to look at Priti and Saad. They both gave me a thumbs-up.

I scanned the list. Which one would be the most useful for me to know?

The one on familiars might be interesting. But there was also astrology and astronomy. My gaze kept returning to simple trickery. That might come in handy and open up further classes later on. I reached out a slightly trembling hand and tapped the button for the class.

"Very good! Simple trickery," the dean said.

From her chair, Tess harrumphed and a scowl crossed her lips.

"Now we will continue with old magic in alphabetical order. When they are finished, new magic will pick in alphabetical order."

The dean called more students up, one by one, until it was Saad's turn. Without hesitation, he tapped simple trickery. As each student went up to choose, Priti's face fell a little more. I got the feeling she wanted to be in simple trickery with us. Apparently, it was a very popular class. By the time the dean got to S, simple trickery was full.

Priti went up to the front and selected astrology and astronomy. She hurried back to her seat and slumped into her chair. "Maybe you could let me read your books for simple trickery," she said. "And I can tell you what I'm learning in astrology and astronomy."

"It's a deal," I said.

By the time they got to Tess and her cohorts, the only elective left was familiars. Tess stomped up to the front of the hall and jabbed the button in the air display. She spun back around, her perfect blond hair lifting off her shoulders, then settling back down again. Hailey and Nia selected the same class with less force. A small smile turned Nia's lips up. At least someone got their first choice.

Tess stormed out of the dining hall, her friends following close behind her.

"Serves her right," Priti said.

"What now?" Saad leaned back in his chair.

The selection of classes was finished. Lunch would be served any minute. After that, we had the rest of the day and the long weekend to do whatever we wanted until classes began on Tuesday. As much as I wanted to hang out with my new friends, I felt like I needed to study before school started. Everyone else was so much farther ahead than I was because they'd known from a young age that magic was real. They'd been exposed to magic their whole lives, some of them anyway. I had a lot of catching up to do.

"I want to go back to the room to figure out my schedule and maybe start hitting the books."

Priti's eyes lit up. Saad frowned.

"You can come with us," Priti offered.

"If you don't mind a lot of girl talk," I added.

We grinned at each other.

Saad shook his head. "Maybe later."

Back in our room, we dumped our snack cache from the dining hall onto our beds. I had opted for actual food, presumably picked or gathered from nearby farms, while Priti chose the snack cards at the exit of the hall. They were pictures of food that merely needed magic to make them whole. Since I'd only performed one incantation, and I wasn't sure if it even worked given the result, I didn't want to risk midnight food cravings going unanswered.

Priti eyed the apple I held in my hand. "You could have carried a lot more with the snack cards." She nodded to the pile on her bed. There had to be at least a hundred there.

"That's okay. I prefer real food. I never did get a handle on the incantation to make food out of thin air."

Despite Priti having my back so far, I wasn't sure I could tell her about my magic being bound. Not that it should matter, since Mrs. Sapienti had unbound it, but I didn't feel much different. I wasn't sure how much magic I had. What if I had almost none? Afraid to test the unbinding, I hadn't wanted to try harder spells or incantations. With classes starting on Tuesday, though, I would have little choice. I was sure I could not get through four years of magic school without performing any magic.

Priti picked a card from the pile, whispered an incantation, and a bowl of strawberries topped with whipped cream appeared in its place in her hand.

"Suit yourself. With these, I can have hot meals without a microwave." She held up a snack card of a cheeseburger.

Should I have faith that I could trust her and blurt out my secret? Or use the spell first to make sure I could trust her? If she ever found out I used the spell on her she might be upset. We would be together for four years. Studying together, learning from each other, laughing together. That was a long time to keep a secret.

My gut didn't lie. And my gut told me Priti was the real deal.

I pushed the food on my bed to the side and slumped onto the duvet. "Truth is I'm not sure I could turn those cards into actual food."

"What? Of course you can."

I shook my head. "Until a few days ago, I didn't even know magic was real. I didn't have any power. I might not have any now. Still. Mrs. Sapienti unbound my power, but I don't feel any different. I might flunk out of magic school by next week."

"Unbound it? Why was it bound?"

I pulled my legs up on the bed and crossed them, took a deep breath, and related the story of foster care, bound powers, and demon assassins.

Priti paced the floor, a worried expression on her face as she covered the distance from the door to the windows and back again. "We have to test it out. If you need any help with anything, tell me. I've grown up with magic. We'll get you where you should have been all along."

"Thanks." Relief coursed through me. No butterflies in my stomach. No unexpected heat rushing through me. No glow on that mark on my arm. My gut had been right.

"You're my roommate. And trust me, one day we're going to be best friends."

I'd never had a best friend before, but at the end of four years, we would either love or hate each other. It would be nice to have a best friend. Someone I could always talk to, confide in.

"I have no doubts." I smiled at her.

"Should we check our schedules?"

"Good idea."

She flopped down on her bed, tapped something on her tablet, and her class schedule appeared in the air above our beds. I pulled out my tablet and found my schedule, then hunted on the screen for something that said display. She came over to my bed and pointed at an icon of a computer screen on the main menu of my schedule. I hit the button and my schedule joined hers in the air.

"I thought all the classes for the first-year students were the same except for their electives," I said.

"They are, but there are so many freshmen that some of them are broken into two or three classes."

We scrolled through our courses, happy to learn we had lunch period together every day. And most of our classes were together too. Relief was becoming a regular thing for me lately.

"I should go to the library before Tuesday to get the textbooks for simple trickery," I said.

Priti nodded. "Congrats on getting that, by the way. Tess was fuming."

"I hope it really is simple." I took a bite of my apple. The tartness made my jaw clench, but I loved the explosion of flavor in my mouth.

"If you have trouble, I can help. Two of my sisters got that as their elective when they were here."

"So all of your family went here?"

She shook her head, then nodded. "Well, it's complicated. They all went to a school almost identical to this one but in India. I'm the first in my family to attend in Canada."

"What did they do after they graduated?"

That was something Damien hadn't been clear on when he found me. And the dean hadn't really elaborated on it either. We were supposed to protect the innocent.

Stop evil from taking over the world or something. But how well did that pay? Did it pay at all?

"They got good jobs in local companies that allowed them to hunt demons on the side. As well as the magic here, in our junior and senior years they teach us math, English, economics. And in the last two years, you can specialize in subjects that don't require huge amounts of study."

"So no doctors or dentists are demon hunters then?"

Priti smiled, but worry crept into her brown eyes. "Not many, no. It can be done, but it's hard to fight demons and go to medical school. Or law school."

"What's wrong?"

Priti shook her head and shrugged her shoulders. "I'm excited about being here. Don't get me wrong, but it's a little overwhelming."

"Tell me about it."

She chuckled then. "I'm sorry. It must be ten times worse for you. I have the perfect thing to help us."

She bounded off the bed and pulled open the mini-fridge door. She pulled out a small pot with a gold elastic around the neck. Tucked under the elastic was a small spoon. After she put the pot on the table between our beds, she rummaged in the cupboard beside the fridge and pulled out various shapes, sizes, and flavors of crackers.

"You have to try this pâté. The herbs my mother uses give me strength and always calm me down. She adds something special to it, but she refuses to tell me what."

She took the lid off the jar, handed me a small plate with crackers, and offered me the spoon. I sniffed and the aromas that teased my nose made my mouth water. Ginger and garlic. And something else that I couldn't quite put my finger on.

"I've never had pâté before."

"Does it sound snooty to you?"

I laughed. "Everything sounds snooty to me when it comes to unknown food."

"You'll like this. When I feel down or weak, this pâté is the food that heals everything."

I spread a thin layer of the dark pâté on a cracker, sniffed, then took a bite. I sighed at the flavors teasing my tongue. A sense of calm washed over me. Feeling rejuvenated, like I'd just had a solid eight hours of sleep, confidence bloomed.

"Wow. We're going to need more of this."

Chapter Seven

A nudge to my shoulder from the darkness promised to pull me out of the shadows. I brushed it aside and mumbled, "Five more minutes."

The insistent nudge stopped and I drifted back to the shadows. From the darkness, long, spindly fingers reached for me. They tore at my arms, grabbed me. I ran. The trees kept snagging me. Bark scraped against my cheek and the copper scent of blood filled the air. I ran faster, but the darkness was never-ending. The trees loomed taller, encroaching on me as I tried to escape.

I sat up in bed, heaving in breaths of air, my arms flailing to shake off the trees. As the dream faded, I shuddered.

I glanced at the clock and groaned. It was already 8:45 a.m.

I jumped out of bed and put on my uniform. Priti's bed was empty and expertly made. How had I slept through her getting up and ready for class? After sharing a bedroom for almost a week, becoming accustomed to each other's routines when school wasn't in session, her getting dressed, pulling out her books and backpack should have woken me up.

She'd left a message on the blackboard on the door.

A

Tried to wake you up, but you mumbled you wanted five more minutes. See you in defense class. Have a great first class!

P

Shit. Of all classes to be late for on the first day, why did it have to be Ethics? The one thing I needed to do right, arrive on time for class on my first day, and I blew it.

My stomach grumbled, but I didn't have time for breakfast. I grabbed an apple from the bowl on top of the mini-fridge. Priti had conjured the bowl before we'd gone to bed, so we had a place for our snacks. Nestled in with the apples and nectarines were the snack cards Priti had picked up. She said I could use them anytime, but I still didn't know how to make them real food.

I grabbed my tablet, my dagger, the spell book, my textbooks and hurried out the door. Why, in this digital age, they insisted on physical textbooks was beyond me.

I ran down the stairs and stopped in the lobby facing the front door, looking left and right, unsure which way to go. I turned left, saw the signs directing me to the pool, and groaned. I spent all weekend finding my classrooms and I was going in the wrong direction.

I spun around and raced down the hallway to Lecture Room B on the other side of the lobby, next to the dining hall.

I paused outside the classroom, took a deep breath, and pulled. A little too hard. The door banged as it hit the wall. Everyone turned to look at me. Heat rushed to my cheeks. I slipped inside and slid into a seat near the back, hoping I wouldn't be stuck there for the whole term. The teacher, Mrs. Bonum, whose name was written in beautiful script on the blackboard, glared at me.

Great, so much for staying under the radar.

Mrs. Bonum droned on and on about the ethical responsibility inherent in being a magical being. Great, I was not a person but a being? I wasn't sure how I liked that. It didn't occur to me that my humanness would be different now that I could do magic. Well, not that I could actually do magic. That remained to be seen. I definitely didn't count the friend or foe spell as successful.

Even though I'd arrived fifteen minutes late, the class turned out to be the longest I'd ever had. Did time move differently at the school once classes started? Could we manipulate time? So many questions and Ethics wasn't answering any of them. Defense class had to be better than this. At least Priti and Saad would be there.

The bell finally rang.

"Don't forget your homework! I want one thousand words on the ethics of changing a caterpillar into a butterfly, based on chapters one to five of your textbook."

Grumbles filled the room as students jotted down the instructions, then hurried out of the room.

At least the gym was close to the lecture room. I raced down the hall, my mind whirling with how I would come up with a thousand words on insect metamorphosis. Being new to magic, I got the feeling the paper was a trap. I needed to read the chapters first, then come up with a thesis.

I pushed through the double doors of the gym to see Saad and Priti were already there. Tess was also there talking to Hailey. Nathan lingered close by, seemingly not paying attention to anything, but he was listening to all the conversations around him. His ears twitched when Hailey said something. His eyes darted when Nia said something.

Damien stood in the middle of the room wearing black jeans and a loose T-shirt. On his feet, black sneakers with thick soles kept him from sliding all over the polished wood floor of the gym.

With fifteen minutes in between classes, the room was abuzz with chatter. Students talked about their first class. Almost everyone from my Ethics class was here. With so many first-year students, the rest would be taught by the other defense teacher.

When the bell rang to indicate the start of class, Damien raised his hands and called for us all to quiet down.

All eyes turned toward him and a hush fell over the room. The most physical of all the classes, most students hated defense class. I was looking forward to it. Being on the streets and then in foster care, I knew how to take care of myself, unless an unknown demon twice my size came charging at me at work.

"Welcome to your first defense class," Damien said. "You're going to learn how to protect yourself, and therefore others, from demons, vampires, werewolves, and other creatures that want to kill you or use you for their evil purpose."

Images from vampire movies flashed in my head. First demons were real and now vampires and werewolves were too. I didn't even want to think about the other creatures he'd mentioned.

My confidence plummeted. I glanced around the room at the nodding heads and the wide grins. Students were eager to learn how to stop evil. But had they ever had a demon attack them in real life? Did that happen to others, or just me?

"We'll be doing some hand-to-hand combat." Damien glanced around the room, his lips moving slightly as he counted the number of students.

"Demons appear in plain sight. What's the first thing you do when a demon is coming at you?"

I shuffled back slightly, behind Saad. Mouth dry, my heart palpitated. Visions of the demon from the coffee shop flashed through my head.

"Alex. What do you do?"

"Don't piss it off?"

Chuckles went through the room. Even Damien smiled at my answer. It was what he'd told me that night at the coffee shop. The only person not smiling was Tess. She raised a hand and gave me a hard glare.

Damien pointed at her. "Yes, Tess, you have a different answer?"

She lowered her hand. "Assess for weapons. External and internal."

"Correct."

Tess beamed a smile that almost blinded me. Then she narrowed her eyes at me like I was marked or something. It was definitely on. It was clear she would be the teacher's favorite if she always answered the questions correctly.

"Lucky guess," I said.

"Studying. You should try it sometime," Tess fired back.

"That's enough." Damien raised his hands in front of his face and steepled his fingers. "It's always important to assess your demon as quickly as possible to ascertain any hidden weapons. Some demons have claws. Some have spears that protrude out from the wrist. Know your demons. Ideally, you want to research before you fight."

A flash of razor-sharp claws from my demon filtered into my mind. There would be worse demons than that? What the hell did I sign up for? Not for the first time, I questioned my being there. I couldn't even fight that demon and save myself. How was I supposed to save the innocent?

"I'm going to divide you into groups so you can practice sparring with a demon."

My heart rate kicked up about a hundred notches. Sweat slicked my palms. Fear of hyperventilating forced me to take in deep breaths. I focused on what he was saying. A teacher wouldn't put students in danger. Not on the first day.

"*Medium apparent daemonium*," Damien said.

Gasps filled the room as half the students took on demonic form. Heart racing, I studied them. Even though they weren't real demons, they were still scary as hell. I glanced around the room and spotted Priti and Saad. At least I wouldn't have to spar with one of them. Tess wasn't there now, at least in human form.

All the feelings from my first encounter with a demon flooded me. Rooted to my spot, I watched as a "demon" charged toward me. I assessed for weapons but didn't see anything. Not like the claws the first one had. Those claws could have ripped me in two with one swipe. A shiver ran down my back. Eyes wide, I studied the "demon" as it hurtled closer to me. In theory, I knew I had to do something. But there were no tables here to hide behind. No counter to jump over. I couldn't use the dagger in my pocket. They may look like demons, but they were still students. The illusion wouldn't make them impervious to harm.

Suddenly Priti stood beside me. She stuck out her foot just as the "demon" got within my personal space. I sidestepped as the demon tumbled down, landing at my feet. The illusion faded, and Tess shot daggers at me with her eyes.

Nathan sauntered over, a grin on his face. "Nice technique. Good thing Priti was with you. What will you do when she's not? Who will save you then?"

Muscles in my arms quivered. Saad strolled over and smiled at me, then he turned to Nathan. "Alex can take care of herself."

"Sure she can." With Tess still glaring and dusting herself off, Nathan reached down a hand to help her.

Despite her fall, she rose with grace. "Priti won't be there the next time."

The threat hung in the air as Tess stalked away to join Hailey and Nia on the other side of the gym. They also looked like demons. Other students were helping fallen "demons" off the floor. Some students still danced back and forth, the spar a draw between "demon" and human.

"Get ready to switch, people! If you were a demon before you'll be a protector now."

Tess kept her gaze on me as Damien uttered the spell again. From my perspective, everything looked the same. My vision didn't change. I didn't feel any different. But hatred crept into Tess's eyes and she focused all of her attention on me. It was clear that if I didn't attack someone soon as a "demon" Tess would be coming after me. I scanned the room for a suitable sparring partner and charged toward a petite freshman with brunette hair, who looked bored out of her mind.

***

To kill time before our next class, spells and potions scheduled for two in the afternoon, we hung out in the lounge, the common area on the second floor. Not many sophomores lingered in the area. I guess most of them were in a class now. And the juniors and seniors had their own common area on the third floor.

I flopped into an oversized chair and put my feet up on the dark wood table nestled in front of a large sofa where Priti and Saad took seats.

My stomach grumbled. I pulled out an apple and bit into the green skin. It was a little too early for lunch, but the apple would tide me over until we went to the dining hall.

"What do you think so far?" Priti asked.

I felt like I was being interviewed for a news story. "I hope it gets easier."

"You'll get the hang of things. You are, after all, from a founding family."

I would never live that down if I didn't get with the program and perform magic perfectly. What kind of scandal would that be among the magical community? It wasn't my fault. If I'd known, if I'd had control of my magic, I would have been practicing.

"I hope it happens before we hit semi-finals. I'd like to move up with the rest of the class and not stay a freshman forever."

After much resting, my nerves relaxed. I didn't jump at the slightest sound. We hurried to the dining hall to have a quick lunch. There was no way I was going to be late for any more classes today.

Pleased to see the dining hall did not contain the Tess trio, I relaxed further, not scarfing down my meal. I took the time to enjoy all the flavors that mingled together to make the perfect macaroni and cheese dish. Sometimes you just needed comfort food.

After lunch, we raced to the second floor for spells and

potions. The idea of them intrigued me. My hand cramped several times while taking notes. I knew we had tablets, but for things to sink in, I needed that hand-to-brain connection. Later I would input my notes into the tablet where I would actually do my studying from.

As the teacher, Miss Carmina, talked about different spells, I wondered if there was one that would make Tess a better person. Probably not. It was magic, not a miracle.

The bell rang and the teacher shouted, "Don't forget to study the spells in chapter two!"

Arcane history was in the lecture room next to spells and potions. We sidled over, and Priti and I took seats in the middle of the class. Saad sat behind us.

I craned my neck around to see who else was in the class with us. Lunch had been bliss without Tess and her friends. But with a minute to spare before the start of class, Tess, Hailey, and Nia sauntered in. They moved down the aisle, looking from side to side at the students already seated. At the second row, Tess paused, fixed the guy sitting there with a withering stare, and lifted her chin in a dismissive nod.

He scrambled to get out, as did the two people beside him. Tess and her friends sat, shifting in the seats until they were comfortable.

I rolled my eyes and sighed. The evicted found seats at the back of the class.

The teacher, Mrs. Rúnda, a fortyish woman with long blond hair wearing a black pinstripe suit with a floor-length skirt instead of pants, stood at the front of the class and smiled. She looked more like a stockbroker than a teacher, but I didn't care as long as I learned about my family's history.

"Welcome to arcane history." Her voice was soft, but it carried to the back of the room. "We'll be starting with the

Salem witch trials to teach you why talking about magic outside the community is forbidden. The trials had less to do with actual witches than they did with fear. Very few real witches died during the trials, but a lot of innocent women, and a few men, did perish."

Everyone took out their tablets or notebooks. I was relieved to see I wasn't the only one going old-school for notes. Another freshman, the petite brunette from defense class, also used a notebook. Hers was bright red, spiral-bound, with a line on the front for her name and a line for subject. I retrieved my green one from my right front pocket and clicked my pen, ready to write.

"After that, we will be looking into magic before the trials and how it started. Ancient magic, medieval magic. We'll discuss how the founding families came together."

My stomach fluttered. I couldn't wait to learn about the founders. I knew almost nothing about my family. Even my parents were a bit of a mystery to me. They died when I was five. Snatches of memory of my mom making cakes, or my dad using empty boxes to build me castles in the living room were about all I had. Memories of my grandmother were even fewer. At least I'd had five years with my parents. I only had two with her. Now that I knew about Nathan's family dying because of me, it hit me that my grandmother also died because of me. Why else would she have been killed?

"Turn to chapter one in The Salem Witch Trials: A True Account."

The shuffle of paper being turned filled the room. Once everyone was ready, Mrs. Rúnda continued with her lesson. She droned on about the trials until I wanted to scream. In high school, we'd learned a little about that time in history, but not in the detail she was covering. My heart hurt for those women, most of them not even witches, who burned alive or drowned because the men in their community feared them. Feared the power they might have had had more enlightening thoughts prevailed.

By the end of the day, I was mentally exhausted. One day here felt like a week from high school. They said college was different, and no shit, this was different.

When the bell rang, everyone sat for a moment, waiting for the teacher to assign homework. She merely smiled and wished us a lovely evening.

At least I might finish homework before bedtime now.

"We're going back to our room to tackle homework before dinner," Priti said to Saad. "Wanna join?"

He glanced at me and I nodded. "Not tonight. I'll catch you at dinner. I'm going to check in with Conrad to see how his day's been."

Conrad, Saad's roommate, was new magic. Though they rarely paired old and new magic together, the school had acquiesced to Saad's request. Conrad and Saad lived on the same block, grew up best friends.

"Tell him to hang in there," I said.

Saad nodded and hurried off.

Back upstairs, I wanted to crash into my bed and sleep for a week. My brain hurt from all the information and now I was going to try to cram more in there before feeding my stomach. But I didn't want to fall behind already. I had no idea how much, if any, homework I'd get from the other two classes I hadn't even been to yet.

I let Priti go first, still wary of that alarm we'd set almost a week ago. She opened the door and stepped inside. I peered over her shoulder at the space. Nothing out of place. No hologram of a demon charging at us. I rushed in and dropped my book bag on the floor at the foot of my bed.

"What's that?" Priti asked. She stood beside my bed, pointing at something on the bedspread.

I shook my head. "There was nothing there when I left."

In the middle of the bed, there was an object that looked like a tarot card, except for the fact that it was thicker than a card. My best guess was two centimeters thick, but the same height as a card. A symbol took up most of the card, with the rest of the area empty space showing the grain of the wood the symbol was painted on.

"Do you recognize that symbol?" I asked.

Priti's brows drew together in thought, then she shook her head. "I haven't seen it before, I don't think. If I have, I don't remember it. It's demon-related, though, I can see that much based on the markings at the side."

I picked up the object, turning it over in my hands. There were markings on the side, nothing on the back, and that symbol on the front. I shook it, but nothing rattled. There were no visible means of opening it, if it was a box and not solid wood.

"How could a demon leave this for me?"

"They couldn't. There shouldn't be any demons on campus. There are wards and protections. Can you imagine if they were able to wipe us out before we had training? Who would be the protectors of the next generation?"

A shiver ran down my spine. It wasn't put on my bed for a prank. It was a message or a threat. No matter which one it was, neither of us had any answers. We needed someone else. Right now, Damien was the only adult I sort of trusted.

"We have time before dinner. We should take it to Professor O'Connor," I said.

"Agreed."

As we hurried to the gym, I hoped Damien would still be there. Who knew where he went after class when there was nothing else scheduled for his day? He could have gone back to his room. All the professors stayed on campus during the school year, living, eating, and socializing with the students. It made the bonds stronger and allowed for more time to teach.

We pushed through the gym doors, racing to the far side of the room, to the office door on the right side of the wall. It was slightly ajar. I peeked inside as I knocked. A flash of movement caught my eye.

"Come in." Damien's voice boomed.

Entering the room, I took in the bookcases lining the far wall, the large oak desk in the center. Damien sat in a high-backed leather chair behind the desk. Two smaller leather chairs sat in front of the desk for visitors.

Damien looked up, surprise lighting his face.

"I wasn't expecting student conferences so soon in the school year. Ladies, what can I do for you?"

We rushed in and sat in the chairs, me closer to the wall, Priti near the door. I placed the block of wood on his desk.

"I found that on my bed after classes today."

He picked it up and examined it, turning it over in his hands to look at each side of the block.

His brow wrinkled. "This is troubling."

Pain in my fingers alerted me to the fact I had been gripping the arm of the chair so hard my knuckles appeared white. I loosened my grip, took a deep breath, and pierced him with a questioning look. Surely it couldn't be that bad.

"Troubling why? It's probably just a joke now that I think about it."

"If it's a joke, it's a bad one." He turned the block

around so Priti and I could see the symbol. "This is the symbol for Malum, Omnis Mali, basically the source of all evil. If he's out to get you, you need to get up to speed fast. I never imagined he'd sent the demon in the shop."

Priti bit her lip. "The shop?"

"I'll tell you later." Great, now I would need to fill her in on things I didn't want anyone to know. It wasn't the end of the world being a foster kid. Or having a demon attack you, especially if you managed by some miracle to survive. But I liked to keep personal things personal.

"You're safe here." He put the block on his desk. "No demons can get into the school without the dean knowing. I'm going to keep this and look into it further."

With the meeting over, there wasn't much more to do but return to the room and spill my guts to Priti.

Back in our dorm, door firmly closed, wards checked again and a magical soundproofing erected by Priti, we sat on our beds facing each other. The space between the beds was like a deep, dark chasm. I shifted away from the edge, crossed my legs, and took a deep breath.

"I have to tell you things about me and I'm not sure how you'll take them."

Priti smiled, light shining in her rich brown eyes. "We all have things about ourselves we don't like. You're a good person. Nothing you tell me will change how I feel about you. We're going to be best friends, remember?"

I remembered. Having never had one, I didn't know what it would be like to lose one. But how would it feel to lose her before we even got to the BFF stage?

"I was in foster care because my parents died when I was five."

"We would have learned that in arcane history. It's not something you should be ashamed of."

"But is it in arcane history that I was in human foster care? Jumping to different ordpops households?"

Priti leaned back, eyes wide. "You grew up with no magic around you at all?"

I shook my head. "Not only that, but because my magic was bound it made me an easy target for the demon Damien was talking about. One found me at work last week and tried to kill me. Damien, Professor O'Connor, got rid of it."

Understanding shone in her eyes. "That's why you froze up today in defense class when Tess charged at you as a demon."

"Yes."

"Well, this changes everything." Priti got up and went to the trunk at the foot of her bed.

A sick feeling churned in my stomach. My mouth dry, I wished for the tallest glass of water I could find.

Priti pulled out book after book from her trunk. She handed a few to me and gathered the rest, dropping them on her mattress. She climbed back onto her bed and smiled. "You're an even stronger witch than I originally thought. I'm more certain now than ever that we'll be BFFs."

Relief washed over me. "What are all these?"

"This is all I have from the home library about demons. My mother thought I should take some with me to school in case the library was lacking."

"She thought a school library wouldn't have enough for you to learn, so she sent more books?"

Priti chuckled. "That's my mom. Always the over-achiever. It rubbed off a little on me."

She leaned over to the music box on the table between our beds. It had been there since I'd arrived, but I hadn't noticed it before. Delicately carved, with intricate lacing around the edge, it would fit into a large pocket. Priti lifted the lid and hauntingly beautiful Celtic music filled the room.

"It helps me concentrate," she said as she opened a book.

The music soothed me. Feelings of love and safety enveloped me. The smiling faces of my parents lifting me up for a hug, patting me on the head, and tucking me into bed filled my mind.

"I like it too."

We pored over the books for an hour and a half before we had to go to the dining hall for dinner. The little I learned about demons and Malum, in general, made my palms sweat. Hopefully, I wouldn't have more nightmares. Turns out I should have been afraid of the dark all these years. There was so much out there lurking, waiting, biding its time that I couldn't believe ordinary people didn't have a clue. How many unexplainable deaths, fires, explosions had been due to demon forces and not nature or man?

Chapter Eight

After waking up on time, having breakfast with Priti and Saad, going over our notes for class, I was on a triumphant high Wednesday morning. None of the information was sticking in my brain yet, but it was a matter of time. Magic was still new to me. I had to learn about whole new systems, a new language to be able to cast spells, a new way of life. It hit me that once college was over, I would be using my magic if I could tap into it all to help people. The world hadn't treated me all that great so far, but I didn't want to see anyone in it come to harm because I couldn't figure out a simple spell or couldn't defeat a demon.

The endorphins plummeted when I arrived at defense class. Nausea churned my stomach. The delicious breakfast I'd had of fluffy pancakes and real maple syrup now felt like lead with a sickeningly sweet topping.

If it was a quiz again, I was doomed. Everyone else had a lifetime of knowing demons existed. Probably even the fundamentals about how to defeat them. I was catching up. Give me a person to fight and I was fine. Usually better than fine. Give me a huge demon and I'd freeze up again. Hopefully, that would fade, but I didn't see that happening today.

Damien stood in the middle of the gym, counting as students piled into the space. When everyone had arrived, he greeted us all, then dove right into the lesson.

"What do you do when you encounter a demon out there?" He nodded his head to the right. "In the real world?"

Hailey popped her hand in the air. Damien nodded in her direction and she smiled. "You fight it."

"Ah, but fight it how?"

Jenny, the petite brunette from yesterday, rose her hand. "A spell?"

Damien frowned and the student's face turned bright red. Seemed a reasonable answer considering we were in magic school, but things were not always as simple as they appeared.

"You can't let the real world know there's magic and demons. There's a reason even the demons use glamours or possess people. Only witches and other magical beings can see through that façade. Again, how do you fight it?"

Most of us shook our heads. But my fingers tingled, anticipating his revelation.

"Hand-to-hand combat. But demons tend to fight dirty. This is one of the reasons why first-year students aren't allowed to leave campus grounds alone their freshman year."

Hope grew. If this was going to be a plain hand-to-hand lesson I might not freeze up. At school and on the streets the bullies stopped picking on me when they realized I could fight back. I looked around the gym. There were no weapons on the walls. The hardwood floor was highly polished, without the usual markings for basketball.

At least that meant possibly no team sport classes. Against the wall on the left, hand and foot holes provided a climbing wall for us that I assumed would come in handy at some point. There was the dreaded rope to climb near the back corner on the left side, away from his office.

"You need to keep up with your physical training. I'm dividing you into pairs. No glamours this time. See how well you do one-on-one. No magic."

I almost rubbed my hands together but stopped, not wanting to appear overly eager. They already thought I couldn't fight because of yesterday. And I wasn't the only one. A sudden acrid stench of fear wafted through the room. I wish I knew who else was worried about hand-to-hand, but maybe it was all of us.

My first "opponent" was Faith. A little taller than me, she also had about twenty pounds more muscle than I did. All the other groups of two charged each other. She waited, sizing me up. It was a good move. As with fighting a demon, you needed to take in your opponent, determine if they might be concealing any weapons.

Finally, Faith surged forward. I kept my breathing under control, sidestepped her, then spun around, waiting for her next charge. Blinded by the goal of getting me down on the floor, she was ruled by adrenaline. As she charged forward again, I bent down, then pushed up with my legs, making sure my shoulder made contact with her chest.

Before she landed on the floor, an inflatable rubber mattress appeared to break her fall. I turned to see Damien pointing at the floor, a smile on his face. He gave me an encouraging nod.

One after the other, I felled all of my opponents. And then Tess stood in front of me. The grin on her face sent a chill down my spine. Perfect makeup, still perfect hair told me she'd most likely won most or all of her hand-to-hand tests.

We circled each other. I shoved all the noise and activity going on around us out of my mind and focused on Tess. She moved her lips and flicked her wrist. A small light flash to my left drew my attention for a second. It threw me off long enough to give Tess an opening. She hurtled forward and I met the floor with enough force to knock the wind out of me.

Tess looked down at me, and I was suddenly thankful there were no weapons around. "You're not all that tough now, are you?"

"Ms. Monroe, were you on time for class?"

Tess's face turned bright red. She spun around to look at Damien, Professor O'Connor, without even extending a hand to help me up. Nathan offered a hand, having been a few feet away with his sparring partner. Saad also appeared at my side seemingly from nowhere and offered his hand. I grabbed Saad's outstretched hand, his fingers circling around mine tightly.

"Yes." Tess's voice was soft, low. Anyone farther away than a few feet wouldn't have heard her.

"Then you heard my stipulation that no magic was to be used during these hand-to-hand sparring matches?"

She stood straighter, but her voice was still low when she said, "Yes."

Damien pointed to the rope at the end of the gym. "Punishment for disobeying is a climb up the rope."

When everyone turned toward the rope, some marching in that direction, Damien whistled, using two fingers in his mouth to emit a high-pitched noise I swear could rupture eardrums.

Everyone stopped, including Tess, and looked at Damien.

"Just Tess. Everyone else, you still have sparring matches."

Nathan nudged my shoulder. "She had to use magic to beat you. You're fucking awesome at fighting."

The unexpected compliment caused my heart to flutter and my stomach to flip. Heat rose to my face. I hated being the center of attention and now everyone was looking at me and nodding in agreement.

"I had to learn early in life."

I left my comment in the air, wondering if he would ask what I meant. Priti gave me a knowing look. It was worse in foster care. On the streets, almost everyone was out for themselves. My foster family was supposed to look after me, keep me safe. What a joke that was.

"Hot girls who know how to fight is a huge turn-on." He leered at me.

I rolled my eyes and inched away from him.

Saad nodded. "Though crude, you know he's right."

"Shut up." I punched him in the arm. "I'm sure a sweaty, scrawny girl is so sexy."

Damien pointed at Nathan. "You think it's so sexy. I'm pairing you with Alex for the next sparring round."

Nathan grinned at me, jumping up and down while at the same time bobbing his head from side to side. "Bring it."

The whole class stopped what they were doing, even Tess, who was halfway up the rope by now, to watch Nathan and me circle each other. I pictured the guy that loitered in the alley near the soup kitchen. On several occasions when he was particularly drunk, he would accost anyone walking by asking for money. Sometimes more if it was a pretty woman. Both times he'd tried with me, I'd incapacitated him easily.

I focused on Nathan. Every movement of every

muscle. Every twitch. When he lurched forward, I knew he was coming before he did. I held up a hand and hit him hard in the chest. The air whooshed out of him. Before he could gain his equilibrium back, I grabbed his arm, turned my back to him, and hoisted him over my shoulder. I went down with him, straddling him, pinning him to the floor.

He grinned up at me and winked.

Narrowing my eyes, I got to my feet again. Jaw clenched until it hurt, I forced myself to loosen the muscles. I tapped my foot. The air around me warmed and I sucked in deep breaths.

"You didn't even try."

Nathan got off the floor and shrugged. "Maybe you're just that good. Wanna go again?"

Damien's eyes were dark with anger. "What if she were a demon? Some of them can take multiple forms. I can include this sparring match as fifty percent of your grade if you'd like. Would that make you take it seriously?"

Nathan held up his hands in a placating gesture. "I was just messing around, dude. Relax. I'll try this time."

Damien took a step forward, his eyes glittering with annoyance. "That is Professor O'Connor to you."

Nathan's cheeks blossomed with red patches. "Sorry."

The second time, he moved a little faster. Dodged when he should dodge. He threw some right hooks that almost connected. A sweep of the leg caught me slightly by surprise, yet I anticipated his every move. Then when he thought he had me, I gave him a left hook and a right hook. While he was shaking that off, I swept my leg, catching his left calf. He tumbled to the ground that was suddenly covered in rubber air mattresses.

Damien smiled down at him. "Better. But it still needs work."

"Your face might freeze like that," Saad said as we left defense class.

Priti rushed past us to get to the observatory in the west tower. "See you at lunch," she hollered as she darted around ambling students.

The grin on my face was starting to hurt my cheeks, but I couldn't help it. "That was the best!"

Nathan mumbled, "Good match," when he walked by.

Tess glared at me, gently blowing on the blisters forming on her red palms. It had taken her the rest of class to reach the top of the rope. Hailey and Nia followed behind her but didn't throw a glance in my direction.

"You did have a good class." A grin appeared on Saad's face.

"I hope simple trickery is good."

The more I thought about the class, the more my stomach clenched. It was the first class where I might have to use magic. And I didn't think I could yet, not without having practiced a little first. I had no idea what we'd be doing first. If it was a quiz like the first class in defense, I was doomed.

We hurried along the corridor from the gym to Lecture Room C on the first floor. Keeping Priti's suggestion for seating in mind, I slipped into a row in the middle of the classroom. Saad took the seat beside me this time since Priti was in another class.

I opened my notebook and put it on the desk in front of me. I grabbed two pens from my backpack in case one of them dried up. Then I found the textbook for the class and positioned it beside my notebook. I took a deep breath and waited for the rest of the students and the teacher to enter.

"Relax. I've heard this class is great. Always the most sought after by freshmen."

Tess's withering look when I picked the class came back to me. I was sure she'd find a way to make me regret getting a spot here and her being shut out of the class.

The scraping of chairs on the hardwood floor, jostle of bags, and the chatter of students calmed me. Except for the magic, this was school. Just school. I was good at school. With the teacher's help, I would pass this class and all of my classes.

A shock of fluorescent pink caught my eye. It scurried to the front of the class, pausing in front of the chalkboard where Professor Wilton now appeared in perfect script.

The tall woman with pink hair, pink blouse, pink pants gave way to a shorter woman with brown hair, brown eyes wearing a peasant blouse and a long, flowing skirt.

"Good morning, class, and welcome to simple trickery. As the name implies, we are going to learn some simple tricks to help in your fight against evil. We will be covering lessons on glamours. Appearance shifting, which is necessary to hide behind sometimes in order to protect yourselves and others from demons."

I took another deep breath and focused on everything the teacher was saying. If I could do what she just did, I would be thrilled. It would have helped a lot in the foster home.

"In defense class, you dealt with glamours of some demons to help you fight. In this class, you're going to learn how to cast a glamour on yourselves and eventually outward onto other people or objects."

Now I was intrigued. Casting glamours on myself was one thing. But how could I cast one on someone else? Or even something else? That too could come in handy in the big wide world once I had to start fighting the demons.

Suddenly I didn't want that time to come. What if after four years here I still wasn't ready? My mistakes could get people killed. The worst mistake I ever made at work never hurt anyone. It left them with a caramel latte instead of a vanilla latte.

I wrote out everything the teacher said, suddenly wishing I'd thought to bring a recording device instead. My tablet had such an app, I was sure, but I hadn't used it yet. I wasn't even sure we could record these lessons. What if someone got a hold of the recordings when we left school? I wouldn't be staying there over the summer. At least I didn't think so. Damien said we'd discuss it later, but I was pretty sure the school wouldn't let students hang around when school wasn't in session for three months.

The teacher paced back and forth at the front of the room as she spoke. "You shouldn't rely on glamours of course, but they can get you out of a tight spot. Watch carefully."

Every eye in class focused their full attention on the professor.

"Damien *simulantior*." As soon as the words were out of her mouth, her appearance changed and she looked like Damien. Even down to what he had been wearing earlier in defense class.

There were oohs and aahs from the students. I wanted to see it again. It couldn't be that easy, could it?

Thankfully, someone behind me, Jenny, shot her hand in the air.

Professor Wilton consulted her class list and smiled. "Yes, Jenny. You had a question."

"Can you say anyone's name? Like could I make myself look like a box office darling?"

Professor Wilton smiled and shook her head. "Ideally, you should use someone you know well. In a pinch, you can use someone you've just met or an acquaintance you haven't seen in a while. Those are the ones easier to hold. You might be able to pull off a celebrity after you've been practicing for a while. But for obvious reasons, you shouldn't."

"Obvious reasons?" Jenny asked.

"The world cannot know magic is real. How would you explain the celebrity being in two places at once? It would draw too much attention. You need to keep things low profile. And remember these glamours should be used sparingly. Only when needed to get you out of a bind."

Another hand went up, this time in a row toward the front of the class.

"Yes, Ian."

"How long can you keep the glamour in place?"

"If you get really good at it, you can hold it for hours. Usually, you won't need to hold it for more than a few minutes. Now, everyone, think of someone close to you. Someone you know very well. Picture them in your mind and say the phrase."

"Do you want to go first?" Saad said as the rest of the class mumbled names along with the word to impersonate someone.

Before my eyes, everyone in the class changed to someone else. Worry frothed in my stomach. I bit my bottom lip. What if I couldn't do it? I shook my head.

"You can go first. Show me how it's done."

Saad nodded. "Conrad *simulantior*."

When he finished saying the phrase, his face changed, followed by everything else about him. No longer was he a tall, light brown guy with black hair and brown eyes. In front of me, he smiled, with a twinkle in his hazel eyes. With dark red hair cut shorter at the back and a little fuller on top, he also had a sprinkling of dark freckles across his nose. Based on where my gaze landed now that he was someone else, this person was also a little taller than Saad.

"Whoa. That's amazing. That's what your roommate looks like?"

"Yes, why?"

It was still Saad's voice. The whole thing was throwing me off now. I couldn't reconcile Saad's voice coming from that face.

"No reason, really. Did you know your roommate is hot?"

His roommate's face frowned at me. The professor hadn't told us the incantation to stop the glamour, but it didn't matter. No one in the class could hold one that long yet, so everyone, including Saad, switched back to normal.

"Never mind that. You try."

I took a deep breath, picturing Lacey in my head. In her work uniform, smiling at a customer. "Lacey *simulantior*."

Saad smiled, then frowned.

"What? What's wrong?"

"You switched for a few seconds, then it went back to you."

"Shit. I'll never get the hang of this."

"You're being too hard on yourself. Sometimes it takes longer for others to get it. You just need to practice."

Practice being someone I wasn't. I'd been doing that my whole life. Being what I thought would get other people to like me or leave me alone, depending on my mood. But now I wanted to fit in, to be able to get this stuff quicker. Partly because being different here would be bad for me. It meant I was closer to normal than this school probably liked. And definitely more normal than the bullies of the school were willing to put up with. It still surprised me that a school of magic had bullies, but Tess was proof.

"Let me try again." I rolled my shoulders, loosened my neck, and closed my eyes. I brought more images of Lacey into my mind this time. Cleaning the coffee pots, making the biscuits. Wiping down the tables. Even images from her apartment when I'd stayed there the night before coming to Hell's Watch.

"Lacey *simulantior*."

"Well?" I asked.

A smile appeared on Saad's face and it didn't turn into a frown right away. "Better. You held it for a little while longer. Still under thirty seconds, though."

"I'll just keep practicing every chance I get."

"That's going to confuse Priti." Saad laughed.

I laughed along with him. It would throw her off if I didn't explain what I was doing.

The hour flew by. Professor Wilton demonstrated again after seeing how good or bad we did with our own glamours. She provided tips on how to hold them longer. Thinking about someone close to us worked for most. I didn't have anyone that I was really close to. I could barely remember what my parents looked like, let alone my grandmother. Lacey was the closest thing I had to a friend, but she was no more than an acquaintance.

The teacher also went over more of the lesson, providing a history of glamours and what they'd been used for. She outlined what else we'd be learning in class. Simple trickery wasn't only about glamours, but also other spells and potions we could use to help us fight and, in some cases, vanquish demons.

When the bell rang to indicate the end of class, I was more than ready to hit the dining hall. My stomach grumbled. I would need something to help me stay awake and alert in arcane history class that afternoon.

Saad and I walked to the dining hall. He pulled open

the heavy wooden door and waited for me to step through. I smiled my thanks.

Halfway to what I considered our table, I spotted Nathan. I smothered a groan. I didn't want to deal with him right now. I still didn't know how to take him. Seriously? With a grain of salt? Was he harmless? He got under my skin and I didn't want to chat with him, especially after defense class.

I mumbled the phrase under my breath as we approached him, hoping he hadn't seen me come in. Saad smiled beside me and kept talking, not missing a beat.

"So who is that?" he asked.

Nathan looked around us, confused. Maybe he had seen us come in. He frowned and went back to pushing his food around on his plate.

Once we'd made it past Nathan, I said, "My co-worker from Toronto."

By the time we got to the table, the glamour had faded, but it had done what I needed it to do. If I could get it to last for more than a few seconds, it could be a great tool.

We sat down to dirty looks from Tess, Hailey, and Nia, who were already at their table. Too bad theirs and ours were so close together. Well, Tess's look was dirty. The others were lackluster. Like they didn't care one way or the other if Tess hated me or not.

Priti bounced into the dining hall and slipped in on the opposite side of the table, blocking my view of Tess.

"How did your class go?" she asked. "Mine was fabulous! Did you know *when* you do certain spells can affect how well they turn out?"

"Did not know that," Saad admitted.

"We learned how to do glamours. Well, Saad did. Mine didn't stick very well. I'm going to need a lot of practice."

"I'll help you," Priti promised.

"Great. And I can show you how to do them too. If you teach us when the right time to do them is."

We agreed on study times over the weekend. With Priti's and Saad's help, I could get through these classes. There was just one more new class and then I would know what the rest of my year was going to be like. We finished our lunch and then headed to arcane history. This time I'd brought a large coffee with me. The professor droned on and on again about the Salem witch trials. While important to know, I wanted to learn about my family. Priti saw my irritation.

"They'll get to your family."

When? Senior year? I didn't want to wait that long to find out what my parents had been keeping from me my whole life.

Chapter Nine

Sunny September slid into crisp October. Chatter abounded about Thanksgiving and Halloween. Most students were heading home for the first holiday but staying on campus for the second. Though the school was a castle, the place was kept at an optimum temperature, so if you didn't glance out a window to see the bright red, yellow, and orange leaves on the trees you wouldn't know what time of year it was. If you were a freshman at least. For us, all classes were held in the main building. Even swimming practice. I was as surprised as anyone when I joined the swim team the second week of school.

Students from the sophomore, junior, and senior classes frequently had classes at some of the outbuildings that surrounded the main castle. I saw them lately bundled with sweaters in the dining hall at breakfast.

Standing in defense class, waiting for it to start, I glanced around the room. Though more confident in defense class, I was still a little wary. Most of the time we practiced hand-to-hand. Everyone tried to beat me, but so far no one could. We'd also practiced archery and used various weapons. Not a whole lot of magic, which I was thankful for. I still couldn't access most of mine, though I'd been able to tap into enough to get by so far. I didn't know how long that would last.

"What do you think he'll have us do for semi-finals next month?" Priti asked.

I shrugged. The last thing I wanted to think about was tests. "No idea, but I know I'll need a lot of help if I want to pass."

Damien pushed through the gym doors two minutes late. He looked flustered, agitated. His eyes darted around the room in a quick head count. He offered no apology for his tardiness, just jumped in.

"Today you're going to work in pairs. I want to see how well you work with others. And you'll be working with strength in the hand-to-hand, and cunning by using some magic."

He hurried over to his office and returned with a bag that sagged low to the ground. Dropping the bag on the floor in the center of the gym, he reached in and pulled out a poppet. A little doll-like thing that appeared to have been made out of clay.

"This is what you'll be fighting."

Chuckles went around the room.

"Don't let looks deceive you. This little guy will look and act very dangerous with a little magic."

Dangerous yes, but they hadn't done anything yet that had hurt anyone. The teachers were careful with the magic used in class to make sure we all got away unscathed. Except for Jenny, who added too much kick to a potion and burned off her eyebrows and eyelashes.

"Pair up. If you don't have a partner, I'll partner with you."

Priti looked at me and I nodded. Saad was already pairing up with Ian.

Damien went around the room and placed a poppet at the feet of each pair of students. He walked back to his spot in the center of the gym, mumbling something in Latin. When he turned and waved his hands in the air, completing his incantation, a hiss filled the room.

A rumbling on the floor made my heart beat faster. All around me, the poppets grew, their shapes changing. Where once they appeared small and cute, now they were tall, lean, muscular demons with hatred in their eyes, claws for fingers, and demonic grins.

I gasped, as did almost every other student there. "I'll handle the magic if you do the hand-to-hand," Priti said.

I nodded, though hand-to-hand with a demon hadn't gone well the first time, or when they were just glamours. *It's not real.* I repeated that mantra in my head as I circled the thing, formulating some kind of plan. The "demon" had at least a foot on me, probably more. Around the room, similar demons waited to be defeated.

Would it move first, or did I have to initiate something?

Finally, the "demon" moved forward. Looked like there was a two-minute limit before indecision bit me in the ass. It lunged for me and I dove to the side. Priti stood behind it, saying something I couldn't hear. No doubt trying to come up with a spell or remember a spell to stop it or turn it back to a harmless piece of clay.

It swiped at me and I jumped back. Getting close enough to punch it wasn't an option. Even if I could punch it, would it do any good? It looked like it was pure muscle. I opted for luring it away again, diving to the side and sweeping a leg under it.

It swung around, pissed. Visions from that night in the coffee shop flooded my brain. Rooted to my spot, I stared as the creature's nostrils flared, arm muscles bunched and the claws growing inches longer. Now it could be farther away from me and still pierce me with a sharp talon. Cold seeped through my body. My tattoo tingled, glowed. I put up my hands to cover my face as the demon swung. An invisible force pushed it back, tumbling it onto the floor.

Priti jumped out of the way so she wasn't taken down like a lone bowling pin. I raised my eyebrows at her, thinking she'd remembered a spell. She shook her head and shrugged her shoulders.

The demon sprang off the floor again. It lunged and Priti put out a hand, uttering phrase after phrase. Her face contorted as if in pain. Her arm trembled with the effort to hold the demon back.

Out of the corner of my eye, I spotted Damien threading his way through the teams, evaluating their progress. After he consulted with them, their poppets turned back to clay.

Finally, he stopped beside me. Beads of sweat popped out on Priti's forehead. The demon attempted to walk but went nowhere, appearing to be on an invisible treadmill.

Damien said, "*Lutum facti*," and the creature became a piece of clay again.

My heart rate slowed. My fingers no longer tingled and the heat that had been surrounding me faded. If there had been breakables around, the gym floor would have been littered with glass. I felt as helpless as I had the night Damien stopped the demon from attacking me.

"How do you think you did?" he asked.

Priti, standing beside me, wiped her arm across her forehead. "I think we held our own."

"From one perspective, I'd agree, but it's still a fail."

"A fail? Why?" I clenched my jaw, and heat rose to my face. "That's not fair."

"I agree. It's not fair that Priti did most of the work and all the magic."

"I did some magic. I pushed it away."

Damien leaned closer so only I could hear him. "That was a fear response and not active magic. You weren't trying to do magic. It was the same response at the coffee shop. You have to get better at confronting the demons head-on, Alex. This will be your purpose in life when you leave here."

"I'm so sorry, Priti," I said.

Damien walked off to evaluate another team.

Guilt turned my insides into knots. My lack of knowledge was going to drag down Priti's grade. I couldn't let that happen. She was an excellent student, but if she kept pairing up with me, she would fail the class. A racing heart brought a wave of dizziness. If I had to partner with someone else, anyone other than Saad, I would be doomed. No one else would understand why I couldn't do the things all the other students could do already.

"It's okay. We'll work on it later. You'll get the hang of it."

Full after a scrumptious dinner of roasted chicken and vegetables, Saad, Priti, and I headed to the gym for more hand-to-hand combat training. I was going to help them with the physical side, and they were going to help me with magic. So far, a lot of spells and potions hadn't been necessary for any of my classes, except the glamours in simple trickery and a few other simple incantations, but that would change soon. Semi-finals would start next month and I had a stone in the pit of my stomach when I thought about how those would play out.

We pushed through the doors of the gym to find it dark. All the lights were off except for the set of track lighting outside the door of Damien's office.

Saad raised a hand and said, "*Luminaria...*"

"Wait," I whispered.

"What's wrong?" Priti asked.

"Someone's here."

I crept over to the back wall near the rope. They followed me without being asked. Then I inched my way along the wall closer to Damien's office. As I did, the voices I thought I'd heard got louder.

"I know I need to flush out the demon," Damien said. "But it's not that simple. The demon likes a certain type of female and a glamour might not work on him."

"He's a higher-level demon, yes. But figure something out," the dean said.

Intrigued, I moved closer. The sound of a chair scraping along the floor forced us to freeze. I glanced around in a panic. There was nowhere to hide in the gym. And not enough time to exit even if we ran to the door.

"Stay still and put your back to the wall," Saad said.

Priti and I complied. My heart raced. We weren't doing anything wrong being in the gym in the evening to get in a little extra training. But it felt wrong now that we'd overheard the dean's conversation with Damien. What demon did he have to stop? How dangerous was it?

Saad said, "Walls *simulantior*." And he swept his arm across all three of us. He squeezed his eyes shut, whispering the words over and over again.

A few seconds later, the dean marched out of Damien's office. Inside the office, the sound of drawers being opened, the jangle of keys, and the flick of the light switch indicated Damien was leaving.

I squeezed my eyes shut, remained still, pressing my

back to the wall harder, willing him to not see us. He closed his office door, locked it, and strode across the gym to the door. When he was out of the gym, we all took deep breaths.

"That was amazing, Saad. Did you really make us look like the wall?" I asked.

"That was the intent. Must have worked. Either that or he was so focused on leaving, he didn't even glance back."

"We should follow him," I said.

Priti's eyebrows rose. "Why?"

"What if he needs help?" I couldn't help focusing on the fact that a glamour might not work for him. If the demon figured out he wasn't who he said he was, how much danger would Damien be in? He'd helped me at the coffee shop. I had to help him if I could.

We followed him as far as the parking area on the left side of the castle, beyond the outbuildings. He clicked the fob on his key chain and a car's lights flashed. I remembered that car but didn't know how it got there. He'd left it at Union Station and boarded the bus with me and the others two months ago. He must have gone back at some point to pick it up.

If he needed the car he wasn't going anywhere close to the school. In Niagara Falls that meant he was probably going to the Strip. Around Clifton Hill. I'd been there once with my parents before they died, but I didn't remember anything about it.

Priti grabbed my arm before I could follow Damien to his car. "He's leaving campus."

"Yes. And he might need help."

"He won't let us go with him," Saad said.

"True." But that wasn't going to stop me.

"Can you do something to cause a distraction while I get into his car?"

Saad and Priti looked at each other, pained expressions on their faces. They didn't understand the debt I had to him. Well, Priti knew, but she didn't understand. She wasn't there when the demon attacked me.

"Okay, but you'd better hurry. And for the record, I think this is a bad idea." Saad rubbed a hand down his face.

Saad and Priti made their way through the cars, talking loudly, drawing Damien's attention away from his car. I thought they would use magic, but I didn't care as long as it worked.

I noticed Saad flick his wrist and the sky lit up like there were fireworks without the sound. Everything he did made me realize how far behind I was with my own magic. I would never pass semi-finals unless I improved. Priti, also way ahead of me, was teaching me things, but they never worked as expected when I tried.

With Damien striding over to Saad and Priti, I beelined to his car and quietly climbed into the back seat. I hunkered down as low as I could, thankful that I was wearing dark colors.

Footsteps, boots scraping against pavement had me holding my breath. If he looked into the back seat before getting in the car, I would be in trouble. But he didn't look. The door creaked open and he pulled it shut. The engine hummed to life and the car lurched forward.

I remained quiet, not wanting to reveal myself until it was too late for him to take me back to the school. The vehicle passed through the magical barrier that hid the school. The sky looked the same. Noises from other cars drowned out any shuffling noises I made as I moved to relieve pressure on my hip.

As we drove closer to the heart of Niagara Falls, the lights got brighter. The noises louder. I sat up a little, peering out the window to see pedestrians walking along the sidewalks. I couldn't hear the roar of the falls yet, but if we got any closer, the sound and mist would drift over us.

The car pulled to a stop.

The driver's side door slammed when Damien got out. I stumbled out of the back seat and found myself in a hotel parking lot between a steak house and a haunted house attraction. Someone opened the door to the restaurant and the scent of grilled steak wafted through the air, making my stomach grumble.

"Wait," I said.

Damien stiffened and turned around. Eyes bulged, staring back at me.

"What are you doing here?" He glanced around as if to make sure no one he knew had spotted him.

"I'm here to help."

He took my arm, frowned, let me go, and pointed angrily to a spot near the hotel's entrance. He stalked over without looking back to see if I followed him.

I hurried to catch up. "What's wrong?"

"You are breaking so many school rules right now."

"I know, but we overheard you might need help with a demon."

Lips flattened, face red, he took a deep breath. "You and your friends were eavesdropping in my office?"

"Not on purpose. We went to train. Saad and Priti wanted help with hand-to-hand and I needed help with magic. We didn't know anyone was still there, but then we heard you talking to the dean."

I filled him in on the rest of what we heard and how we remained undetected when he and the dean left the office.

"Saad should get good marks for simple trickery."

"I'm already here. Let me help."

"Every demon will know you. You can't stay looking like that." He waved in my general direction.

"Like what?"

"Like you. That block left on your bed was from one of Malum's followers. We don't know how it got there, but he will have every demon in Niagara Falls looking for you."

"Then I won't look like me." I walked into the shadows of the hotel between the lobby and the first-floor rooms. "Tess *simulantior*."

I took a deep breath and came out of the shadows.

"Fine, you look like someone else, and that will have to do for now. I don't have time to ferry you back to school and return here in time."

"In time for what?"

"The demon I'm looking for is attempting to taint a person before he can choose good or evil. He doesn't know he has magical abilities and when he finds out, things could go either way."

"Just like me?"

Damien shrugged. "A little like you. He's also an orphan, but his parents weren't killed by demons to get to him."

"How is this demon going to taint him?"

"Mammon is a bookie in his civilian 'life' and he's trying to get Cole to throw a game. It's the first step to choosing wrong over right. And after that first step, the rest get easier."

"Until he's completely bad?"

"Something like that. I want to stop the demon before he can do that."

"What do I have to do?"

"Well, you are his type, especially looking like Tess. He hangs out in The Haunted House. I need to get him out of there and to the park." He nodded across the street.

Across the street and to the left was a splash of red, yellow, and orange from a park. Fallen leaves littered the ground, crunching underfoot as the few people milling about walked along the path. October, though warm during the day this year, was cooler at night, keeping most people away. The prime time for tourists was the summer months. In October, not many ventured to The Falls unless they were devout gamblers.

"How do I do that?"

"I don't even want to go there." Damien grimaced. "Tell him something that will get him there. I'll take care of the rest. He's meeting Cole in thirty minutes. We have to take that meeting instead."

No pressure. How the fuck was I going to tempt a demon away from a meeting with someone he wanted to corrupt? What if I offered to be corrupted?

"Okay, I think I've got it. What does the demon look like?"

So close to Halloween, the demon could walk around looking all evil and no one would bat an eye. A shiver went down my spine at the thought of confronting him on purpose. But if it was to help Damien, to help another person, I had no choice. After all, this was what they were training us for at Hell's Watch. Nothing like field experience.

Damien nodded at a man about six feet tall, wearing jeans and a T-shirt with a cat meme on it. "That's him."

"The demon?" The guy looked completely normal. No claws that I could see. A little scruff on his jaw. Brown shaggy hair that needed a trim.

Damien nodded.

"But..."

"He doesn't look like a demon?"

"Yes."

"They don't always appear demonic. Demons have magic too. And sometimes they possess people instead of showing their true visage to the world. Right now, our demon is possessing a ticket taker."

Great, that wasn't something they'd gotten to yet in demonology class. When were they going to spring that little surprise on us? So far, all the "demons" we'd been fighting in defense class looked like demons. Down to the cloven hoofs, horns, claws.

If the guy was being possessed, wouldn't hurting the demon hurt the guy?

"Okay, I've got this," I said with more confidence than I felt.

Damien inched back into the shadows and I turned the corner and walked into The Haunted House.

My mark was standing in the lobby of the place, looking around for Cole. Too bad I couldn't glamour into him, but I hadn't ever seen him before. And it was hard enough keeping the Tess glamour going.

I smiled at the demon and boldly walked over to him. "You look like you're waiting for someone."

Startled, he flashed black eyes at me briefly but quickly changed back to the guy's normal brown eyes. "I am."

"I'm here."

"You're not who I was waiting for."

I leaned in closer to him. Close enough to smell the guy's aftershave. "How do you know until you try me?" I whispered.

Lust flashed in his eyes. "What did you have in mind?"

"Follow me and I'll show you."

I walked away from him, swaying my hips in an exaggerated motion I'd seen women do when trying to attract a man. I'd never wanted or needed to attract a man before. It's not that I didn't like them. They were fine, but I had other things on my mind like getting out of that foster home.

With Tess's looks, I hoped the demon wouldn't be able to resist. Despite her nature, Tess was the prettiest girl in Hell's Watch.

I heard the guy growl, then the sound of footsteps fell in behind me. I grinned.

Thankfully, the night was chilly and the sidewalks were empty. I quickened my pace, eager to get the whole thing over with and get back to the safety of the school. Now that I had a demon following me, one I enticed, I was rethinking tagging along with Damien. Despite his insistence that he might not be able to lure the demon on his own, he would have thought of something.

"You smell great," the demon said, as he fell into step beside me.

"Thanks, I try."

"Smells like fear."

I paused, giving him what I hoped was a disappointed look. "That's disappointing. I'll return this perfume and try one with more pheromones."

I sashayed my hips as I dashed across the street in front of the park. Hooking a finger, I gestured for him to come over.

Yellow pylons with flat tops blocked most of the entrance. Red lettering along the side indicated there was danger beyond. On the other side of the park along Falls Avenue, there were more yellow pylons. As we walked into the park, I touched one of the pylons with my foot. Solid, not illusion.

I turned so I was facing him, backing up with a seductive smile on my face. Wiggling my hips, I used both hands to lure him closer. The demon's lips curled into a lascivious grin that made my skin crawl.

Movement from the shadows drew my attention, giving me Damien's location, and I inched closer to him. Before the demon could attack me, Damien emerged from the darkness, uttering something in Latin. The demon gagged, growled. Suddenly, black eyes glared at me. The demon clutched at his neck like something was strangling him. He collapsed on the ground, bucking and squirming. Damien's voice got louder. The demon's back arched. Ugly green smoke, vaguely humanoid-shaped, spewed from the demon's mouth, blended into the darkness, then it fell down and was absorbed into the ground with a pathetic groan of pain.

"Whoa, dude, what the hell was that?"

On the ground, the guy was coughing, shaking his head. He glanced around, eyebrows squished together.

"When they're hitching a ride, we send them back to hell." Damien bent to help the guy up. "You're going to be okay."

"I want to do that."

"In time. Probably senior year." Damien jogged over to Falls Avenue to pick up the yellow pylons. "How did you get him here so quickly? I almost didn't finish setting up."

"He might have been a demon, but even they think with their private parts."

"What?" the guy asked.

Damien put an arm around the guy and directed him toward the entrance of the park, bending to pick up the pylons there. "I don't want to hear that."

I grinned. "Tess is attractive." I spun around, impressed with myself that I was still holding the glamour.

When we crossed the street, Damien pulled out some money and shoved it in the guy's hand. "Get something to eat, hydrate, and don't leave the restaurant until I talk to you." He nodded to the steak house.

A minute later, with the pylons safely ensconced in his trunk again, we waited inside The Haunted House for Cole. The image of the demon spewing out of the guy's mouth played in my head over and over again. The fact that demons could possess us hadn't been discussed in demonology class yet. Maybe that was a second or third-year thing. Maybe even a senior tidbit they threw at us before graduating and going out into the world to hunt these things. Be careful out there because they can totally possess your ass and make you do things you don't want to do.

I glanced at my watch. "Maybe it was a rumor that a demon was going to prey on some poor kid."

Damien shrugged. "Intel isn't always correct, but I've had my eye on this kid for a while. He's struggling and demons take advantage."

"Not just demons," I said. Damien glanced at me questioningly. "Nothing."

Finally, a few minutes later, a tall boy wearing a high school letter jacket approached the place. He glanced in all directions before stepping inside. He sat in a seat by the door used for customers that needed to wait their turn before venturing into The Haunted House.

Damien walked over to him. "Cole?"

"Who wants to know?"

The bravado was laughable. His face pale, he held his hands in his lap to control the shaking. If he stood, I swear I would see his knees knock together.

"It's okay, Cole. We know you're here to see Mammon. But we've taken care of him."

"Taken care of him?" Eyebrows raised, he cocked his head to the side.

"Yes. Play your best. There's no need to throw the game. Don't do something you'll regret."

He straightened his back, shaking his head. "I wasn't going to throw anything."

I put on my best Tess smile, one that she reserved for Hailey and Nia, and actually meant it. "It's really okay. We know he had something on you or was threatening you. He's not going to be able to hurt anyone anymore."

Relief slumped his shoulders. "Is it really okay? I didn't want to let the team down, but he was going to hurt my sister and make the rest of my school life miserable."

Damien nodded. "We can't tell you exactly everything that's gone on, but rest assured that he is no longer a problem. To anyone."

"Thanks, mister. Miss." He shot out of the chair and out the door like the devil himself was after him. And he sort of was before we put a stop to it.

"How long will he be safe? Will other demons come after him?" I asked.

"Others might. We have surveillance on him just in case. We only need to keep him from picking the wrong path until he gets into Hell's Watch. He has to choose to go there once he gets his acceptance letter."

"But if he doesn't know magic exists, won't he think it's a scam like I did?"

"He's seen magic. He just doesn't realize it. We'll do our best to convince him. But the choice will be up to him."

Back at the car, I pulled open the passenger side door. At least I wouldn't have to go back to school hunkered down in the back seat.

"What are you doing?"

"Aren't we going back to the school?"

"Yes." He pointed to the back seat. "The same way we came. I have to sneak you back in. I can't have you sitting up front like we were on a field trip. And do not do this again."

I frowned, slammed the passenger front door, and opened the back door. "You needed help."

"I would have handled it." He got in the car and started the engine.

The next morning, before the sun had fully risen, I stood at the edge of Hell's Watch pool, waiting for the swim team coach to blow the whistle that would send all of us into the tepid water. It was never too cold, but also never warm. If you stopped swimming, a chill would follow you until you moved again. It always worked way better than coffee at waking me up on the days we had practice.

Swim team, like all other sports at the school, was meant more to help us with our physical fitness than anything else. There weren't many schools we could compete against, seeing as the world didn't know about magic. We had arrangements with a few schools in the area that we would compete against, with powers strictly forbidden. But those competitions didn't happen until junior year when we could be trusted more.

Coach Natar blew her whistle and the seven of us dove into the water. The initial shock of cool quickly gave way to warm as I swam through the water. I loved the feeling of the water as it sluiced over my body. Tranquil, I relaxed into the swim, pushing my muscles harder with each stroke. We ran through some drills until the practice hour was over. That's what I liked about swim "team". Unlike other team sports, this one didn't require a lot of interaction with other members. I swam, touched the wall, and a team member dove into the water, swam to the other side, touched the wall. Rinse and repeat for as long as Coach had us in the water. Our times were getting faster, so I knew we were getting stronger.

She blew the whistle and we left the pool. I lingered until everyone was finished in the change room. When I peered into the room, the steam from the showers still hung in the air, but the room was quiet. I hurriedly got ready for the day, pulling on my uniform after a quick shower. On practice days, I ate early so I could dash to class right afterward. I grabbed my backpack from my change room locker and raced out of the room.

A few minutes later, I settled into my seat for magical ethics. The question of whether or not to use magic intrigued me in every class. The situations presented were always different, and the answer wasn't always what you thought it should be. Despite the purpose of the school being to teach magic, they wanted us to avoid using our power if at all possible, especially when ordpops were around.

"Don't forget to read chapters ten and eleven of To Magic or Not for tomorrow's class. We'll be getting into some pop quizzes soon."

A collective groan warbled through the room.

The bell rang and I was out of there before the chime finished. Not that I was overly eager to get to defense class. How would Damien treat me after last night? Would he still be angry? I'd only wanted to help, but breaking the rules was super frowned upon here.

Defense class had been more like gym class lately. They were big on keeping us physically fit so we could take on demons more than twice our size. And of course, size didn't matter. The tiniest of the girls could still take down a huge demon if she kept her cool and used the knowledge she had.

Today, magically painted lines on the hardwood floor indicated we would be playing basketball. The whir from the air conditioner filled the room.

Damien stood in the center of the court, a bright orange basketball in his hands. "Today, you're going to need to change into shorts, T-shirts, and running shoes. Check your locker. The quartermaster should have already sent the garments to you." He waved to the far right wall, past his office.

We all jogged over, the women continuing right for our locker room and the guys veering left for theirs. I'd wondered why the locker room was here the first time I'd had class because we'd never needed to change clothes before.

Tall metal lockers, two sets of them back to back with wooden benches in between, took up most of the locker room. To the left of the lockers was a shower area offering six spots for us to rinse off the sweat of class. Beside the shower area were six stalls with toilets. And in front of the shower stalls, sinks with mirrors.

Each locker sported a name written on tape at the top. I found mine, yanked out the new gym uniform, and pulled it on as quickly as possible, surreptitiously checking to see if anyone was watching me. Still shy about my body, I didn't want anyone to see me in my bra and underwear.

We hurried out again to find the guys trickling into the gym. When we were all present again, Damien smiled.

"I'm sure you all know how basketball works. I'm dividing you into two teams. First to twenty points wins."

He flicked his hand at each of us, moving us into one team or another. For the ones that didn't make a team, they sat on benches against the wall to watch.

Priti grabbed my hand. "We're on the same team!"

Saad moseyed over to me as well. At least I knew I could count on some of my teammates.

Nia ended up with us. Tess, Hailey, and Nathan were on the opposing team. Great. At least with them not on my team, I wouldn't have to worry about them screwing things up for us.

"Everyone, take positions."

Damien tossed the ball into the air and we jumped into action. Saad managed to hit the ball to me. I dribbled down the court, blocking everything out of my mind, my only goal to get close enough to the basket to throw it and get the points.

From out of nowhere, Tess was there. She charged at me, hitting me in the shoulder as she tried to steal the ball. Every move I made she mirrored, swiping with her hand when I bounced the ball on the floor. The closer she got to me, the more annoyed I got. Heat kicked up around us. Tess's face flushed. If I pushed my hand out, without even touching her, I knew I would send her flying across the court. Though I liked this ability, I didn't think it would bode well for my academics if I used it against a student.

I sucked in a deep breath, pulled the heat back, and glared at Tess. I turned my back to her, dribbled the ball a few steps, then jumped to throw. The satisfying swoosh made me smile. I turned to Tess and threw her a smug look.

The rest of class went by smoothly, with Saad and Priti blocking most of Tess's attempts to get close to me. Nathan encroached a few times, but I dodged by him, making a basket each time.

At the end of the class, before the bell rang, we all ran to the lockers to get changed. There was plenty of time for me to linger in the shower since I didn't have another class until the afternoon. I loved Fridays. Even the fact that Tess had lunch at the same time didn't bother me on Fridays.

I rushed through the shower anyway. There was still a lot of catching up to do on my part. Priti and Saad usually helped during the time between classes and before lunch. It wasn't study hall exactly, but close enough if you wanted to put a label on it.

"We're meeting Saad in the library," Priti said as she twisted her hair, ringing water out of the dark locks.

"Great. I need to brush up on magical ethics. It's like all the questions are trick questions."

Priti nodded. "I know. It's like we can never use magic. Except when we can."

I laughed. "I hope all this gets easier."

We finished dressing and rushed out of the locker room. Some students still lingered in the gym. Damien was gone, probably in his office. He hadn't done or said anything differently today, so maybe he'd forgiven me for stowing away in his car last night. I didn't want to give him a chance to call me over, so I grabbed Priti's hand and dashed for the gym doors.

The rest of the day flew by. Test pop quizzes in the library with friends, lunch where Tess shot daggers at me with her eyes. Arcane history where we'd left the Salem witch trials, but still hadn't gotten to anything about my family yet. It was still early October, so I had hope we'd get to it soon. At least it was a little more intriguing now that we'd gone to the middle ages. Medieval magic was fascinating. And of course there were plenty of persecutions, but the whole point wasn't witch trials.

After dinner, we all sat upstairs in the second-floor common area. Despite wanting to be alone some of the time, it was nice to sit and chat with people who were becoming my friends.

Priti lounged in a plush chair on the left side of me. Saad and his roommate took up the entire sofa in front of us. On the table, arranged in three distinct categories, were drinks, savory snacks, and sweet snacks.

"What happened after you followed Damien last night?" Saad asked.

I shrugged. "I helped him with the demon."

Priti's eyes grew wide. "Did you fight?"

I grinned. "I lured it into a park using Tess's whiles and Damien took care of it."

"Impressed you could hold the glamour long enough to do that," Conrad said.

"I was motivated. I figured if I helped enough I wouldn't get in as much trouble."

"How much trouble did it cause?" Saad asked.

"I don't know. I avoided him after defense class. He hasn't called me to his office yet. I think he's disappointed in me and that hurts more."

"At least we're not stuck in here all month. Anyone going home for Thanksgiving next Friday?" Saad grabbed a handful of peanuts.

Priti and Conrad nodded. Everyone turned to look at me. I shook my head. Priti squeezed my hand and gave me an understanding nod. My heart clenched. I took a deep breath and sighed. If I could trust anyone else at school, it was Saad and his roommate.

Before they could ask why I wasn't going home, I held up my hand. "My foster family isn't family. They never made me feel welcome. I'd have a better time here with the other students who have nowhere to go during a holiday."

"I'm sorry. I should have remembered. Your intro at the beginning of school was different than most others," Saad said.

I nodded. "Never really knew my parents. At five, I

wanted to play, run around. I do remember my mother reading stories to me at bedtime. It's all such a blur now. The longer it's been, the harder it is to picture them."

Nathan appeared at the top of the stairs and sauntered over to our group. He smiled at everyone, even me, and I wondered what he was up to. He'd been cozy with Tess in class earlier. Had she turned him into one of her minions?

"What's up?" He looked directly at me.

"Nothing. We were talking about the pop quizzes coming up."

There was no way I was going to keep spilling my guts with Nathan around. Besides, he'd learn the basics of my family just like everyone else. A tiny bit of anger curled in my stomach that my parents never told me anything about magic. We were a fucking founding family and I had no idea magic even existed until a little over a month ago. How could they keep that from me?

"We should get back to our room," Saad said, nodding at Conrad.

"Yes, get in some studying for those pop quizzes." Conrad smiled.

Priti stood and stretched. "Good idea."

"I'll meet you back in the room." I wanted to be alone for a while. Someplace I could think without all the noise from other students competing for space in my head.

Priti nodded. "Okay, I'll get some snacks ready."

Priti dashed off down the hall, and I smiled at Nathan. "Bad timing. Have a great night."

Sadness clouded his eyes and I felt a slight twinge of guilt for taking off on him so abruptly. Maybe he wasn't a spy for Tess. Maybe he was just being nice. Maybe he wanted to fit in as badly as the rest of us. There was something about him, though, that I couldn't put my finger on.

It didn't help that I hadn't been able to do the friend or foe spell on him.

"Sure. I'll catch you guys next time."

It was a simple phrase, but the way he said it made it sound ominous. Like we should run from him.

He stalked off to the left, presumably to his room. I dashed down the stairs and raced down the hallway to the library. After dinner, so close to bedtime, the library was usually empty. I pulled open the heavy wood door, stepped inside, and took a deep breath. The scent of the books always calmed me. I wished I could bottle it and take a whiff whenever I felt stressed.

I marched to the back of the library, to the reference section that held the books not placed in their expected slots on the main shelves. I'd searched through the shelves at length before, looking for any tomes that talked about my family, with no luck. My last resort was the reference section.

I combed through the titles, finally finding one that looked promising. After a quick glance around, I pulled the title from the shelf, smoothing my hand over the weathered leather. Flipping it open, I looked at the back to see who else had checked the book from the stacks. It wasn't allowed to leave the library, but we could read in another room. My mother's and grandmother's names jumped out at me.

Tears pooled in my eyes, making the text blurry. My throat ached. Other names with the last name Kavanagh were listed too, none of them familiar to me. How many in my family had gone here? I realized how powerful my family was. I couldn't let them down. I needed to do better, be better. As a founding family, it was our duty to help protect the world. There was no way I was going to let my family down.

Wishing I could take the book with me, I put it back on the shelves. I could visit it anytime I wanted while I was here. The risk of taking another book from the library that shouldn't leave the room was too great. I ran my finger down the spine as a tear escaped and trailed down my cheek.

It was time to stop feeling sorry for myself and apply everything I'd learned. If the magic didn't happen like it should, I would see the dean about doing another unbinding spell.

Chapter Ten

The Friday before Halloween, excitement lingered in the air everywhere I went in the school. Chatter filled the hallways about the "holiday" and who was dressing up as what. For Thanksgiving, I'd had the castle almost to myself. Everyone save the professors and a few students had gone home for the long weekend. But for Halloween, everyone stayed on campus. There were parties, costumes, shows of magic. I'd never liked Halloween before, never had a sweet tooth, but it was always an excuse to get out of the foster home for hours without anyone thinking twice about my absence.

Arcane history was finally getting interesting. Due to Halloween being around the corner, arcane history and demonology had synced up to talk about vampires, demons, creatures at the same time. Learning about things I always thought were myths and legends made me question everything I knew. Did that mean Bigfoot existed? What about mermaids? So many questions and not enough time between both classes to learn it all. I suspected I would be taking out books from the library to do some extracurricular learning in the next few weeks. Since the two classes had synced up I'd only needed one coffee to get through arcane history.

I couldn't wait for AH class, but first I had to get through defense class. I stood in the gym with the rest of the students, waiting for Damien to fill us in on what we'd be doing today. He hadn't brought up me stowing away in his car, so I didn't mention it either. The disappointed looks he shot my way gradually stopped, especially when I did something particularly well in class.

"Today we'll go back to hand-to-hand combat, but in groups of four. You can pick your own teams."

Panic rushed through me. With four of us, the chances that I'd be stuck with Tess in my group rose. But if we could pick our own, I already knew who I'd be with.

Priti grabbed my hand and pulled me over to Saad and his roommate. Safety in friends.

"One of you will be the witch, and the other three will be the demons," Damien said. "No glamours this time, but pretend you have three demons coming after you. After all, some of them may look like regular people."

The image of the sickly green smoke spewing out of the guy in the park flashed through my mind. Black eyes in the smoke had followed my every move until they disappeared into the ground. A shiver raced down my spine. I wanted to learn how Damien had exorcised the demon. But apparently we didn't learn that until senior year. We needed at least two years of Latin first. And we didn't get to study that until our sophomore year.

"Who wants to be the 'victim'?" Conrad asked.

Priti's hand shot up. She was getting better at hand-to-hand but thought she needed even more practice.

We all nodded, then rushed her at the same time. She jumped out of the way with the quickness of a cat. She turned, ready for another approach, her gaze flitting back and forth between us. Waiting our turn wouldn't be realistic. How many demons would wait while she dispatched one of them before attacking?

Priti used a combination of spells, glamours, and old-fashioned fighting techniques to keep us at bay.

Saad huffed, bending over to suck in some air. "You've been practicing."

Priti grinned, nodding at me. "Alex is an excellent teacher."

"Okay, teach, I think it should be your turn next," Conrad said.

I rolled my shoulders, craning my neck from side to side to loosen up. "You're on."

We moved out a little, putting more space between us. I focused on the three of them, watching every move they made, every draw of breath. Saad moved first and I jumped out of his way. Before I knew it, Priti moved in. I dodged the other way. Conrad, quick on Priti's heels, landed a blow to my shoulder. I shook it off and spun around.

The three of them moved as one then. All coming toward me at the same time. A small burst of light and noise from my left drew my attention long enough for Saad to take me down. As we fell, an inflatable rubber mattress slid into place under us. I landed hard, and Saad rolled off the mattress so he didn't put his full weight on me. Winded, I lay there, trying to pull in lungfuls of air. I sat up, looking over my shoulder to see Tess grinning at me. Hailey laughed. Nia and Nathan remained indifferent.

Damien shook his head. Anger, fetid and ripe, coursed through me. We'd been too close to Tess's group. I had to remind myself that we should never be within magic shot of her or any of her friends. For some reason, her dislike of me grew with each passing week.

That wasn't the only problem of course. I was letting myself get distracted. I knew better than that. Tess had pulled similar tricks on numerous occasions, and I fell for it every time. I needed to zone out everything around me and focus on the task at hand. In order to survive in here and out there, I needed to hone my ability to know what was going on around me. Things were different in this school than in the real world. Nothing was as it seemed here. Complacency, because most people were nice here, wouldn't help me pass semi-final exams.

The bell rang and I breathed a sigh of relief. One more class to get through and it was the weekend, which meant my likelihood of seeing Tess went down to almost nil if I stayed in my room instead of attending any of the parties on campus.

I'd waited until almost seven to make my way to the dining hall. The longer I waited, the less likely I was to run into people planning parties, inviting people to parties, shunning other people from parties. If all the formalities had already happened, I didn't risk getting invited and saying no. Or worse, not getting invited to any parties at all. As much as I didn't want to spend Friday and Saturday night mingling and making small talk with my classmates, it would be devastating to not even be invited.

Priti and Saad humored me and were waiting by the doors of the hall. I'm sure the two of them had already been invited to more parties than they could attend anyway, but a smidgen of guilt crawled up my spine.

"Finally the weekend!" Priti's smile brightened her whole face.

Saad opened the door and held it for us. "You guys going to any of the parties?"

Priti nodded. I shrugged.

"I'll probably check out a few," Saad said.

Inside the dining hall, a few students lingered, but it was mostly empty. They served dinner until seven-thirty every day, but by this time on a Friday evening, most students were off getting ready for their weekend.

Two days a week, I had blissful lunches without having to deal with Tess. In the evenings, I wasn't so lucky. Tonight, she walked toward us, a smirk on her face. Priti moved away to make room for her. Heat began to rise in me before Tess even got close. Instead of walking by, she hit my shoulder with her shoulder, even though there was plenty of room for her to walk.

She leaned into my ear and whispered, "Your roommate is always covering your ass. How about I tell Professor O'Connor she's cheating?"

I glared at her, heat rising around me. My mark tingled, then glowed. Tess's eyes went wide in mock surprise. The smirk came back.

"Freak."

I gritted my teeth, my jaw aching. A dull throb in my head kept time with my racing heart. Tess moved closer and I put my hands in front of me, pushing the air to keep her back.

Tess went flying through the air a few feet and landed beside an empty table littered with dirty plates and cutlery. Castle staff hadn't been by to whisk everything away for cleaning. I imagined they just zapped it out and zapped clean dishes in.

A few teachers at the front of the dining hall turned at

the commotion. Mr. Keen, our demonology professor, stormed over with a frown on his face, the elemental magic teacher, Miss Brand, and Mr. Walch, the Latin professor, close behind. They all glanced at Tess with concern.

Miss perfect shook her head, still not a hair out of place.

Mr. Keen helped Tess up. "Are you okay?"

Fake tears shone in her eyes. "I think so. She's crazy. I didn't even do anything."

Mr. Keen pointed at the two other teachers. "Take her to the infirmary." They nodded and both wrapped an arm around Tess to guide her out of the dining hall.

"She started it," I said, then clamped my mouth shut.

"Really? What did she do?" Mr. Keen tilted his head with a raised eyebrow.

I crossed my arms over my chest.

"That isn't like you." Priti's eyebrows pinched together. "What did she say?"

"It's nothing."

Priti gave everyone the benefit of the doubt, and so far Tess hadn't targeted her with any of her hatred bullshit. Obviously, there was just something about me Tess didn't like. I didn't see her picking on anyone else in the school.

"It's not nothing," Priti insisted.

"If it's nothing, then you need to leave the dining hall. You're confined to your room for dinners for a week." Mr. Keen pointed to the door. "Go. Now."

"But I haven't even eaten yet."

"You can eat in your room."

I turned, took a few steps toward the door, and Priti and Saad followed me. I shook my head. "I want to be alone."

Priti sighed. "I'll be up later."

I stomped out of the hall, thankful that most students

were getting ready for whatever party they were going to that night. The lobby and common area were relatively empty.

Shadows enveloped me when I stepped into the room. I half expected the phantom demon alarm to come at me, but since we'd fixed the alarm, it hadn't happened. Something in the air felt different. A shiver went through me. Something was wrong.

"*Luminaria.*"

The lights came on and I scanned the room. Nothing looked out of place. About to sit on my bed, an object in the center stopped me. A chill crept up my spine. The now familiar symbols of Malum taunted me. The cube was a little bigger than the last one. I thought about bringing it to Damien, but he was still looking into the last present someone left for me. If there was something in the cube, I wanted to know. But I couldn't see a way to get into it. Rumors of a forbidden library, deep in the main library, nagged at me. If the rumors were true, I might find an answer there. Except the entrance to the forbidden section was hidden from all students.

The spell book I had contained a lot of useful information and I thought I remembered a spell to reveal things. At the time I hadn't thought of any practical uses for it, but now, maybe, it would help me find the forbidden library.

I shoved the cube into a pocket, grabbed the spell book out of my backpack, and shoved that in beside the cube. At the door, I picked up the chalk to leave Priti a message. If I told her where I was going, would that make her an accomplice if I got caught? The less she knew about Malum and my attempt to find the forbidden library, the better. I put the chalk back and left the room.

The hall leading to the library was dark. I imagined shadowy arms reaching out for me as I walked, trying to stop me from my task. At this hour on a Friday, no one manned the desk. Students were on the honor system after hours when taking books out of the library. If that failed, the school had a way of tracking which students had what books.

The jar of candies on the check-out desk was half full now. A layer of dust covered a sign that said, this time, that the librarian would be back Monday morning. Lights came on as I moved farther into the room, chasing some of the shadows away. I paused, waiting for the swoosh of the door as it closed. I closed my eyes and listened for any sounds that might indicate I wasn't alone. Whispers, rustling of pages, footsteps. Nothing but the beating of my heart, still pounding after my confrontation with Tess.

Where would you hide a forbidden library? In plain sight of course, but where was the likeliest place in here? The door on the left, behind section 000, looked promising. I hadn't tried the knob before, but would a forbidden section be that obvious?

The aisle that never ended might be a good spot, perhaps a set number of steps from the start of the aisle, but if you needed to get to it in a hurry, you could make mistakes. I turned to the card catalog behind the desk.

I pulled out the spell book and turned the pages until I found the reveal spell. Grandmother Julie had a spell for almost anything. I hoped this spell worked the way I thought it would.

Standing in front of the tiny filing cabinets, I uttered the spell, stumbling over the Latin. The air felt different. If candles had been lit they would have flickered, I was sure. The hair on the back of my neck rose and I spun around to make sure no one had entered the library without me knowing. It was still as quiet as before.

I turned back to the catalog and repeated the spell.

Either I had the wrong place or I didn't have enough magic to get the spell to work. After a third try, the image of a door shimmered into existence for a split second, then vanished.

"Shit."

No matter how many times I tried, I wouldn't gain access to the forbidden library. They must have something else protecting it besides a magically hidden doorway. At least now I knew for certain where it was. Accessing it would be another story. Maybe by the time I was a senior, I'd be able to penetrate the magic keeping it from me.

I tried one last time, dropping the book into my pocket as I said the spell. The outline of the door glowed again, then faded.

"What do you think you're doing, Miss Kavanagh?" Mrs. Sapienti's voice boomed in the silent library.

Heart pounding, I spun around, heat rushing to my face. "Studying?"

With a stern face, eyes glaring at me over her glasses, she pointed at the library door. Shoulders hunched, I skulked out. She walked beside me as I navigated the hallway to the stairs leading to the second floor.

When I stormed into the room, Priti spun around in her chair. She sat at her desk, poring over her tablet, presumably her notes for a class. She sprang out of her chair, eyes wide.

"Are you okay?"

"I'm fine." I ambled into the room and plopped onto my bed.

"I didn't know where you went." She wrung her hands. "You were acting odd in the dining hall. I thought you might do something rash."

Heat rose, flushing my cheeks. I sprang off the bed. "So you narced on me?"

Crestfallen, she flinched. "I'm sorry. I was worried."

Mrs. Sapienti cleared her throat. "Alex is the one who should be sorry. She was trying to sneak into the forbidden library."

Mrs. Sapienti left, pulling the door firmly closed behind her. I half worried she would lock us in, but they wouldn't punish Priti for something I did. What was the big deal anyway? It wasn't like I'd actually been able to get into the forbidden library. Did they really expect us to not even try?

Priti sat at her desk again, swiping on her tablet too fast to be reading anything. "I am sorry."

I sighed and sat at my desk. "It's not your fault. I'm a horrible person, remember?"

She turned to face me, shoving the tablet away. "No, you're not. You had reasons for what happened in the dining hall, even if you won't tell me. And reasons for wanting to get into the forbidden library."

Hope shone in her eyes. And I was tempted to tell her everything, but I didn't want her to feel the brunt of Tess's bullying if at all possible.

I turned in my chair to face her this time. "You know you're my best friend, right?"

She smiled. "Okay, forgiven. Want me to zip down to the dining hall to get you something to eat? You missed dinner."

Though my stomach grumbled, I shook my head. "I'll raid the snack stash. That will tide me over until breakfast."

Priti hit the power button on her tablet and put the device in her backpack. "I'm studied out. Gonna get ready for bed."

"I think I'll do some more reading first. I need all the studying I can get."

I rummaged through the mini-fridge and pulled out a small tub of cappuccino ice cream. Maybe the caffeine in it would help me stay awake.

Blocking out Priti's padding around the room, leaving for the bathroom and coming back, I focused on my written notes. Despite the notes, I had also made sure my tablet recorded all the classes in case I had to go back over them. Sometimes I couldn't read my own writing, I wrote so fast.

While going over my notes for demonology class, I started drifting off to sleep. The writing swam in front of me, blurring the more I tried to concentrate. Faceless demons chased after me in class. Teachers used dark magic to pick off the students, letting the demons roam free. Nathan and teachers emerged from the trees in the forest behind the school.

Chapter Eleven

By mid-November, with semi-finals around the corner, my ability to access my magic was stronger than it was when I arrived at Hell's Watch. But I still didn't think it was enough to pass them. Before any of the tests, I planned on going back to see Mrs. Sapienti about testing to see if the unbinding spell actually worked. After the incident in the dining hall and the library, I had steered clear of her. It hurt more that she seemed disappointed in me and I didn't want to face that if I didn't have to.

I wasn't sure how many of the other professors knew about the binding, but Damien did. After a discussion with him, if he said I wasn't as far along as I should be, I couldn't put off a trip to see Mrs. Sapienti and the dean.

The week of having dinner in my room had been blissful. No crowded dining hall, no loud chatter, no possibility of Tess interrupting my meal with her petty attacks. Priti and Saad kept me company. They'd turned Priti's desk into a larger table with the help of a transmogrifying spell.

Magical ethics had proven to be more interesting than I thought it would be when classes first started in

September, and I left the lecture room with my mind swirling with magical dilemmas. Defense class always helped with that. The physical activity of the class often cleared my mind.

I entered the gym, ready for hand-to-hand combat training. Priti and Saad waited for me on the left side of the room. The class had gravitated toward various cliques that almost always trained together. Damien rarely broke us up, but I figured that wouldn't last. We were comfortable with each other. Knew the strengths and foibles of our usual partners. In the real world, fighting actual demons, we wouldn't have the same luxury. Any day now, I expected Damien to split us into different groups. Panic raced down my spine at the thought of that change happening for the semi-final.

Damien walked into the gym from his office, carrying a large plastic container filled with the training poppets. They were great for taking out your frustrations on and I couldn't wait to practice some punches and high kicks.

He dropped the container on the floor, pulled out a poppet, and tossed it to Nathan. He continued to pull them out and toss them to people. In the end, we were working on our own with a poppet.

"This is your last chance to hone your hand-to-hand before semi-finals. One-on-one with your poppet. You have five minutes to prepare yourselves. Space yourselves out. Then I'll cast the spell to bring them to life."

Priti, Saad, and I stayed on the left side of the room near the rope. We spaced ourselves out so we had enough room to fight and not interfere with each other. We put our poppets on the floor in front of us and waited. Priti's foot tapped, and her gaze darted to the gym's door.

"You okay?" I asked Priti.

She nodded, but her pallor belied her response. "Can't wait to get in more practice."

Saad shook Priti's shoulder. "You'll do great. You've been practicing a lot."

Before we could talk further, Damien uttered the spell. The poppets all around the gym sprang to life. Various forms of demons attacked. Some with claws, others with razor-sharp teeth. Tall ones, short ones.

Mine looked much like the demon that tried to kill me months ago. Fear snaked up my body. Even though I knew it wasn't real, couldn't really do damage, my heart raced. My arm tingled. I fought the feelings. I needed to take an active part in my defense, not reactive.

Out of the corner of my eye, swift movements pulled my attention away. Priti darted, punched, and kicked like a pro. Her poppet fell to the ground, turning back into clay with its defeat. Priti huffed over it, sweat dripping down her face, a grin tugging at her lips.

Grunts and groans all around me indicated not everyone was finished with their combat. I turned my attention back to my demon as it barreled toward me. I dove out of the way to the right. The demon spun around and bore down on me again. I jumped back up, took a fighting stance, legs apart, hands up to protect my face.

A huge hand, claws thankfully retracted, punched me in the side. Shooting pain exploded through me. I sucked in a breath, darting away before he could hit me again.

As he came forward again, I threw a punch, hitting him in the neck. A blow to the face wouldn't bring him down. I wasn't strong enough yet. His hands clutched his throat. I danced around him and smashed his leg with my foot. He screamed as if in pain, but I knew these things weren't real.

Heart racing, I jabbed where I thought kidneys might

be. Did demons have kidneys? They had hearts, but I didn't know where in the body any of the organs were. Damien's advice to research your opponent before facing them came back to me. Good advice. But we wouldn't always have that opportunity.

The demon whirled around, the blows to his side not even fazing him. His lips curled up in a snarl. He snaked out a hand so fast I didn't see it in time. It connected with my jaw. Pain throbbed in my head. The metallic taste of blood filled my mouth.

I shook my head to clear it.

A few quick punches to the demon caused it to stumble backward. I swept my leg across the floor, hitting his feet. He crashed to the ground.

"Time!"

I looked up. Everyone was already done, their poppets back to clay in front of them again. Damien uttered the phrase to change the remaining demons back. Only mine needed the help.

Nathan strolled over, a grin on his face. "What happened, Red? Priti was amazing today. Better than you."

Priti smiled, straightened her back, and squared her shoulders. "Thanks."

Tess sashayed over. "She's also better than you at any kind of magic. You don't even have all the tools you need to be a proper witch."

"What does that mean?" I bristled.

"What are you going to wear once school is out? The same two tops alternating every day?"

Tess snickered and glided out of the gym, her shoulders gently bouncing with laughter as she went.

Heat rushed to my face. The uniform made me fit in with everyone else, but they all knew I didn't have any money if they were keeping track of my weekend attire like Tess seemed to be doing.

Why did it even matter? Why did Tess care what I wore on the weekends? Or what I would wear in the real world. The demons wouldn't stop coming for me because I had nice clothes. As long as my tops and jeans made it easy to move and fight, that's all that mattered.

"Don't listen to her," Priti said. "Coming to lunch?"

"I'll be there after the library. I want to talk to Damien."

"About what?" Saad asked.

Priti frowned. "That's none of our business." She grabbed Saad's arm and dragged him toward the door.

I waited for the rest of the students to trickle out before I approached Damien.

He was picking up the poppets and returning them to the plastic tub. I picked up some of the clay dolls as I walked and dropped them into the tub.

"Thanks. What can I do for you, Alex?"

He picked up the tub and walked to his office. I followed close behind, screwing up my nerve to ask what I wanted to.

Inside his office, he put the plastic tub down in the corner, pulled out his chair, and sank into it with a sigh. On his desk, beside a cream-colored parchment, was a mug that I was sure once contained hot coffee. He picked it up.

"*Calor*," he said into the mug. Steam rose from the liquid.

He waved at the chairs in front of his desk and I plopped into the one closest to the door.

"Did you find out anything about the block Malum left on my bed?"

A frown crossed his face. He shook his head, placing

the mug back on the desk without taking a sip. Avoiding eye contact, he said, "Nothing yet."

If what he'd learned was so bad he felt he couldn't tell me, that didn't bode well for my safety. Even at a school warded against demons and the forces of darkness.

"Maybe this will help." I hadn't decided until that moment to give him the second object left on my bed. But if more data would help him gather information, I was all for it.

I plunked the box in the center of his desk.

"When did you get that?"

"A few weeks ago." I recounted the day it happened. How I'd been caught by Mrs. Sapienti trying to find the entrance to the forbidden library.

"That's why you were trying to get in there? It's forbidden, especially to freshmen, for a reason."

"I know." And the more I was told I couldn't go in there, the more I wanted to go in there.

He picked up the new block, checking every side. "This might help. I'll talk to the dean."

"Whatever it is, whatever it means, you can tell me. You can't protect me all the time. I need to know things. I'm still new to all this. I worry that I'm falling behind in everything because all my classmates had a lifetime head start."

With an understanding nod, he leaned closer, reaching out a hand. He patted the desk, my hands too far away. "You're doing fine. Especially in defense class. Your teachers haven't mentioned troubles in any of your other classes."

Maybe that was because Priti and I were good at hiding how much I didn't know and wasn't able to do when it came to magic. Not hiding as well as I thought. Tess knew, or at least suspected, that I could barely perform active magic. So far my need for self-preservation had kicked in when it needed to and I'd passed whatever test the teacher had us perform. In the real world, I couldn't rely on that. I had to be on the offensive. I would need to see Mrs. Sapienti soon about trying another unbinding spell.

"Is there a way to tell how much magic I have access to?"

"You can ask the dean. He has a way to determine if the unbinding worked to restore all of your magic."

"Thanks."

"You're welcome. Come see me anytime during office hours. I've got to get ready for my next class."

I bolted off the chair. "Right. Sorry."

Outside the gym, Saad stood against the wall, looking like a bored, lone warrior. I frowned.

"Priti had to pick up something from her astrology and astronomy teacher."

"Don't you have class?"

He gave me a sheepish grin. "Yeah, but I didn't want you to come out here and find no one."

"I'm a big girl. I can handle my friends having a life." I faked a sob.

Saad laughed. "Okay. See you at lunch."

I watched him race off. This would be a perfect time to grab more of my books and find a place to study. Every little bit extra I did gave me the confidence I might pass my semi-finals.

Back in my room, I sat at my desk relishing the quiet, contemplating staying there to study. It had everything I needed. My books, snacks, silence. But the silence was oppressive sometimes. And with the stunning view of the forest behind the castle, I might daydream about what hid in those trees.

I was trying to be less solitary. Well, not too less, but I liked to be seen around the campus at least. I still tried to avoid Tess every chance I got, and that was another mark in the pro column for staying in my room.

My room didn't have all the books, though. Sure, I had my regular textbooks. The spell book I "borrowed" from the library. Dozens of Post-it notes marked spells I wanted to look at later. And the map of the school. But what if I needed another book? What if one of my textbooks sent me down a rabbit hole of information and I needed more? I'd have to leave anyway.

I tossed my simple trickery and demonology textbooks into my backpack, made sure the map of the school was still in the side pocket, and threw in some snacks. Real ones, not cards I needed to use magic on to get actual food.

I surveyed the room to see if I'd forgotten anything. Threw in a few pens. Something on my bed caught my eye. Heart racing, I held my breath.

I plodded over on shaking legs and peered at the object nestled in my bedspread. The box was different than the others. It was about the size of a mass-market paperback, but four centimeters thick. Dark wood with no discernible opening. What looked like a crest was painted on the top. The crest looked vaguely familiar and I recalled seeing it in the house when I was younger. Mom had a book with the crest on it. And I was sure I remembered seeing a similar book with the crest at my grandmother's house.

My mark didn't tingle or glow, so I figured the box was safe. I picked it up, looked at it from all sides, then put it in my backpack. If it was a puzzle box, it would take some figuring out. And I wanted to get in some studying before lunch.

With most of the freshmen and sophomores in class and some of the juniors, the corridors and common areas only had a handful of people. Still, those areas weren't necessarily supposed to remain quiet, so I continued to the library.

I pushed through the door and Ms. Leaber, the librarian, smiled at me. In the few months I'd been at the school, I'd only seen the woman a handful of times. I usually came here later so there would be more of a chance I'd have the place to myself.

Today, students occupied most of the reading nooks. There were students in the aisles. A few by the door at the end of aisle 000. Though the chatter was in whispers, it was still too crowded for my liking.

I huffed and left the room, pulling out the map from my backpack. I hadn't yet tried the basement. The old castle had to have one. The dean had mentioned a dungeon when we arrived, so I knew there had to be at least one level lower than the ground floor.

Beside the library, an unmarked door was located in the exact spot the map indicated there would be a staircase. Figuring it would be locked, I dug in my bag for the spell book. I recalled seeing a spell in there about obstacles.

I flipped through the Post-it notes I'd used as bookmarks and found the spell I wanted.

"*Resigno.*"

This would be a test of how much magic I had available to me. I didn't want to rely on magic, because what if I performed too much and it took days to replenish? It wasn't unlimited. How easy would life be for all the witches out there if they didn't have to work for anything? Just say a spell and boom, they had whatever they wanted.

Magical ethics talked a lot about the rules of when and where to use magic. And the consequences for using it. It was like a muscle that you had to hone, train. But if you used it too much, that muscle would strain and let you down. Sometimes when you needed it most.

The lock clicked and I turned the handle. Rewarded with a cloud of dust as the door swung open, I coughed and squinted in the dim lighting. Sconces on the wall every few feet cast dim yellow light on the stairs.

With a glance over my shoulder to make sure no one saw me, I slipped through the door and closed it firmly behind me. I should have thought to bring a flashlight.

The stone stairs were old, but not crumbling. Small cracks in the wall gave it a rough texture. My hand pressed against it to guide me down the steps. No hand railing meant nothing to grab onto if I lost my footing.

At the bottom of the stairs, two corridors spread out to the left and right. In front of me, with about five feet of space, was another wall. Possibly of a room. There was no visible door.

I took the left corridor. More sconces lit the way. About ten feet from the stairs, I came to a nook carved into the stone wall, complete with a stone bench and a sconce burning, casting the whole area in a pleasant yellow light.

I sat on the bench, dropping my bag at my feet. Wiggling around a little to get more comfortable, I pulled my feet off the ground and rested them on the bench. A few throw pillows and some snacks and this could be my new studying place.

I pulled out the box that had been left on my bed. With the spell book still in hand, I flipped through to find the reveal spell. It hadn't worked on the forbidden library, but the box was smaller. If I couldn't get it open right away, at least I could see what was in it. Make sure it wasn't something dangerous. The familiar crest could be a trap to lure me in.

I uttered the words to the reveal spell. The box in my hand glowed, then turned invisible for a split second, revealing a pair of throwing stars.

Beyond the nook, a spot in the wall glowed as well.

Startled, I leapt off the bench and dropped the box. It bounced off my foot. Holy fuck. What did I just do? Curiosity about where the door led got the better of me and I stepped forward.

That's when I noticed dark shadows on the wall. They didn't dance and flow like shadows from a flickering light. They scuttled. Moving closer, I widened my eyes, wishing again that I'd thought to bring a flashlight. One of the shadows leapt from the wall. It wasn't until it was in mid-air that I realized what it was.

Eight hairy legs and a plump body hurtled toward me. I shoved my hands out, and my defensive magic kicked in. But more shadows jumped. There were too many of them.

Spiders rained down on me. I shrieked. I didn't care who heard me. I wanted everyone to hear me.

I flung my arms around, trying to get them off. Stamped my feet, hoping to shake them off. I felt them crawling in my hair. I clamped my mouth shut after another shriek, worried they would get into my mouth.

A shiver raced up my spine. At least I hoped it was a shiver and not a spider that had made it down my top.

A sharp pain in my shoulder pulled a yelp from me. Were they *biting* me?

Fresh panic seared through me. My only thought was to get them off me. I pictured myself running up the stairs, into the pool area, and jumping. Would that get them off me?

Footsteps on the stairs filled me with some relief. A few

seconds later, Mr. Wozniak, the caretaker, appeared in the corridor. The grimace on his face caused my legs to tremble.

Another sharp pain in my wrist made me woozy. The room spun. Suddenly, there were three caretakers, all with the same disturbed expression on their faces.

Fire traveled up my wrist and down my arm from the puncture wounds. What kind of spider caused this kind of pain?

I swayed back, reaching my arm out to steady myself against the wall. Head throbbing, I bent over, sucking in dank, moist air. Featherlight tickling along my cheek made me hold my breath. Claw at my face to fling the spiders away.

Legs once able to kick a demon in the stomach and topple him now turned to jelly. I could barely stand. I inched toward the bench. Why wasn't I moving faster?

Before I could fall, Mr. Wozniak caught me.

"Whoa now." He eased me onto the bench and sprayed me with something that smelled vaguely of mint.

The spiders fell to the ground, creating a soft plop as they landed. Stunned for a moment, they lay on the ground, looking dead, but they quickly righted themselves and scurried back over to the wall.

"Thanks."

"You shouldn't be practicing down here. There are dangers in the basement you know nothing about."

I think I nodded. I couldn't feel parts of my body. And other parts tingled.

"They came out of nowhere."

"Magical spiders. Guarding..."

He didn't finish and I wanted to know what they were guarding. Someone? Something? The dungeon? What was in the dungeon that needed to be guarded by magical jumping spiders?

"Guarding what?"

"Never mind. I need to get you to the infirmary."

About to protest, I acquiesced instead. Then the nook and everything around me went black.

A fresh but medicinal scent of pine teased my nose. Crisp sheets under my arms were cool, comforting.

"Is she going to be okay?" the dean's voice held a hint of concern.

Papers rustling, then, "She'll be fine. Only two bit her. Likelihood of metamorphosis minimal." The female voice wasn't familiar, but I knew it must be the doctor. Who else would tell the dean I wouldn't turn into a giant spider?

Another shiver coursed through me at an imaginary spider racing across my arm. I gasped out of the semi-sleep I was in and rubbed my arms with trembling hands.

"She's awake."

Dr. Dotair scurried over, pulled a penlight out of her lab coat pocket, and shone it in one of my eyes, then the other.

"Normal pupil response."

She put a soft hand to my head, moved it a few times, then smiled at me. "How do you feel?"

"Okay. A little queasy."

"That's normal. The spider's poison can do a number on your system. Light meals for the rest of the day and turn in early. Sleep will help with the healing."

"Would I have turned into a spider?"

The nervous laugh churned my stomach. "My, no. We would never let that happen."

Nostrils flaring, eyes bulging, the dean stalked over to the bed, his face softening when he saw me up close. "The dungeon is off-limits."

"I know. I wasn't looking for that, I swear. I wanted to find a little nook to study and I was doing a spell and suddenly the door glowed. I didn't mean for anything like that to happen."

"Okay, don't worry about it now. We should have more wards in place around the door, I suppose. None of the students ever wanted to venture down to the basement before. They are content with all the places they are allowed to go. The quad, the pool, all the common areas, the dining hall, library, observatory, greenhouse, gym."

"I'm sorry. I spent so much time crowded in with other people in foster homes, I wanted a little nook for myself."

Nodding, he squeezed my hand gently. "Understandable. I'll have Mrs. Sapienti strengthen the lock and warding surrounding the basement."

The loss of my secret spot paled in comparison to the fact that I was almost turned into a spider.

"I've reversed the magic and cleared your body of the poison. If you feel up to it, you can leave as long as you take it easy."

Throwing my legs over the side of the bed, I tentatively put them on the floor. Slightly wobbly, but strong enough to hold my weight. Wanting to avoid any further reprimand, I hurried out of the infirmary as quickly as I was able.

The door swooshed shut behind me and I breathed deeply for the first time since the spiders attacked. After a few lungfuls of air, I realized I didn't have my backpack with me. If Mr. Wozniak hadn't brought it with us, I'd have to ask the dean to get it for me.

I ambled back into the room to find it empty. The

doctor and the dean must have gone to her office. Spotting my bag on the side of my hospital bed, I grabbed it and shrugged the straps over my shoulders.

"I don't think she knows anything," the doctor said. Her voice carried through the quiet infirmary.

"Good. We need to keep it that way. I'll beef up security as soon as I get back to my office."

Afraid I would be caught eavesdropping, I raced out of the room again and stopped in the hallway to catch my breath. Lightheaded, I waited for the world to stop spinning, then I checked the time.

It was already after lunch and halfway through spells and potions. I would wait for Priti and Saad outside Lecture Room F and tell them everything before arcane history class started.

Chapter Twelve

Two days later, sitting in the freshman common area in between classes, I still pondered what it was I didn't know. Saad and Priti wondered too. I thought they might have more insight, since they knew about the school long before I did. And Priti's family had gone here. Surely if there was a secret, one of them would have spilled it by now.

It had something to do with the basement. Convinced that the dungeon held the secret, I wanted to check it out again, but the memory of spiders raining down on me pulled a shiver from me.

"The spiders again?" Priti asked.

Kisha, Priti's friend from astronomy, shuddered. "I can't imagine."

Gabriela from Priti's ethics class shifted in her seat, pulling her legs up to sit cross-legged on the sofa. "I would have freaked out."

Saad nodded. "What do you think the dean meant?"

After an early lunch, Priti, Saad, Kisha, Gabriela, and I sat discussing what the school could be hiding. Priti and I sat in chairs beside each other. Saad and Gabi sat on the sofa with only enough room between them for a small child, so Kisha sat on the floor in front of the sofa cross-legged.

I shook my head. "No idea, but he seemed worried that I knew something. I still have no idea what. I saw a door, which I assume is the dungeon, but the dungeon isn't a secret."

"My sisters told me about it," Priti said. "That it was there, but they never mentioned what was in it. All the magic schools have one."

Conrad arrived, backpack slung over his shoulder. He nodded at Saad. "Dude, we studying?"

"Later, ladies." Saad vacated his spot on the sofa and Gabi stretched out her legs to take up the entire length.

Kisha tapped Gabi's legs and she moved them out of the way so Kisha could slip into Saad's spot.

Priti leaned forward. "This is the last weekend before semi-finals."

"That's right." Kisha grabbed a handful of jellybeans. "All-nighter?"

"I'm in. Sounds like fun," Gabi said.

"All-nighter?" I clasped my hands to stop the sudden shaking.

"My sisters told me about it. They used to pull all-night study groups the weekend before semi-finals," Priti said.

Didn't sound all that scary, but something was still making my stomach churn. Around Priti, I could be myself, and she knew my magical limitations. But I wasn't as close to Kisha and Gabi. I wasn't sure I could trust them. In high school, I didn't have any friends, so having Priti and Saad was new for me. Two I could handle. Kisha and Gabi had potential.

Hailey and Nia entered the common area. The four of

us remained quiet while they walked by. Hailey shot me a dirty look as they went. They settled into the chairs in the nook beside us. Where they were, Tess wasn't far behind.

"Pajama party!" Gabi clapped her hands. "I love it. We can get comfy in our PJs, stock up on snacks and caffeine."

Sucking in a calming breath, I pressed a hand to my stomach to stop the fluttering. "Pajamas?"

Priti leaned closer to me and whispered, "You can wear something of mine if you don't have something you can wear."

Used to taunts about my lack of fashionable clothing, Priti's offer surprised me, though it shouldn't have. She'd never made me feel like I was less than everyone else due to my lack of financial means.

"Yes!" Kisha fist-pumped the air. "But we have to actually study."

Priti laughed. "Of course. We can study in the observatory. It's beautiful up there and quiet."

The opportunity to see the campus from such a vantage point was exciting. Maybe we could even take a look through the telescopes they had up there. I knew they were there because Priti raved about seeing Jupiter.

"Okay, sounds great," Gabi said.

Priti's tablet pinged, the sound of a Hollywood kiss emanating from her backpack sitting on the floor in front of her chair. A blush crept across her cheeks and she fumbled to get the tablet out before another text came in.

"That's Renato. Can I catch up with you guys for the all-nighter? He's begging to see me to help him with one of his classes."

"Have fun but be careful," I said.

Priti laughed, pushing my shoulder. "It's not like that."

I nodded. "Sure. I've seen the way he looks at you."

They met in astronomy class and hit it off right away

but didn't start "dating" until after Halloween. He looked at Priti most times like a lovesick puppy. But there were those other times, times I didn't tell her about, where he gazed at her like a lion stalking his prey. Whether he saw her as a conquest or an actual girlfriend, I had no idea. I hoped he genuinely liked her, but my trust in people didn't go much beyond Priti, Saad, and Damien.

An image of Nathan popped into my head as if to say *What about me?* I almost laughed out loud. I didn't trust him as far as I could throw him. He hovered in between cliques at the school, not a part of any in particular, but part of all at the same time. Even Priti and Saad seemed to like him. There was something about him, though, that I didn't quite trust. Everyone hid something they didn't want others to know, but I worried that his secret was dangerous, though I had no proof. Gut feelings got me through a lot in life.

Renato had always been nice to me. Never looked down his nose at me like Tess and her friends. But he never made me feel like he was listening to me either when I talked. He always seemed distracted, on his tablet, or nodding at whatever I said, even though his focus was on something besides me.

Was I jealous that she had a boyfriend? I examined that for a minute and dismissed the idea. I wanted Priti to be happy and if having a boyfriend made her happy I was all for it. On a personal level as well as a magical one, I didn't have time for a boyfriend. All my focus needed to be on developing my magical abilities so I could pass my semi-finals and then finals.

"He wants help with astronomy and astrology." She blushed again. "He said he can't concentrate in class because I distract him."

The logic of her helping him with the subject when she

was a distraction didn't make sense. He would be all moony-eyed the entire time they were together.

"Make sure he learns something," I said.

Priti picked up her backpack, dropped her tablet into the bag, and slung it over her shoulder. "I will."

"See you tonight," Gabi said.

Priti leaned over to whisper in my ear, "Check out my dresser for any set of pajamas you want to wear."

I nodded, sure I would find something that fit me. None of my clothes would have sufficed. Threadbare nightgowns, battered jeans, old T-shirts never bothered me before. But I couldn't show up at a pajama party in any of them. Sorry, a pajama all-night study party.

"We should head to class." Kisha nodded at Gabi.

We all stood, picked up our backpacks, and headed to the stairs. I looked over my shoulder to make sure I hadn't forgotten anything. Hailey and Nia still sat huddled together, like they were making plans of their own.

After dinner, I returned to my room to get ready for the overnight study session. Priti wasn't there, and there was no message on the blackboard on the back of the door. She was probably still with Renato. I'd hoped we would head up to the observatory together, since it was more her territory than mine, but I could go on my own if she didn't return soon.

Uncomfortable about going through Priti's drawers without her here, I sat on the bed, tapping my foot for a few minutes. I couldn't wait forever. If she didn't return soon, I would have to rummage through her clothes, get changed, grab my stuff, and meet her in the observatory.

Fifteen minutes later, I sighed and got off the bed. I

pulled out my tablet to see if she'd sent a message and there was nothing on the screen except for a reminder for the study group. I shoved the tablet in my backpack again.

Her side of the dresser was organized, top to bottom, with bras and underwear, T-shirts, and pajamas and night-gowns. My side of the dresser needed no such organization. I had five tops and two pairs of jeans, plus my undergarments. Jeans went in my closet, and the tops and other stuff went in my top drawer. I yanked open the bottom drawer on her side and pulled out the first thing that looked like it would fit.

She called them her comfy pajamas. Flannel, baggy on her, and the bluest blue I'd ever seen. The material so soft it was like a fluffy blanket on your skin. Though all areas of the castle, even the observatory, were heated, I didn't know how well insulated the tower would be.

I quickly donned the pajamas. At least I wouldn't need a coat while I was up there. And I suspected someone would bring a blanket. November was cool at the castle, and the observatory might be cold, especially at night. It wasn't like we could light a fire to chase the chill away. They frowned on that here. Plus, we might set something on fire by accident. I wasn't even sure any of the freshmen witches could create fire out of the air yet. That was something we'd learn years down the road.

I gathered the items I would need to get me through a night of studying. My spell book, map of the castle, text-books for demonology and arcane history. Though I needed help in all of my classes, there was only so much information I could stuff in my brain in one night. I needed to focus on the two most troublesome classes and worry about the others later. There was the rest of the weekend to study, plus Monday and Tuesday. Semi-finals started on Wednesday.

I shoved everything into my backpack, grabbing my tablet from the depths of the cavernous bag to settle it on top.

My tablet chimed with an incoming text. I picked it up and frowned.

A

Studying with Renato going longer than expected. Study group location has changed to the roof near the greenhouse. Meet you there soon.

P

It was an odd change. We weren't supposed to be near the greenhouse, but I guess if we weren't going into it, being on the same level as it was okay? One of the other students must know something I didn't. A loophole maybe that said we were okay to be up there. The roof had plenty of space, so we didn't have to be anywhere close to the greenhouse. It would also provide us with an unobstructed view of the night sky. Priti wouldn't have telescopes to look through, but maybe she wasn't planning on studying astronomy and astrology tonight. She was doing that now with Renato.

I fired off a quick text back.

P

Okay, see you there. Don't forget more snacks.

A

I surveyed the room to make sure I hadn't forgotten

anything, then left. Instead of going left at the stairs in the middle of the common area, I continued walking to the end of the hall and up the stairs on the sophomore side of the floor. The only way to get to the roof.

The stairs were old, curving, and there were no lights on the wall to guide my way. Old-fashioned sconces with candles burned down to nothing lined the wall. Either no one ever went up to the roof this way and there was some other entrance I didn't know about, or everyone used magic to light the stairwell.

I made a note to study the map of the castle again. After a few months here, I thought I knew the entire layout. I must have missed something. They wouldn't risk the juniors and seniors getting hurt due to lack of lighting.

I pushed through the door at the top of the stairs and dragged in a huge breath of the chilled night air. The dust from the stairs made me cough. I glanced around in the darkness. No one was there. I couldn't be the first to arrive. I hated being the first to arrive. It always left me anxious, wondering if everything had been a big joke and no one else was coming. But Priti was coming. She'd sent the message to tell me of the change in location. She must still be with her boyfriend.

A section of the pajamas around my left arm, just below my shoulder, brightened. Even though I couldn't see the vaccine mark, I knew it was glowing. The hairs on the back of my neck rose.

I spun around. The only person I saw was Nathan, on the ground, looking up at the roof. He pointed, might have been saying something, but I couldn't hear him.

I ventured closer to the greenhouse. The lights on inside the enclosure spilled out onto the roof, creating a small area of illumination. Everything else was still swallowed by the darkness.

A sound, pebbles tumbling down a slate roof and pinging off the concrete below, drew my attention. The mark on my arm glowed again, providing more light in the dark.

A shadow moved. Without getting closer, I couldn't be positive, but my gut told me it was Tess. She smiled in the dark. Her voice, calm, floated through the blackness of night.

"Glad you got the message," Tess said.

As she advanced on me, the chatter of teachers floated up. Angry, concerned voices, with Damien's most prominent, followed by the dean.

"What are you doing here?"

"What better place to practice? You think you can prevent yourself from falling over the edge?"

A blast of magic hit me, a force pushed my chest, and I stumbled backward. Magic Tess had never used before, at least not in class.

Heat raced through me. The lights of the greenhouse flickered. I moved away from the enclosure, closer to Tess. If I had no control over the magic, I might blow up the greenhouse. How much trouble would that get me in? Expelled for the rest of the year? Kicked out of the school altogether?

"What are you doing?" Was Tess just trying to scare me?

Even in the darkness, I still noticed when she flicked a blond lock over her shoulder. "You know, if your roommate dies during the school year, you get an A in everything. Automatic pass. Think Priti could use any more As?"

More chatter reached us.

"Expelled, both of them," the dean said.

Tess dashed away, a beam of light marking a path for her to follow. She'd brought a flashlight or used magic.

Either way, it didn't matter. As soon as she disappeared, the gentle click of the lock engaged. My chances of getting off the roof without help plummeted.

The message. It had been faked. But how? Magic? Priti would never participate in a prank, especially not one with the potential to get me into trouble for being in a forbidden area. Not to mention the fact that I needed all the study time I could get. And it was slipping away the longer I was up here.

I glanced down. Nathan still stood there, but there were no teachers. No dean. He was alone, still pointing at the roof.

I breathed a small sigh of relief. If the sounds of teachers had been an auditory glamour, there was a chance I could get out of this without getting into trouble.

The only thing standing in my way was the locked door.

I rushed forward, almost tripping on pebbles that littered the rooftop. I slowed my progress and pulled out my phone to use its flashlight feature. Fully charged, there was no way it would conk out on me when I needed it most. I rarely used it. Who did I have to call? Most communication in school was through email or texts to the tablet. I roomed with my now best friend.

How much of a best friend was she, if she'd tricked me into coming to the roof? I had to give her the benefit of the doubt. There was no way she would help Tess trap me up here. I had no idea what the bully's plans had been. Had trapping me been her only objective? Or did she want to take me out of the school permanently? The magic she'd used to almost push me into the greenhouse shouldn't be possible for her yet.

At the door, I grabbed the knob and turned. Tried to turn. The knob didn't budge. I shone the light where a keyhole should be and found nothing. Locked from the other side, I had no way of picking it open.

I dropped my backpack at my feet, rummaging around for the spell book. Maybe there was something in there that could help me.

I flipped through the pages, glancing over each spell. Halfway through the book, I found one that looked promising. My grandmother had made a note in the margins.

When you don't have a key

I uttered the phrase in the book three times, as instructed. "*Reserare ostium, reserare ostium, reserare ostium.*"

I grabbed the knob again. It didn't turn.

Stomping feet on the stairs caused my stomach to churn. Teachers? Tess back for more after discovering there were no teachers watching us on the roof? Something else, happy I was trapped up here alone?

Despite what the professors and some students had said, I felt deep down that there were monsters here. Maybe they were students, like Tess. Maybe something else.

"Alex?"

Priti's voice came through the door. She sounded far away, not on the other side of a wooden door.

"I'm here. The door's locked and I can't get it open."

"Hold on. I don't see a key anywhere around the door," Priti said.

"Can we try magic?"

I told her about the spell I'd found. It hadn't worked for me, but if my magic wasn't completely unbound as I suspected, that could explain why it failed.

"Okay, we'll all say it together," Priti said.

"Count of three?"

"Yes."

I counted us down. When I hit three, Priti, Saad, Nathan, and I recited the spell.

The lock clicked. The door swayed open, then caught on a gentle breeze, banged against the wall beside it. Inside the top of the stairwell, my friends and Nathan sighed.

"Let's get out of here before any teachers come by," Priti said.

We hurried down the stairs, Nathan lighting the way with his phone. At the bottom, I hugged Priti.

"Thanks."

"You're welcome. What were you doing up there? If Nathan hadn't told us you were there, we wouldn't have even thought to check the roof."

"I got a message from your tablet telling me the study group meeting place had changed."

I turned to Nathan. "I guess I should thank you too."

He shrugged. "I didn't want anyone to have an advantage during semi-finals."

"Thank you."

Me being expelled might have altered the class average. Would my demise have helped Tess in any other way? I would have to find out. There was more to her bullying than being a bully. Tonight was the first time I was convinced she wanted to do actual harm to me. There had been malice in her magical push. Hatred. Despite not fitting in all through high school, I never thought anyone there actually hated me. I only got that from my foster sisters. Tess's dislike was more than that.

"I'm going to get her back to our room. Thanks for helping, guys." Priti nodded at Nathan and Saad, then looped her arm through mine.

I sighed with relief back at our room, falling onto my bed.

"What about the study group?"

"When I left and didn't know how long I would be, they decided to finish studying in their rooms. It was a tad nippy up there."

Disappointed she had missed out on bonding more with her classmates, I frowned. "I'm sorry."

"Not your fault." She sat in the middle of her bed, crossing her legs underneath her. She clasped her hands in her lap. "You know I didn't send that message, right? I would never do that. I would never help Tess hurt you."

The niggly doubt in the back of my mind disappeared. The concern on Priti's face, the worry lines on her forehead, melted through my frozen heart.

"I know."

"Someone must have spoofed my tablet or something."

"Or something."

"What does that mean?"

I shook my head. Realization of what must have happened gnawed at me. Priti had a right to know I suspected Renato, but I didn't want to test our friendship. I'd seen many high school girls pick their boyfriends over friends they'd had for years when loyalties were questioned. Priti was the first true friend I'd ever had and I didn't want to blow it if I was wrong about Renato.

"Nothing. We'll figure it out. I'm worried it will happen again, though. How will I know now if I can trust texts that come through? From anyone?"

"I'll put a spell on your tablet."

I shrugged, bent to grab it from my backpack on the floor, then handed it to her.

She waved her hand over the tablet. "*Amicus et inimucus in tabula.*"

She handed it back. "There. Now if it's me, Professor O'Connor, or Saad texting you, the message will glow green."

"What about the dean and other teachers?"

"It should work for them too if they have your best interests at heart. We can test it tomorrow."

"Nice. Thanks."

She blushed and waved away my gratitude. "It's nothing. What are we going to do now? We still need to study. And I have all these snacks."

She dumped the contents of her backpack onto the bed. Among the books, pens, and highlighters were dozens of snack cards.

"I'm too wound up to sleep, so I say we study for as long as we can keep our eyes open."

We launched off our beds. Priti grabbed some of the cards, and we went to our desks.

I pored over book after book from demonology class and arcane history. Events muddled together in my mind until I wasn't sure what happened when. Demons walked the Earth, then witches came to stop them. Or witches formed, then demons came to wreak havoc. Iron counteracted the demons' magic, but could also affect witches if they got too close. I yawned. Shook my head to clear the cobwebs.

Images danced in my mind, not of spells and defense moves, but of my parents. Smiling, laughing, then anguish and horror. Bright red light surrounded them. My mother keeled over, blood spilling out of her body until the sidewalk supporting her turned a sickly rust red. A scream startled me awake. Sweat trickled down my neck.

Priti rushed over from her bed. "Are you okay?"

I shook my head, glancing around to orient myself. Books open on my desk depicted various demons and their vital information and the history of magic we'd studied so far. Despite not getting to information about my family, I'd read ahead to see if there were any mentions of my parents. I must have pieced together things about their death and they manifested in a nightmare.

"I'm okay. Nightmare."

Priti's eyebrows drew together, her head tilting to one side. "Maybe you should put the studying aside for the night and start fresh in the morning."

Rolling my shoulders, I shook my head. "I'll study for a little while longer, then go to bed. I need to pass these semi-finals."

Priti nodded and returned to her bed. "Okay, but wake me if you need anything."

Though I nodded, I knew I wouldn't wake her. Unless I had another nightmare because I'd fallen asleep at my desk. The only thing I needed was to soak in all the knowledge I could. Later, after semi-finals and finals, I would find out what exactly happened to my parents. If the demon who had killed them wasn't already dead, sending him back to hell would be my life's mission.

Chapter Thirteen

The night before semi-finals, restless, I paced my room, waiting for Priti to come back from wherever it was she'd disappeared to. I hadn't seen her most of the day and I suspected she was with Renato. Dinner in the dining hall hadn't been the same without her. I liked Saad and his roommate, who had started to join us, but I missed my best friend. Odd feeling, actually missing someone I saw every day.

If she didn't return soon, I would start studying without her. I had a few hours to drill information into my brain and I didn't think there was room for anything else in there. Thankfully, the few days before semi-finals were earmarked for studying, so we'd had no classes with new information that we needed to absorb. Everything we needed to pass the exams had already been taught. And mostly understood.

My pacing brought me to the window at the back of the room between our two beds. Movement at the edge of the grounds, before the thick trees of the forest began, caught my attention. Priti. Her bright fuchsia top was unmistakable in the light of the moon. In three nights it would be full, but even now it shone moonlight onto the two people at the edge of the trees.

Priti shook her head, turning to walk back to the castle. Renato said something and Priti turned around, though she stood her ground.

Though I wanted to check out the forest, explore its secrets, and I knew it must have them, I stopped myself every time the urge took hold. Why else, if not for secrets, would it be forbidden for freshmen to venture into the trees?

I pulled my tablet out of my backpack and checked the time. It was well past curfew. A double whammy if Priti got caught at her current location.

Renato pointed to the trees, nodding, jerking his head in the direction of the forest. His feet shuffled closer to the edge.

I willed Priti to leave him there. To return to the safety of the room.

He grabbed her arm and pulled. She jerked forward, then yanked her arm out of his grasp. I didn't have to see her face to know she was shooting daggers at him. Her eyes, usually blue-green and beautiful, could turn on a dime when angry.

He held up his hands in a placating gesture. Shoulders slouched, head down, he still moved closer to the forest. He was probably saying something to her, trying to convince her to follow him. To what end? Why would he want to go into the forest now?

Tess's taunt about a dead roommate came back to me. Clenching my fists, I took quick, shallow breaths. Heat rose around me the longer I looked at him. He reached out a hand again, but Priti moved backward.

I grabbed my tablet and the castle map and shoved

them into the front pocket of my uniform. Even though we didn't need to wear them in between classes and semi-finals, I still wore mine. It was comfortable and flexible, and better than most of my own clothes.

I raced down the stairs, out the back door of the castle, through the courtyard. The gate surrounding the courtyard was open, so I pushed through, the clang of the metal fence hitting the steel lock making me cringe. The courtyard was empty, but who knew how many prying eyes watched the spectacle I was making of myself. Any one of them could inform the dean or one of the teachers.

When I reached the spot where Priti and Renato had been no one was there. I slid to a halt and spun around, glancing in every direction for any sign of them.

Beams of moonlight revealed the brown grass around me and under my feet was well trampled. Other people had been here. I hadn't been seeing things.

Relief lifted the weight off my shoulders. I breathed a little easier, despite the race through the castle. Defense class had the added side benefit of getting me in the best shape I'd ever been in. Who needed a gym, just learn to fight monsters.

Halfway back to the gate at the back of the castle, my tablet buzzed with a text. I paused to pull out my tablet. Priti might be back in the room, wondering where I was. In a rush to help her, I hadn't left a message on the black-board behind the door. A shadow moved, and my heart leaped to my throat. Was Renato still there? Someone else who wanted to do me harm? Mr. Wozniak waited until I was through the gate and then locked it with a shake of his head at me.

I took a deep breath to calm my racing heart. Then checked out my tablet. A message from Damien appeared on the screen. A slight green glow around the message indicated Priti's spell had worked.

Ms. Kavanagh

My office. Now

Professor O'Connor

Dejected, I sighed and dropped the tablet back in my pocket. I hated when he called me that. So formal. So in trouble. It wasn't the caretaker's fault, though he didn't really have to tell anyone I'd been near the forest. I should have been more careful. Paid more attention to who was present when I raced through gates to where I shouldn't be.

I dawdled on my way to the gym. Why rush punishment? The longer it took to get there, the longer I would be punishment-free. What would it be this time? Confining me to my room during semi-finals wouldn't be much punishment. It would give me more time to study. And though they harped on the rules, I couldn't imagine them doing something that would prevent me from studying. Despite me breaking the rules, they still wanted me to do well in my classes.

The gym was dark when I pushed through the doors. A triangle of light from the crack in his office door spilled onto the hardwood floor. Why was he even in there so late? He had a room on campus that must be more comfortable than a stuffy office.

Before I could knock, he said, "Come in, Miss Kavanagh."

I peeked inside, pushed the door open all the way, and entered. Slumping into the first chair available, I folded my hands in my lap and waited for the barrage of fury.

He finished writing something, put his pen down, and looked at me. The disappointment in his eyes was like a punch to the stomach.

"Ms. Kavanagh, what you did was extremely foolish. You need to approach the forest with caution. Don't go barreling in. As a freshman, you shouldn't ever be that close to it unsupervised."

"I know. I..." Even though I had a good reason, at least to me, I couldn't tell him Priti had been there. There was no point in both of us getting into trouble. Roommates didn't rat on each other. I thought about mentioning Renato, but Damien might think Priti was with him. Everyone knew they were seeing each other.

"You what?" Damien folded his hands on top of his desk. He regarded me with raised eyebrows, arms crossed over his chest.

"I promise not to go back there again unsupervised."

Contrite was the best option. I had no argument that wouldn't get my roommate in trouble. And I wanted this little meeting to be over so I could return to my room to make sure she was okay.

He leaned back in his chair. Lips pursed, he shrugged. "Fine. See that you don't and I'll keep this between us."

"Promise." I gripped the arms of the chair, ready to push myself off as soon as he gave the word.

"Dismissed."

I bolted off the chair and yanked the door open. "Thanks."

I raced out of the gym before he could change his mind. At this time of night, the halls were quiet. Chatter from the common areas floated in the air, hushed whispers filled with questions and facts.

I took the stairs two at a time, hurried down the hallway of the second floor, and burst into my room. Priti, sitting at her desk, hunched over a textbook, let out a yelp.

"Alex, you scared the hell out of me. Where were you?"

"I couldn't concentrate, so I went for a little walk around the castle. Clear my head." I sat at my desk and opened the first textbook I found. "We missed you at dinner."

"Sorry about that. Renato wanted to go over stuff before semi-finals tomorrow."

"What about you? You think you're going to pass?"

Priti huffed, slumping back in her chair. "I'd have to say it's a solid maybe."

I grinned. "Then let's study for a while before bed. A few test quizzes should put your mind at ease."

When Priti was ready to talk about what happened with her boyfriend she would share. For now, we both needed to cram our minds full of ethical reasons to use magic.

If I listened hard enough I swear I could hear the ticking of a clock marking the passing of each second. It was my imagination of course. There were no analog clocks on the wall in the lecture hall, just a digital one on the corner of the desk relaying the time. Telling me how many minutes I had left until the exam was over.

I went through my paper again to make sure I hadn't forgotten anything. All the multiple-choice questions had an answer circled. All the true/false questions had one of the options selected. The essay questions were well thought out. At least I hoped they were.

The necromancy questions had me stumbling a little.

We didn't discuss it much in class, but I had pored over the chapters in the textbooks. Years ago, had I known it was a thing, would I have wanted to bring my parents back? Even then it would have been too late. And had I learned at five that it might have been a possibility, I didn't have enough magic to bring them back.

A buzzing noise from the desk startled me. "That's time, everyone." Mrs. Bonum shut off the alarm.

All around me students groaned, giggled, gasped.

Chairs scraped across the floor as students got up from their desks. I couldn't wait to compare notes with Priti and Saad about the exam. With two ethics classes for freshmen, the exam was held in two rooms.

When I reached the common area on the second floor they were already in their usual spots in the first nook. Priti and Saad on the sofa. Conrad and Kisha were also there in chairs facing the sofa. I fell into the spot between Priti and Saad.

"How did you guys do?" I grabbed a handful of peanuts from the table. Now that the stress of the exam was over, my stomach grumbled for food.

Priti beamed. "I think I did pretty well."

Saad nodded. "She whizzed through all the questions. Me, I think I did okay."

"I'm sure you all did fine." Conrad leaned over to investigate the available snacks on the table. After a few moments, he picked up a fun-size chocolate bar leftover from Halloween. "My ethics grade is iffy. I hope I passed."

"Do people die forever?" I asked.

Conrad choked on the half eaten chocolate bar, his face turning an angry shade of red for a split second before he cleared his throat. "What made you ask that?"

"The necromancy questions on the exam. Before, I figured dead was dead. Loved ones who died were gone forever, alive only in memories and pictures. But I never believed in magic either and it turns out that's real."

"Necromancy is an ethical question, though," Priti said. "That was the point on the exam." Her face scrunched with worry.

"Relax. I got the ethical dilemma of it all. But the fact remains, ethical or not, that we can bring people back if we have the knowledge, enough magic, the ingredients for the spell. How often does it actually happen? Has anyone missed someone so much that they threw ethics aside and brought back their mother or father?"

"No." Priti's firm negative drew everyone's attention. "At least I haven't heard of anyone doing that."

Saad nodded. "Sure, but it's also pretty much forbidden, so even if it did happen, the Bureau of Magical Discourse would bury the story."

"Bury the story?" I asked.

"For the ordpops the BOMD would spin the story so it's something innocuous. Grave robbing, maybe. But underneath that story would be the magical story, the one only we can see, giving us a magical explanation. But they wouldn't say it was necromancy."

The philosophical question of necromancy flew off my radar at the knowledge there were hidden messages in newspapers. "Wait, in newspapers there are two layers to a story?"

"On the internet too. The underlying magical story, if there is one, will be indicated on the page. You can click that button and see the magical story."

Head spinning, I grabbed more peanuts. How had no one mentioned this before now? True, we hadn't talked about the outside world much since school started. There was no reason to, really. Especially for me. I had nothing out there that I missed or wanted to get back to. In truth, I was dreading the end of the school year. And I hoped the school would let me stay on campus during the Christmas holidays.

"On that note, it's clear I have a lot more to learn before tomorrow's exams. I'm going back to my room to study."

Priti jumped up from the sofa. "I'll come too."

I was glad for her company. Studying with someone meant we could quiz each other, test small spells, get more comfortable with magic in general.

The guys and Kisha stayed behind, their conversation fading to barely audible as we walked down the hall to our room.

Inside, I settled into the chair at my desk, dropped my backpack on the floor, and thought about what I should study first.

"How do you keep track of everything? There's so much to know, and so much we probably won't know when we finish school."

Priti pulled out her chair and sank into it. She adjusted the monitor on the desk, tilting it up and down until she was happy with the angle. "Most of us have the advantage that we've grown up with this stuff." She yanked open the bottom drawer of her desk. Both hands disappeared into the depths and she pulled out a large, thick tome with a light brown leather cover. A ribbon sewn into the spine acted as a bookmark.

She dropped it on my desk. The cover had an elaborate symbol on it. I raised an eyebrow.

"The crest of my family."

I opened the book and it naturally fell about two hundred pages in. A list of items took up the left side of the page. On the right were a few paragraphs of text with a word at the top in a darker script, underlined. Beelzebub.

"What is this?"

"My Book of Shadows. Everything I've learned from my family I document in here. What works, what doesn't work. Favorite spells. Information on demons. I add my own notes to stuff that is already in here."

"That's pretty hefty. You can't travel with that every day just in case you encounter a demon."

Priti laughed. "Of course not. It's a good starting point. And I have it scanned into my phone so I can reference it when I'm not near the book."

I flipped through a few more pages, wondering if the demon who attacked me was in here. "Does it have all demons in it?"

Priti shook her head. "Only ones I or my family have encountered mostly. A few I'd heard about, so I made a quick note."

"I have so many questions. Was it already started when you got it?"

"It was passed down to me from my mother. Each of my siblings received one too. With some of it already filled out with what the family knows."

Disappointment settled in my stomach, a knot churning. If my family had a similar book, it was long gone. I'd never seen anything like this in our home that I could remember. And my grandmother never mentioned anything either.

"I guess I should start one. They haven't mentioned anything in any of the classes yet. I would think arcane history would at least mention it."

"They might later. I can't remember if my sisters said anything about that. I started this when I was fourteen."

I leaned back in my chair and blew out a breath. "I am so behind the times here. I have so much to catch up on.

And I need to make sure I don't overexert myself so my magic isn't drained completely."

A pain in my jaw forced me to unclench my teeth.

"You'll start one when you're ready. There's still plenty of time. You won't truly need it until we graduate and start hunting demons."

"I hope so. Because right now I feel like I know nothing."

"You know a lot more than you think you do. Like the demonic hot spots. Do you know where you're going to settle when school is over?"

I shook my head. "Do we have to settle in a hot spot?"

Priti shrugged. "Maybe. There are only eight of them. All the demon hunters probably won't be needed in those places. They're focused on places of sin."

"I guess with two casinos here, Niagara Falls qualifies. But I don't want to stay here forever."

"I think because of the school, even though it's a hot spot, the demon population is under control."

"When are they going to teach us about that stuff?" I envied Priti's advanced knowledge of most things demon. A pang of sadness hit me as a flash of my mother's smile filled my head. Taken before she could teach me anything about our heritage, I wanted to kill the demon who had taken her from me.

"We should probably study a little more before bed," Priti said.

I nodded, handing her book back. I reached into my backpack and pulled out my arcane history textbooks.

Despite probably acing my ethics exam, I still wasn't sure of my abilities. I was testing my magic more each day to make sure I could do simple things, the things we were supposed to do in class or for homework. Time and my exam scores would tell if I was actually getting anywhere.

Chapter Fourteen

After checking my answers for my last semi-final for the third time, I put my pen down and glanced around the room. Most students were still heads down, scribbling answers on the page, their brows furrowed in thought. Others, like me, were finished, but waiting for the exam time to be over. Technically, I could have left when I finished the test, but I didn't want to disturb those still working on their answers. Plus, I might want to go through and check it one last time. You never know what you might find in the proofread. Especially for arcane history. There was so much history to know, so many trials, so many famous demon battles, that I wanted to make sure I hadn't missed anything important. The first two times I'd gone through my answers, I'd added three paragraphs.

Now that the last semi-final was almost officially over, a weight lifted from my shoulders. Despite my late start in the magical world, I believed I passed all my exams, and some of them I even aced. Glad they were over, I vowed to study more for the next round. These were just semi-finals.

The next exams were finals and a big chunk of our marks depended on how we did.

A little disappointed that the exams dealt with mostly theory and the lecture material instead of practical application, I found myself wanting to flex my magical muscles. I tapped into the magic when I could, straining the bindings that reined in my power. Despite Mrs. Sapienti declaring the binding broken after a second unbinding before semi-finals started, I knew I didn't have access to all my magic. Something still held it back.

The timer at the front of the class buzzed.

"Pens down everyone," Mrs. Rúnda said.

Shuffles of paper and groans from students floated through the room. The pens were magical. With a spell on them, they prevented each student from cheating. If the student had the answers somewhere, the pens would not work. If the student tried to look at someone else's paper, the pens refused to let the ink flow over the paper. With the ability to use magic, spells to make you smarter, potions to help you remember, it was tempting to cheat. But then we'd only be cheating ourselves. In the real world, we weren't supposed to use our magic unless we had no other choice.

I dashed out of the room and hurried to the common area. It was now our usual meeting place instead of the dining hall. The nooks were more intimate, the floor less crowded, especially in between classes, or in this case in between exams. The sophomores still had one more mid-term to get through, but the freshmen were done.

When I hit the top of the stairs I smiled. Saad, Priti, Kisha, and Conrad were already there. A few nooks over Hailey and Nia laughed about something. I couldn't help thinking it was something about me.

I plopped into an empty spot on the sofa between Saad and Priti.

"It's over!" I leaned my head back to rest on the sofa.

"How did you do?" Priti asked.

"Okay, I think. What about you guys?"

Nods all around said confidence, but Priti's eyes darkened.

"You did great, Priti."

My roommate sighed. "I hope so. I don't want to disappoint my family."

Bonus of being an orphan, I had no one to disappoint except for myself.

"Enough talk about semi-finals. They're done. Let's talk about celebrating not having to cram for exams until the spring." Conrad put his feet up on the table, almost knocking over a bowl of pretzels.

"It would be nice to blow off a little steam. I feel like I've been studying forever," Priti said.

Saad leaned forward. "What should we do? There's not a lot in the way of steam blowing here."

For those who lived on campus, a school with the usual amenities at least had pubs or a new city to explore. And if you didn't live on campus, you had the rest of your world to kill time and entertain yourself. Being cooped up in the school as freshmen seemed like cruel and unusual punishment.

Kisha raised her hand. All eyes turned toward her. "Sorry, used to class. We could check out Clifton Hill."

Alarm bells went off in my mind. Sneaking out of the school could result in a lot of trouble, but what else were we going to do?

Saad shook his head. "I don't know about that. We're not supposed to be in town." He looked pointedly at me.

"I was helping the last time."

Conrad grabbed a handful of the pretzels he'd almost toppled. "It's a time honored tradition. We would be remiss if we didn't continue."

I glanced over at Priti, who nodded. "He's not wrong. My sisters snuck out their freshman year after semi-finals."

"Did they get caught?" I asked.

"No. Made it out of the school, to one of the beach resort bars, had a few laughs, and returned with no one the wiser."

"I like the sound of a few laughs." I leaned back against the soft cushions of the sofa, my mind swirling with fun possibilities.

"We could all use some," Conrad agreed.

"I think we should go," I said. "We can stay for a couple of hours and be back before curfew."

Saad shook his head. "I don't think it's a good idea."

I pouted. "I thought you were more adventurous."

Saad straightened, anger flashing across his face. "I'm adventurous."

A smile spread across my face. "Prove it. Come with me, us, this time."

"Fine. But I want to go on the record with the fact that I think this is a bad idea. Very bad."

"Noted." I turned back to Conrad and Priti. "How do we go about slipping out without anyone seeing us?"

"Let's meet in the lobby after dinner. We'll have to glamour before reaching the lobby so the security cameras don't recognize us."

The more I thought about freedom, the more anxious I was for dinner to be over with. My adventure with Damien left me wanting to explore more of the city. And it would be a lot more fun with friends.

In the lobby, after dinner, a group of people congregated by the door. All but one were familiar to me. Conrad was the only person in a glamour I recognized from his older brother's picture. I sidled up to them, wearing a facade of Lacey's face. It was the only person I knew well enough to hold the glamour long enough. It was too bad Tess was a freshman. I would have used hers since I'd done well with it the last time.

I pointed at Conrad. "You, I recognize. The others, I have no idea."

A petite Indian young lady moved to the front of the group. She had long black hair that fell to her shoulders in waves. Light brown eyes twinkled when she smiled. She leaned closer and whispered, "It's me, Priti."

"Sister?" Despite being roommates, I had not seen any pictures of her family.

Priti nodded. "My oldest."

The rest of the introductions were made. Saad was a sophomore that he and his roommate had spent a lot of time with. Kisha had glamoured into her cousin, who had also attended the school and had graduated last year.

"Who are you?" Priti asked.

"Co-worker. Well, former co-worker."

"Not even magical. Nice," Conrad said.

Priti waved her hands in a circle and moved closer to the door. "Gather around me as close as you can get."

When we'd all moved in until we felt like sardines she put her hands up in a stopping gesture.

"Good. *Ingerere nos silentio.*"

"What was that?" I asked, moving back again.

"Cloak of silence."

"I want to try." I waited in the opening of the doorway, pointed at the surveillance cameras. "*Caligo et nebula.*"

A cloud of fog hovered in front of the cameras.

Saad nodded in approval, a grin turning his lips up. "Nice. Getting in some practice at obscuring video cameras."

Though we weren't supposed to take Latin until our sophomore year, I had borrowed some books to learn the basics. Basic spells anyway. Class would teach me a lot more about the language itself, but I didn't need to know how to conjugate a verb to use Latin in a spell.

"Let's go before someone sees us." Kisha clutched her hands in front of her and looked over her shoulder like a criminal escaping prison.

Half expecting a siren to ring in the parking lot past the gates of the ward, I followed Conrad as he ran to his car, the rest of the group close behind me.

Since no one had declared shotgun, I yanked open the passenger door and climbed into the car.

"Ready to have some fun?" Conrad started the car, revved the engine, and put the vehicle into drive.

The drive seemed shorter than the last time I'd ventured to Clifton Hill, most likely due to the comfier circumstances. In Conrad's car, I didn't feel every bump in my hip or lurch to the side with every turn.

He pulled into the same parking lot beside The Haunted House. On a Wednesday night in November, the area was even more deserted than it had been before. A few tourists, braving the cold, huddled into their coats, speed-walked along the sidewalk. They disappeared into the steak house. I could almost hear the sizzle as they warmed up the moment they stepped inside.

To the left, lights dripped from the trees in the park across the street. Groups of tourists meandered along the sidewalk, bulky coats blocking out the cold. They carried steaming cups of coffee or hot chocolate and stopped every so often to comment on a storefront. Or, for the tourists loitering near the park, they pointed at the lights, their faces reflecting the soft white of the glow. Their breaths misted in the cold November air.

Excitement filled me at how alive the area was compared to October.

"Where do we want to go?" Priti asked.

To the right was a stretch of sidewalk lined with shops, tourist attractions, museums, and restaurants. With the occasional hotel thrown in for good measure. The sidewalk leading left stretched down to Niagara River Parkway and closer to the Falls.

"Depends. Are we hungry? Do we want to check out a wax museum, play laser tag, be frightened in a haunted house? Or do we want to check out the lights down near the Falls?" I pointed left.

Saad shrugged. His demeanor hadn't changed since we left. There was something still bothering him about being in the tourist area. Maybe part of why the rest of us liked it so much was the fact it was taboo.

I looped my arm through Saad's and gently pulled him in the direction of the Falls. "Let's check out the lights."

We meandered, moving aside when a group of tourists approached. As we passed the park, images from the last time I was there flashed through my mind. The demon, his eyes so full of hate, crumbling before me when Damien recited the exorcism. I shuddered and pulled my coat tighter around me.

A shadow on my left caught my attention. I spun around. A different group of tourists followed us. All of them absorbed in the light display from the park or chatting about something I couldn't hear.

"What?" Conrad asked.

"I thought I saw something."

Priti looped her arm through mine so the three of us made a chain. "Saw what?"

I shook my head. "Not sure. It was probably nothing. Maybe I'm worried about getting caught."

Conrad and Kisha maneuvered around us so they were in front. Conrad walked backward so he could face us as he talked. "We won't get caught. They expect us to do this."

I pinned him with a stare. "Did your brother do this his freshman year?"

He blanched. Shook his head. "No way, man. He didn't want to get caught." He grinned.

An unexpected laugh escaped my lips. "We're only going to be a couple of hours, right?"

He'd turned around again so he wasn't in danger of backing into another pedestrian. "Promise."

At the intersection of Clifton Hill and Niagara River Parkway, I glanced around again, trying to pick out anyone in the crowd that shouldn't be there. It was our job to fight the demons, but first, we had to find them. Was I imagining danger where there was none? Niagara Falls was a tourist destination and I heard nothing in the news over the years about tourists being killed or possessed by demons. Of course, that's not something they would put on the website.

Pedestrians waited for the light to change as cars zipped by. As a group, we huddled closer together, the professors' lectures about the off-limits nature of the town running through my mind. Would they know we'd left? Every trick we used to evade detection might be old hat to them. Especially if leaving the castle after semi-finals was the normal rebellion freshmen went through.

Hairs on the back of my neck rose, warmth flushing through my body. If I'd been wearing short sleeves, I knew

I would be able to see my tattoo glowing. I spun around. A group of guys, looking guilty solely because they were trying to look nonchalant, snagged my attention.

As men went, there was nothing remarkable about any of them. One was tall and thin. Another short and muscular. A third guy was tall and muscular. Tall being relative to my own five-foot-six. It was the intensity of their gazes in our direction that set off alarm bells for me. The slight smirk on their faces, all the same, as if they were wearing masks of people that hid something sinister underneath.

"Alex, come on." A pull from Priti on my arm refocused my attention. The light had turned green and we joined the mass of people hurrying to the other side.

A quick glance over my shoulder confirmed the group of men were close behind us. That didn't mean they were following us. They could be here taking in the Festival of Lights like most of the tourists. But they didn't glance at the lights in the trees. Or in the direction of the red-and-green-colored water of the Falls on their left. Their gazes remained straight ahead, as if they had a singular focus, on us.

More crowded than I expected, we zigzagged through the mass of pedestrians. The task was made harder by tourists who stopped in the middle of the sidewalk to look at the Falls instead of going down the steps and viewing the wonder from behind the barrier.

In front of the zip line, I literally bumped into a guy in a letter jacket.

"Sorry," he said.

"That's okay. I'm sorry." Recognition dawned on me. "Hey, how did the game go?"

Continuing along the sidewalk, Cole stopped. "How did you know about the game?"

"My friend Tess told me about it. She said she ran into

you last month." Putting Tess and friend in the same sentence left a bad taste in my mouth.

His face lit up and he walked back to me. "It went really well. We won."

"In large part thanks to you, I'm guessing."

The smile on his face widened. "Yep."

"Congratulations."

"Thanks." He walked away with a nod.

At least that part of our mission had been successful. The demon who wanted to corrupt Cole was back in hell or wherever they went. As long as another one didn't take its place, he should be safe.

But would we be safe?

I followed Cole's departure, searching the crowd for the guys who had been following us, at least in my paranoid mind. For a moment, I chalked it up to Damien's warnings about how dangerous the city was for us. Inventing danger where there was none wasn't unheard of. But then I spotted them pushing their way through the crowd.

"What is it?" Priti asked.

Not caring if the guys knew I knew they were following us, I nodded at them. "They've been following us."

Saad stepped closer to me. Our arms had become unlooped when I started talking to Cole. "Are you sure?"

"Pretty sure."

I focused my attention on them, studying them. The clothes they wore were lighter than the weather required. Clouds of mist every time they exhaled puffed in front of them. The guy on the left clenched his hands by his side. I focused on his fingers. Were those claws?

My gaze snapped up to their eyes. This far away, it was impossible to tell what color they were. Based on Cole's demon, I would bet these guys had the same black-green eyes.

"I don't want to alarm anyone, but I'm pretty sure those guys are demons."

Conrad scoffed. "They don't look like demons."

"Trust me. Not all demons look like demons."

The guy in the middle snarled. On the right, the tallest of the guys raised a hand at us that didn't look like a hand now. It was clearly a claw.

Without knowing what kind of demons they were, it was impossible to know how to fight them. And we'd never fought more than one at a time. True, there were five of us and only three of them, but I still didn't like our chances.

"I say we run," I said.

We pushed through the crowd at a more leisurely jog. After a few hundred meters, close to the Niagara Parks Police Service, the crowd thinned out enough for us to increase our speed. The other side of the street had fewer pedestrians because most of the tourists wanted a closer view of the Falls.

Priti puffed out air beside me. "We need to get back to the car."

Some people up ahead were crossing at a crosswalk. If we got there before they finished crossing, we could be on the other side and backtrack to the car. Otherwise, we'd have to wait for traffic to stop again on both sides of the street or continue until we found traffic lights.

I increased my pace, hitting the crosswalk while there were still people crossing. We rushed ahead, careful not to bump into anyone. As I passed people, I glanced at them to make sure there were no other demons lurking in plain sight.

On the other side of the street, Conrad gathered us together. "Hold hands." When we complied, he said, "*Invisibilia daemonibus.*"

As soon as the words were out of his mouth, we dashed

along the sidewalk. I glanced across the street and saw the three guys closing in on the crosswalk. Four more had joined their ranks. Now the demons outnumbered us. How many more would they pick up along the way? Where the hell were they coming from?

We raced back up Clifton Hill, huffing and puffing from our exertion. Definitely wasn't ready for calisthenics so late in the evening or the cold.

Halfway back to the car, I spotted Damien and Nathan. Damien held his phone at his waist, gaze lowered to view something on the screen, like he was following directions.

As we approached, he looked up and let out a huge sigh.

"What the hell were you thinking?" His nostrils flared.

"We didn't think it would be a big deal." I crossed my arms over my chest.

"We have rules for a reason."

Priti nodded to his phone. "What are you doing with that?"

"Tracking your magic."

Saad raised an eyebrow. "You can do that?"

"When you're glamoured, I can." With a sweeping hand motion, he pointed to everyone but me. "I recognize you guys." Then he pointed at me. "You, I don't, so you must be Alex."

"Busted. But in our defense, we felt cooped up. We wanted to take in the sights a little. It will be winter soon and we wanted to stretch our legs, walk around something that wasn't the castle or its grounds."

His eyebrows drew together. "Right now we need to get you out of here."

I turned around. The gang of demons had grown to ten.

"What do they want?" I asked.

"Besides finding out where the school is? Some fledgling witches to sacrifice to their boss. Or maybe just a tasty treat. A founding member would bring in quite a reward."

My body turned cold, not from the weather, and my heart raced. The foolishness of our youth was about to come back and slap us all in the face.

"What should we do?" Priti wrung her hands in front of her.

"I can't take them all on, even with your help. Your magic isn't fully developed yet." He waved behind him. "Go to the parking lot and stand against the doors of the first-floor hotel rooms. Go! Run!"

We ran. Heavy footfalls followed us, with Damien and Nathan close behind. They watched our flank, making sure the demons didn't see us go into the lot. Whispers of Latin on the cold night air reached me and I didn't have the energy to translate. Presumably, he was cloaking our retreat, somehow obscuring us from the demons' vision.

In the lot, we pushed ourselves hard against the wall on the first floor of the hotel. Darkness concealed the doors to the rooms.

Damien and Nathan caught up to us. Damien muttered more words in Latin. "*Abscondere a daemonibus.*" Then he and Nathan also stepped into the darkness with us.

I held my breath. We all held our breaths. As the demons raced past, claws, red eyes, and flaring nostrils came into view. Or I imagined those things. It was impossible to see that well in the dark.

Once they were past us, we waited for ten more minutes before Damien stepped into the lot again. "Into the car. I'm following you back."

Still worried about the demons, we inched our way out

of the shadows, glancing both ways to survey the sidewalk. As far as I could tell, the group of demons was gone and only humans passed by, oblivious to the magic going on around them.

Damien's car was parked beside Conrad's. I yanked open the passenger side door of Conrad's car. Before Nathan could get into Damien's car, I said, "Did you tell him where we were going?"

His eyes widened. "No. Why would I do that?"

"Someone told him."

Damien's lips pursed and he raised an eyebrow. "What makes you think someone told me and I didn't figure it out?"

"Why would you even be looking for us at school unless someone blabbed?" I asked.

"Get in the car. I want to see you in my office when we're back at the school."

Damien and Nathan got in Damien's car and waited for us to leave the parking lot.

I huffed, got into the car, and slammed the door shut. If Nathan hadn't said anything, then who did? I searched my memory for our discussion of our little jailbreak. Hailey and Nia had been sitting a nook over from us. Though not obviously eavesdropping, they could have picked up snippets of conversation. I wouldn't put it past Tess to tattle on us, especially if she thought it would get her into the school's good graces.

Heat flooded my body. One day, I would figure out a way to get back at her. Right now I worried about my meeting in Damien's office.

"Take a scenic route. I'm in no hurry to get back to school," I said.

Sitting in Damien's office in the chair closest to the door, closest to escape, I fidgeted under his intense stare from across his desk. The stony expression on his face morphed into flaring nostrils and a jaw muscle that twitched. Finally, he let out a heavy sigh and rubbed the back of his neck.

"Are you trying to get yourself killed or captured?"

"No." My voice sounded small, and I hated that, but it hurt that I'd disappointed him. He was the only person I'd known from the school before I arrived there. That history felt enormous.

"Then why did you go there without supervision and proper magical protection from the school?"

There had been talk of field trips to the core of the tourist area later in the year for sophomores. Freshmen were denied that adventure. Low man on the pole, we didn't get much in the way of perks. I didn't want to sound ungrateful, but it wasn't fair that we were cooped up in the school.

"We're all sorry. I'm sorry. I convinced them we should go. I'm used to no one caring where I am."

He frowned and leaned back in his chair. "Don't think you got away with it, even though I won't tell the dean what happened. As far as I'm concerned, you're all on probation."

I nodded. "Totally fair."

He leaned down. The squeak of a filing cabinet drawer being opened piqued my curiosity. He slammed down a thick, large leather book. I recognized it as a book of shadows. For some reason, I couldn't picture Damien having one, but I guess everyone in the witch community did.

"This is why you need to be more careful." He opened the book to a page. Flipped to other pages. Page after page of demons with information on each one. He stopped at a selection and pointed. A fierce-looking demon with red eyes, claws the size of steak knives but curled at the end, stared back from the page. "This is one of the demons that trailed you tonight."

I leaned closer to read the description. A singular focus, the Maga demon preyed on fledgling witches. As part of Malum's inner circle, he frequently hunted for bounties his master sought. Rewarded with the kill once Malum was done with his prey.

"So, he's sending bounty hunters for me now?"

"I don't think that's anything new. He's just one of the demons you'll encounter. I'm just trying to keep you safe. You're in a precarious position, like our friend Cole, but it's different for you. As a founder of magic, evil is much more interested in swaying you to their side. Or killing you so you don't get in their way."

Averting my gaze, I nodded.

"You're lucky he wasn't one of Malum's lieutenants. Bounty hunters aren't as close to Malum, on the outer edge of his inner circle. You have to wait until you have more power, more control, more experience before going to a hot spot like that."

"I'm sorry. I really am. I won't do it again."

He closed the book and pushed it across his desk. "This is yours. It has a lifetime of my notes in it on every demon or creature I've encountered so far. Any I've heard mention of. And ways to vanquish them if I know how to do that."

Dumbfounded, I stared at him. When I finally found my voice again, I swallowed to get the lump out of my throat. Tears welled in my eyes and I blinked them back. "But don't you need that?"

He shook his head. "I created this one for you. I knew you would need one someday. Today is that day."

Vision blurred, I reached out and wrapped my hands around the book, pulled it to my chest, and clutched it like it was a lifeline. It was the most important and best gift anyone had ever given me and I vowed to not let him down.

"Thank you." I dashed away tears before they could fall.

"You're welcome. Now get some rest. Be ready for classes when they start on Monday."

With a brief nod, I got up, fighting the urge to rush around the desk to hug him. Instead, I took a deep breath and smiled.

"See you in class."

I raced out of his office.

In the last two weeks of the year, the school became quiet. Gone was the echoing of footsteps in the hall. The chatter of students. It was as if the castle breathed a sigh of relief from its reprieve from the wear and tear of two hundred students who didn't appreciate its beauty.

I reveled in the time during the holidays when all the students went back to their families. What I liked most was the lack of Tess. Entering the dining hall each day she was gone felt like a vacation. No weight to shrug off my shoulders. They'd only been gone since Saturday, but already my muscles were more relaxed.

I missed Priti and Saad. I wouldn't see them again until January 3 when all the students returned. All the students who had homes to return from, that is.

Though it would have been blissful to have the entire castle to myself, that wasn't feasible. Some of the staff stayed to clean up after those who remained behind. And a few of the professors chose to stay on campus. Most likely to make sure the few of us who were here didn't get into more trouble. Since our trip in November, we'd all been on our best behaviors.

Monday evening I wandered into the dining hall. With no one else there, the space looked enormous. I could be a rebel and sit at the tables usually occupied by the seniors. A thrill of excitement raced through me at the thought. To see the dining hall from their perspective might give me insight into how things would be once I became a senior.

Though there were only a handful of students still at the school, the entire castle was decorated for the holidays. In the dining hall, garlands hung around the thick wood beams that criss-crossed the ceiling. Bright red poinsettias adorned every table.

Despite my thought about the senior tables, I took my usual spot in the freshmen section. I sat where Priti usually sat, facing the entrance to the hall.

Much to my dismay, Nathan sauntered in a few minutes later. I was still trying to decide what I wanted to eat. If we chose, we could have Christmas dinner with all the trimmings every day. Giving in to that temptation would mean about a thousand extra laps in the pool. Or a lot of time in the gym. With a break from training for the swim team and a break from defense class, I wanted to enjoy doing nothing. At least during this first week.

Nathan grinned and sat across from me.

"It's a huge hall with a lot of empty seats," I said.

A frown crossed his face, and the sparkle in his eyes dimmed. He stood.

"No, it's fine. Stay."

Since coming to my aid after semi-finals, I'd avoided him like carbs before prom. When classes had started again, I kept my distance, saying barely ten words to him. The smug air about him still rubbed me the wrong way. And I wasn't convinced I could trust him yet.

He sat back down and scrolled through his tablet to see what was on the menu. Though the full Christmas dinner was available every day, the rest of the selection was limited. Most of the food was magically prepared, but they still couldn't create it out of thin air. They needed to get the energy from somewhere, so they kept food in store that they could transform.

No one else from any of the other classes was around for dinner, though I knew there were a few from each class who stayed behind. And Nathan made sense, being an orphan as well. I was surprised, though, that he didn't go back to his foster family.

About to order my meal after deciding on the holiday dinner with all the trimmings, the swish of the dining hall door caught my attention.

A gaggle of students from various classes rushed in. Their boisterous chatter boomed in the quiet. Following the sophomores, juniors, and seniors, Nia walked in. She marched over to the table she usually shared with Tess and Hailey.

Almost as soon as the girl sat, food appeared in front of her. She looked around, as if searching for people she knew, then sighed. She picked up a fork and stabbed a piece of broccoli.

I sighed, stood, and marched over to her table. "Do you want to join us?" I pointed over at Nathan, who waved, a silly grin still on his face.

Startled, Nia dropped her fork. She looked around at the few sophomores, a couple of juniors, and the handful of seniors, then shrugged.

"Thanks." She grabbed her plate and cutlery.

When we settled in at our table, Nathan and I put in our order and an instant later, food appeared in front of us.

"So what did you think about semi-finals?" Nathan had a piece of turkey dangling from his fork in mid-air.

"Glad they're over," I said.

Nia laughed. "You and me both." She put her fork down and pinned me with a stare. "I heard about your adventure."

I bristled. "I guess everyone's heard by now."

"I admire you for it. Wish I'd had the courage to leave school like that. Sorry Tess narced on you."

I banged my hand on the table. "I knew it was Tess."

Nathan raised an eyebrow at me. "Really?"

"Eventually, I knew."

"You were pretty quick to blame me when I was the one who came to help rescue you."

"Rescue? We were doing fine and didn't need rescuing."

Nia sat back and watched our exchange, pushing her chair back a little farther with each comment.

"You had a horde of demons after you that you couldn't fight with just the five of you."

I blew out a breath, glared at him, then popped a forkful of mashed potatoes dripping with gravy into my mouth. When the gravy had worked its soothing magic, I said, "We would have found a way."

Nia threw her hands up between us. "What's done is done. She's sorry she suspected you, but, dude, you have been kinda hard to read good or bad guy wise."

I settled back in my seat and devoured the rest of my dinner, saving the stuffing for last. It was, after all, the only reason to have a turkey dinner with all the trimmings in the first place.

"Fine. Sorry I suspected you first." I glared at Nathan.

"What should we do tonight?" Nia's voice was hesitant, hopeful.

Like myself, she'd been without her usual friends for two days and probably didn't want to spend the third day doing nothing. I had no idea if Nathan even had friends. He moved from group to group in classes, during lunch. I never saw him with one distinct group for very long. Maybe that's how he liked it, or maybe he'd pissed off everyone else in the school as much as he annoyed me.

From my pocket—I'd ditched the backpack for now because it was the holidays—I pulled out the map of the school. With it so empty, it was easier to explore. Less likely to get caught since most of the teachers and the dean were away, giving us the opportunity to find more nooks and crannies we weren't supposed to know about. But I wanted to relax for a change. Kick back, do something indulgent, be a normal teenager.

I slapped the map down on the table and pointed to the space by the library I'd been dying to check out since I noticed it. "I say it's movie night!"

"Is that what that room is?" Nathan picked up the map to examine it.

"I'm assuming that's what the media room is for. It's not like it's for the media to wait for official comments from the school or anything."

Nia chuckled. "True. I'm up for a movie."

"Great. I wonder what they have," I said.

Nathan handed the map back to me. "Where did you get this?"

Shrugging, I put it back in my pocket. "I found it. It fell out of one of the spell books my grandmother used a lot."

With our dinners finished, we pushed away from the table. As soon as we stood, our dishes vanished and the table shone as if wiped down with vinegar.

"Lead the way." Nathan waved a hand toward the dining hall doors.

The library and the media room took up the entire length of the floor on the east side of the castle's main floor. Both rooms were huge, but where the library appeared to go on for ages, the media room had definite boundaries. The seats did not spread out forever like a bad dream where you think you're moving forward, but nothing seems to change.

The room was huge. Laid out theater style, a large movie screen took up the whole wall at the front of the room. Positioned in front of the screen with room to move between rows, were at least two hundred chairs. Each row slightly higher than the one before it so everyone had a decent view. At the back of the room, high up on the wall, was a window for the projector.

"It looks like every movie theater I've ever been in." I couldn't keep the disappointment from my voice.

At a magic school, I was expecting something magical about the media room. Maybe the movies played out in real 3D in front of us, like holograms.

"But it's not like every other theater," Nathan said.

We took seats in the center of the theater, in the middle of the row.

"Now what?" I asked.

He pressed a button on the armrest. Popcorn and a drink magically popped into existence, resting in the appropriate cup holders. Another press of a different button produced a list of movies projected in the air in front of us.

I leaned forward, scrolled through the movies, and stopped on a classic Christmas one, about a misunderstood and overlooked boy. Before I touched the title, I glanced at my companions. With nods from both of them, I selected the movie and sat back in my chair.

"How did we not know this was here?" Nia asked.

"I had no idea this is what it meant by media room," I admitted. Had I known, I would have been here a lot more. Movies were more than an escape for me. They were comfort when things were going bad, which was most of the time. They let me get lost in their worlds, worrying about characters instead of worrying about what was happening in my life. In Toronto, I couldn't afford to go to the movies much except on cheap Tuesday.

The opening credits rolled and calm settled over me. The antics on screen made me smile. The character would learn that being alone wasn't all it was cracked up to be, but in the meantime, he would have the time of his life.

After that movie, we watched one of the sequels. Then Nathan picked a slightly darker movie that still went with the Christmas theme. How a serial killer picking off people around the holidays was his idea of a Christmas movie was beyond me, but it was his turn to pick. At least he hadn't picked the third movie in the series we'd started with.

When the third movie ended, I yawned. I pulled out my phone to check the time. It was almost midnight. Time really does fly when you're having fun. And I was surprised to realize this was one of the best times I could remember during the holidays.

"That's enough fun for me." I stood and stretched.

"Maybe we could do a whole day marathon tomorrow." Nia's words rushed out of her mouth in one breath.

Smiling, I nodded. "Sounds like fun."

When we were back on the second floor, we parted ways in the hallway as each of us reached our rooms. I walked the remainder of the hall alone. A sheet of melancholy settled over me, but I forced it away. The emptiness of the room wasn't forever. Two weeks. Fourteen more days until everyone would be back.

I pushed open the door and gently closed it behind me,

hoping for a message on the chalkboard, knowing there wouldn't be one there. Eerily quiet without Priti, the room was just a place to sleep now. I didn't like to hang out there without her. It reminded me I was alone.

"*Lumine on.*"

Light flooded the room, making it a bit cheerier. Settled in the middle of my bed was a pile of presents. My heart jumped. My throat ached. Waiting until Christmas morning to open them would prove impossible. Patience might be a virtue, but I was sorely lacking when it came to presents. I wasn't used to getting any. Sure, my foster family had one trinket under the tree for me every year to keep up appearances. But it was always something small, something I wouldn't care about.

When I sat on the bed, the presents wobbled. I picked up the first one, a small elegantly wrapped box from Priti. With care, I removed the paper so it wasn't ruined. Before opening the box, I took a deep breath. Trembling fingers lifted the lid and a protection crystal winked at me. I grinned.

The next was from her family. The kindness of the gesture brought tears to my eyes. I opened that box to find a small jar of Priti's mother's pâté. Though my roommate wasn't there, the room was suddenly filled with love and caring. I never wanted to go back to the real world.

I placed the crystal on my desk for now. And the pâté in the fridge.

After wrapping Priti's gift, a book of fighting techniques, I placed it on the bed. "*Libera sarcina.*" The gift disappeared in a poof. I hoped Priti liked it.

Chapter Fifteen

Once January hit, our classes went into overdrive. The work seemed to double. They were preparing us for final exams that were scheduled for mid-May. In February, the work doubled again, with more lectures, more information thrown our way, and more practical labs than before the holidays.

If the first term was getting us ready for anything, it was to expect the exams to be harder than we thought possible. Where the semi-finals were mostly written, with multiple-choice, true/false questions, and essays, the finals would be that and more. From our first defense class when all the students returned, Damien drilled into us the practical nature of our finals.

That meant magic.

Even after five months, plus a week in February, of learning I still wasn't happy with the amount of magic I produced. It seemed to be in line with everyone else, but something in my bones told me I could do more.

I stood in defense class with Priti and Saad, waiting for Damien to go through today's lesson. Hoping it didn't involve too much magic. In between classes, studying, and socializing, Priti had been teaching me about spells and how to tap into my power. But I was still rusty and more comfortable with the physical aspects of defense class.

An array of weapons at Damien's feet drew the attention of everyone in the gym. He stood with his feet shoulder width apart and pinned each one of us with a serious look.

"Today we will be focusing on weapons training."

A few shouts of glee went up. A couple of groans followed. I moved my gaze over the group. Tess grinned, eager to pick up weapons. Jenny looked at the ground, wringing her hands in front of them. Nathan, his face impassive, glanced at me and winked.

Since the Christmas break, he'd been a thousand times more pleasant. Even Nia smiled at me more and chatted when Tess and Hailey weren't around.

I glared back at him. I'd be damned if I winked, especially in front of the class, but smiled before turning my attention back to Damien.

I reached into my pocket, my hand circling the dagger Damien gave me in the coffee shop.

"We'll be using rubber-tipped weapons with dulled blades right now. Wouldn't want you to hurt yourselves or me."

Frowning, I dropped my weapon back in my pocket.

"I'll be doing an assessment first to see where you're at. Then for the rest of the month, we'll be practicing. Your goal is to end the situation before it becomes untenable. It's always best to fight hand-to-hand instead of using a weapon. Weapons can be unpredictable. Watch your fellow students as I go through the group."

He started with Jenny, who, predictably, based on her lack of enthusiasm for weapons, did not fare well when

Damien glamoured into a demon and attacked. Had the weapons been real, Jenny would be missing an arm and dying from a stab wound in the heart.

When he got to Priti, Saad and I took a few steps back to give them room. Priti held her weapon without conviction, like it was something not a part of her. Every time she attempted to stab Damien as a demon, she missed. He, on the other hand, connected with her a number of times in blows that would have maimed her. At least none of the stabs would have killed her.

Confident I would do okay, I waited for my turn.

"Not too bad so far for most of you. Any problem areas will be discussed and worked on during the term."

When Damien turned to me, I picked up one of the weapons from the pile all the students had to choose from. I found one that looked like my dagger, though it was lighter and far less lethal. Resisting the urge to bend the blade back and let it go again, I held it in my right hand, took a defensive stance, and waited for Damien to glamour into a demon.

Before my eyes, Damien's height changed. His arms grew longer, claws appearing at the end of long fingers. His transformation into the demon that had attacked me sucked all the breath out of me. A chill ran down my spine. Uncontrollable shivers plagued my legs. Still, I threw my hands up to protect my torso, blade swaying in front of me from the trembling limbs.

Damien took a step, then another. I sucked in a breath, my heart racing. Panic raced through me. I knew it was Damien, but I had flashbacks of flying onto a table, crawling along the floor to hide behind the counter. I couldn't use the dagger then to stop the demon. What made him think I could use it now? Especially a fake one.

My entire body chilled. Damien stopped advancing,

though I noticed him struggle with moving his leg. The glamour faded away. He dropped the weapon he'd been carrying.

Warmth returned to my body. My hands stopped shaking, my legs stopped trembling. I kicked his weapon away. It slid across the gymnasium floor a few feet, then stopped.

"At what point do we call this?" I asked.

Damien frowned. His eyebrows drew together in concentration as he looked at his legs. He swayed as if trying to get them to move. "It's supposed to be a weapons challenge."

I nodded. "I disarmed you. Isn't that the first thing we should try to do? Disarm them so they don't have a weapon against you. Or in your case an extra weapon. The claws were a weapon too. You didn't say we couldn't use magic."

Though I noted that no one else had used magic during their assessments, I hoped I was right. I hated to fail this early in the weapons module.

"Fine. We'll call it a pass for now, but I will test you again. You need to be able to call the magic on purpose."

"Fair enough."

At least if I knew he was going to glamour into the demon again, I wouldn't be caught off guard. It was like he was testing my ability to fight that one demon. Maybe because it was my first. The thing that introduced me to a magical world in the first place. What a way to learn about being a witch. Almost getting killed by something you always thought was make-believe.

He continued with the rest of the class until everyone had been assessed. When the bell rang, I breathed a sigh of relief.

Most of the students raced out of the room like a demon was still after them. Priti, Saad, and I lingered. Priti was obviously still upset by her performance. I was still in shock. Though heat had returned to my body, I didn't think I would ever be truly warm again.

Damien gathered the weapons from the floor, where everyone had discarded them before they left, and put them in a large sack.

"Priti, if you want more help with your knife skills, I'm here. You just need a little help with blending magic and weapons. Alex seems to be able to blend the two even if she isn't trying."

I glared at him. Had he known what my fear response would be before we started? I doubted it, since he had been just as surprised as I was that I had somehow frozen his magic.

Priti nodded eagerly. "I would love that."

Damien smiled. "You're good, but you need help if you meet a high-level demon. I'm not going to go easy on you either."

She shook her head. "Of course not. I wouldn't expect you to."

"Okay, meet me after your last class and we can get in some practice before dinner."

With her tutoring set, the three of us escaped the gym. I needed to relax before braving the dining hall and the lunch crowd. Tess would be there and I did not relish dealing with whatever she was going to pull next.

Back in our room, I sat on my bed, a large gift basket pushed onto my pillow. It wasn't there when I'd left for classes that morning.

"My mom sent it. She mentioned she would. For exam prep."

"Doesn't it feel like we just had exams?"

Priti nodded. "Mom's baskets are great."

I ripped into the plastic wrapping, shredding the ribbon that tied it together. Inside the basket were two jars of her mother's pâté, my favorite ginger snap cookies, soothing bath salts, and herbs to increase magic. I sniffed and began to relax as the scents calmed me. But it wasn't enough. I was still jittery after class and Priti wasn't making me any calmer.

She paced the large space, shaking her arms. I watched her reach the wall, spin around, and retrace her steps. The arm shaking died down until she was only twitching her hands. The entire time, she sucked in breaths of air and forced them back out again.

"I can't wait until after arcane history for more practice. I'm going to go find Saad to see if we can practice now."

"Okay. But this is getting used right now." I held up one of the bath bombs. My nerves were still shot. I needed something to calm them. A warm bath to chase away the remaining chill was exactly what I needed.

"Enjoy. If I can convince Saad to let me attack him, we'll be in the courtyard."

After Priti left, I gathered my toiletries, dropping them all into a satin bag with a cinch. I found my biggest, fluffiest towel, grabbed the CD of forest sounds, and left the room. At this time of day, the women's bathroom would be empty since most of us showered in the morning. For in between classes, there were bathrooms on all levels of the castle.

I found one of the tub enclosures, pulled the curtain aside, lowered the lights, and started the bath.

Dressed again after my bath, feeling refreshed and much less stressed, I grabbed my jacket and shrugged into it, then left the room in search of Priti. February was cold, but the castle had a spell that kept all parts of the grounds above zero degrees so we could still train outside. Almost real world conditions and all that. We wouldn't always, or probably ever, be attacked in a gym. She hadn't returned during my soak, so I assumed she found Saad and convinced him to help her with weapons training until she had a proper tutoring session with Damien.

Not wanting to distract her, I opted for the second-floor balcony overlooking the courtyard to observe. If that's where she was. If she wasn't there, I would check the gym.

Halfway down the corridor on the right side of the floor, I stopped at the French doors that led to the balcony. I entered the balcony and spotted Priti and Saad circling each other, weapons up. They used the same rubber-tipped weapons from defense class. This time, they also sported pads on their arms and a chest plate.

Priti's moves were lithe and focused, but the blade still looked unnatural in her hand. As if she didn't know how to hold it. It wasn't an extension of her arm, but something foreign that she didn't know what to do with.

She stabbed the air when Saad approached her instead of swiping in one fluid motion.

From the corner of my eye, movement caught my attention. It wasn't another student. The ones who were in the courtyard sat at tables closer to the castle doors, drinking coffee or having an early lunch.

A demon popped into my line of vision. The large, monstrous fiend zeroed in on Priti, its eyes narrowing when he spotted her. My heart raced, the hair rose on the back of my neck until I remembered Damien's parting words to Priti about the tutoring. He wouldn't go easy on her. He was glamoured into a different demon this time. One I hadn't seen him mimic before. But what did I know? There were hundreds of demons out there, some with such minuscule differences a novice might think they were the same demon. I had seen him as so many creatures already it was hard to tell if this was one he'd used before.

The demon blew out a breath, the air around him misting with the exhalation. A smile curled his thin lips. Long, sharp teeth glinted in the bright afternoon light.

A student from one of the tables screamed. The demon's focus didn't falter.

Something about the demon sparked a realization. That was not Damien here for a lesson in weapons.

Denial settled in my stomach for a moment. With the wards and spells, all the protections the school had, not to mention the cloaking of its location, how had a demon breached the walls? A sickening thought came to me. Had we somehow led it here when we snuck out after semi-finals? Damien warned us that was one of the reasons the pack of demons followed us. To learn the location of the school.

I shook my head. If that were the case, they would have found a way to get past the protections long before this.

The demon sprinted across the yard, right for Priti.

Saad got in the demon's way and the creature sent him flying. Saad landed six meters away, shaking his head. He stood and raced back to Priti, who was darting across the courtyard toward the gate leading to the back grounds.

The demon never wavered. Saad opened his mouth, yelling at the creature, but it kept its focus on Priti. It was as if she had some sort of tag or homing beacon that the demon was locked onto.

Mind racing, I came up with and dismissed numerous

strategies. I needed to help Priti. There was no way she would survive without weapons against a real demon.

Priti reached the gate, pushed against it, but nothing happened. She spun around, horror in her eyes as the demon closed in on her. She darted around him, back toward the main part of the courtyard.

Students stood motionless, faces frozen in shock.

Saad had his tablet out, presumably texting someone. Damien, I imagined.

A newcomer arrived on the patio. Her coffee cup and saucer crashed to the ground, a scream escaping her lips at the sight of the demon chasing Priti.

It would take too long for me to run down the hall, take the stairs, and get to the courtyard. I checked the sides of the balcony to determine which one held the thickest vines from the climbing rose. The ones on my right looked more promising.

I climbed over the railing and grabbed onto the plant. Thorns bit into my palms. I sucked in a breath but kept going. Blood trickled out of small wounds, making the vine slick. I lowered myself as quickly as I could without losing my grip.

Priti screamed. I craned my head to look over my shoulder. The demon closed in on her. Saad got in its way, but the creature pushed him aside like he was no more substantial than a piece of paper.

Halfway down the vine had to be far enough. I couldn't waste another second getting to Priti. As I let go, I said, "*Bheith* Priti."

I rolled as I landed, but I still turned my ankle. Shaking off the pain, I rose from the ground and yelled at the demon.

"Over here, you big stupid bully."

The demon looked at me, then at Priti, then back at me. Frozen, he didn't know which one of us to go for.

I looked at Priti. "Get behind Saad."

With the demon's gaze following Priti, I reached into my pocket and withdrew my dagger. I darted away.

"She's over here!" I waved my arms in the air.

He turned to me, took a few steps, then stopped. Spinning around, he focused on Priti again. This time he was more hesitant, taking another look at me before breaking into a run toward Saad and Priti.

While the demon had its back to me, I assessed what I could. Thick claws that could probably tear a person apart with one blow. Lean legs for increased speed. Tall. If there were any weapons on his body, I couldn't see them.

"Priti, get behind me!" I yelled.

She raced over. With her behind me, we backed up, inching closer to the doors of the courtyard. The students had scrambled away. Some retreating inside the castle, others running to the far end of the yard.

The demon zeroed in on me this time. He puffed out his chest. A grin curled his lips. Those sharp teeth, like razors protruding out of blackened gums, caught the light. A shiver ran through me.

A soft bang of the door hitting the stone wall of the castle drew my attention. Damien entered the courtyard and froze. Eyes widening, his face paled.

If the defense professor was stunned, that didn't bode well.

"Priti, run for the door as fast as you can." He held out his hand, urging her forward.

With a small squeak of fear, she dashed from behind me and to the door. The demon looked at her. Turned in her direction.

"I'm still over here!" I waved my hands.

The demon glared at me. Then barreled forward.

Before the demon reached me, Damien mumbled the same phrase he used in the coffee shop. I ducked as the creature reached me. It fell over my back and landed with a poof of smoke.

Rolling onto my back, I sighed. Cold from the grass seeped into my jacket. The school could make the air warmer, but the ground took more magic than they wanted to expend.

"Is it dead?" I asked, accepting Saad's hand to help me up. I dropped the glamour of Priti.

"I sent it back somewhere he shouldn't have been able to escape from. They'll fix that so it doesn't happen again."

Dusting off my clothes, I shook my head. "Maybe he had help escaping."

Damien frowned. "They'll look into that too."

"Is it safe to come out now?" Priti's voice was soft, tiny.

"It's fine." Damien waved her over. He turned to me. "You shouldn't have been able to distract him even looking like Priti."

I shrugged. "I'm just glad it worked. It was like she had demon GPS on her or something."

"That's my point. If that demon was tagged to only recognize Priti, you shouldn't have been able to distract it with a surface glamour. It would still know you weren't her."

"I used a different spell. One I found in a spell book of my grandmother's. It was *bheith* instead of *simulantor*."

"Huh. You invoked the magic from its origin. Be Priti, instead of imitating Priti. We use *simulantor* in class because we've found most students can't call the founding magic."

Pride welled up in me. Not only had I been able to save my friend by distracting the demon, I'd invoked the founders' magic. Despite my magic being bound, some of it was leaking out. Some of it was still connected to the founders. It gave me hope that I would pass my classes.

I had to believe I had enough magic to make it through the school year despite my numerous attempts to get Mrs. Sapienti to unbind more of my power. I'd gone to her twice since she performed the unbinding spell and each time she'd said there was nothing she could do.

"Cool. Glad I could help."

"Get inside. I'll check the castle for any other rogue demons."

"Saad, are you okay? He tossed you around there," I asked.

He shrugged. "Bit of a headache, but it'll be fine."

"How about you, Priti?" I looped my arm through hers as we entered the castle again.

"I'm glad you were there."

"Me too. Let's get some lunch. Turns out surviving mortal danger makes me hungry."

After lunch and an intense arcane history class, Priti and I, still shaken up over the demon attack, sat on our beds. My mind returned to the courtyard, picturing the demon's intense focus on Priti.

I shifted on my bed, antsy, wanting to pace, but the room wasn't big enough for me. For this kind of energy, I needed the length of the castle.

"That demon haunted my dreams since I was a kid. To see it in real life threw me off guard." A violent shiver racked her delicate frame. She drew in a quivering breath.

A lack of demons in my dreams during my formative years left me unprepared for the possibilities that were out there. Since I didn't know the creatures existed, my mind didn't conjure them when I slept. My nightmares focused on real threats. The evil that people wrought. I couldn't remember a single foster home where I didn't have nightmares. They didn't happen every night, but they did happen.

"I imagine the demons are going to make a habit of that when we get out there hunting."

Priti wrapped her arms around her body and hugged herself, rocking back and forth on the bed. "I thought I made him up."

"Maybe your parents mentioned him?"

Priti shook her head. "I don't think so. They were vague when it came to specific demons. They didn't want to freak us out at an early age. We knew demons existed, of course, just not what they looked like."

"At least he's gone now."

With a nod, Priti bolted off the bed and paced the room like a caged animal. She paused in front of her desk, pulled up a media player on her computer, and clicked a few more buttons. Wind rustling leaves, the crunch of twigs, all accompanied by classical music, brought a soothing ambiance.

"I hope you don't mind. I need something to calm me down."

"Not at all. I like the sounds of the forest."

A bird called out. Light rain hitting the leaves brought to mind a soft summer rain.

I left my bed and sat on the floor. Still a little shaken after the encounter, I needed more than music to calm my frayed nerves. Even the glamour was different for me. I almost experienced the same fear I imagined Priti going through as I tried to distract the demon.

Priti joined me. It would help if we lit some candles, but this would have to do.

We assumed a cross-legged position and took a deep breath.

"Ten minutes meditation?" Pulling out my tablet, I waved it at her.

She nodded.

I set a timer on the tablet, one that would gently vibrate instead of a harsh alarm that would undo the calming meditation.

Ten minutes later, we took a last deep breath and opened our eyes.

Priti frowned. "I'm not ready for this. How am I going to fight demons for a living if I can't defeat one demon?"

"You will. We're not supposed to be perfect. And we're not even supposed to be really good at it yet. We have at least three more years of schooling to teach us what we need to do."

"I hope you're right."

With more confidence than I felt, I smiled. "I know I am."

Chapter Sixteen

Friday, the day before Ostara, with spring in the air, even the professors didn't care about teaching lessons. At least most didn't. Excitement buzzed through the halls of the castle as the spring festival approached. Freshmen speculated on what it would be like, having never taken part in one in school before. Sophomores, juniors, and seniors reminisced about past celebrations of rebirth.

Saturday afternoon, on the festival grounds in the back of the castle, the entire school would take part in the celebrations, ending with a huge feast in the dining hall.

Decorations to commemorate the passing of winter and the arrival of spring adorned the hallways. Christmas and Halloween hadn't created this much excitement in any of the students.

After a few laps in the pool in between classes, I was famished. Coach was working us hard to prepare for invitationals later in the month with local area schools. To them, Hell's Watch was like any other university, except none of the events were held here. We used another school as a proxy.

Loud, crescendoing chatter spilled out of the dining hall when a student entered in front of me. I grabbed the door before it closed and slipped inside. Conversation stopped. As I walked toward the table where Saad, Priti, and Nia sat, murmurs flowed through the room.

Tess sat with her boyfriend, Owen, and Hailey a few tables over. Tess grinned at me, her gaze glued to my approach. A chill snapped up my spine. Something was most definitely up.

I hefted my backpack off my shoulder and dropped it at my feet as I slipped into a space beside Nia. Not that I'd needed the backpack. None of the teachers cracked a textbook. They all went on about the festival and how it related to their subject. Even defense class had been light on actual defense.

Conversation returned to normal levels after a few minutes. All students turned back to their own interests.

"She's up to something." I jerked my head in Tess's direction.

"What do you think it is?" Priti asked.

Pinning Nia with a stare, I raised an eyebrow.

Nia shook her head. "She stopped telling me things in January. She barely talks to me now."

Stranded in the castle for two weeks with Nathan and Nia was a bonding experience. More so for me and Nia than Nathan. He was still around and I didn't suspect him as much as before. But Nia and I had grown closer. The second Tess saw Nia with me, she'd blackballed her. Not that Nia seemed to care.

"I need to find out what she's up to."

Tess's boyfriend hung on her every word. The three of them huddled together as if hashing out a great conspiracy. Tess's gaze darted over to me a few times, whether on purpose to make me wonder or by accident didn't matter.

It told me part of what I needed to know. She was plan-ning something for me. With only two months left of school, I needed to find out what it was. Soon.

"Worry about it after lunch," Saad said.

We ordered our meals. Though delicious, my mind wasn't on enjoying the flavor combinations of lemongrass and ginger. It was fixated on Tess's plan. In order to foil whatever the blond bully had in store for me, I needed information. I had no shot at getting anything out of Hailey. The two were like twins, always together, and I would never be able to convince Hailey to spill the tea.

My attention turned to Owen. While loyal to Tess, he was still just a guy. Guys could be tempted.

When we finished lunch, we hurried off to arcane history class. The room, like the rest of the castle, was decorated to celebrate spring. Lush green garlands drip-ping with yellow flowers adorned Mrs. Rúnda's desk. And she wore a yellow and purple spring dress. It was the first time I'd ever seen her in anything but trousers.

She grinned, waiting for us to take our seats. When the class had settled, she leaned against her desk.

"For many of you, this is spring as usual. Your families would have taught you the importance of spring. For some"—she looked at me—"this is your first Ostara cele-bration."

She walked away from the desk, picking a flower from the garland and putting it in her hair.

"The festival grounds border the edge of the forest. The spirit house is in the forest and this will be the only time during your freshman year you can go into the forest. Professors and other school staff will, of course, be nearby."

Even with a festival in the mix, we still weren't allowed in the forest unescorted. It made me want to investigate the secrets among the trees that much more. But after leaving school and breaking curfew in November, I wasn't going to disappoint Damien again.

"After the festivities outside, we'll have a feast in the dining hall to welcome spring." A smile on her face to rival a clown's, she clapped.

Still not as excited as I thought I should be, I glanced over at Tess. Hailey sat beside her. Owen, though, a sophomore, did not. What class did Conrad have right now? I searched my mind, sure he had mentioned it on more than one occasion. He was taking some sophomore classes so he could have a lighter load next year. Necromancy. Tess's boyfriend would be in there as well.

If Tess didn't wait for him after class, I had a shot at talking to him without her around.

The shrill clang of the bell prompted everyone to scramble out of their seats and race to the door. Priti stood. Halfway to the door, she stopped and looked over her shoulder.

"You're not coming?"

"I'm going to wait for a bit. I have something I have to do in a few minutes."

Mrs. Rúnda had already left.

"I'll wait with you."

When ten minutes were up, I gathered my bag and left the room, Priti close behind me. Her curiosity was palpable.

We dashed down the hall and stopped in front of Lecture Hall G.

Classes were staggered so the halls didn't overflow with students. Freshmen finished classes first most days. Necromancy didn't let out until three-thirty.

Finally, the bell rang and the door burst open. Students streamed out like they'd been held back by a dam that had suddenly burst. Standing on my toes, I swayed from side to side, trying to see around each student. Conrad smiled as he left and I smiled back.

"Red, what are you doing here? Couldn't wait to see me at dinner?" He grinned and shoved my shoulder.

"Funny. I have a mission." I nodded in the direction of the lecture hall where Owen was gathering his things and meandering down the aisle.

Priti's eyes grew wide. "He knows her plan. Let me find out." She squared her shoulders. Full of confidence, back straight, she looked fierce. She'd matured a lot over the six and a half months we'd been at school. But I couldn't let her barge in and try to strong-arm Owen into telling us Tess's plan.

The guy required some finesse, coaxing, maybe a little flirtation. Not that I was an expert at cajoling the opposite sex into anything, but I had been practicing my powers of persuasion. And I would catch more flies with honey than with Priti's less than subtle vinegar.

"I've got this," I said.

The determination on Priti's face hardened. Her eyes flashed with conviction. "I won't let her hurt you after everything you've been through. She's a bully and she needs to be stopped."

"I know. And I'm going to stop her." Grabbing Priti's hand, my chest tightening, I whispered, "*Reo i bhfeidhm.*"

With Priti stopped, for now, I pushed through the crowd of retreating students before Owen had a chance to leave. I had no idea how long the spell would keep Priti where she was, so I had to work fast.

Before Owen saw me, I glamoured into a cute junior I'd noticed him staring at in the dining hall a few times. She usually sat two tables over with a group of friends. Heart racing, I sidled up to him and smiled.

"Hey, you're Owen."

He flashed a grin. "That I am. And you're Sarita."

I tilted my head and smiled. "I like that you know that."

Chuffed, he puffed out his chest and his grin grew wider. "What can I do for you?"

"Word around the castle says something is going down tomorrow at the festival." I leaned closer, touching his arm. "And that you know what it is."

His smile beamed. "I do."

I glanced around to make sure everyone had left. Priti still stood near the door, lips pinched together. Focus.

Touching his shoulder, I whispered, "That excites me." Batting my eyelashes at him, I touched my lips with the tip of my tongue. "I don't suppose you could tell me."

He looked away, rubbing his chin with the back of his hand. "I probably shouldn't."

Keeping my hand on his shoulder, I pouted. "I understand, but it would have been so fun to have a little secret." I leaned in closer and whispered in his ear, "Just between the two of us."

If he didn't cave soon, I'd have to try a truth spell, or raiding Tess's room somehow. Not that I thought she wrote the whole plan down somewhere, but you never know. Bullies weren't known to be geniuses.

He leaned closer to me, eyes sparkling, the scent of tacos from his lunch making my stomach roil. "Okay. I like secrets. Tess is going to ambush Alex in the spirit house. Tie her to the Maypole with a spell Alex herself will perform inadvertently."

"Wow, that's amazing. How is she going to get Alex to do that?"

He glanced around the room and waited for a beat

before he said, "The objects for the usual ritual will be cursed." He let out a belly laugh. "Isn't that clever?"

"Super clever," I agreed. I kissed his cheek, half hoping Tess decided to stop by his class today. Would she be the jealous type? "Thanks for confiding in me. It will be our little secret." With a wink that left him staring mutely at me, I smiled. Then I walked away, swaying my hips like I'd seen my foster sisters do when they wanted a guy's attention.

Outside the classroom, the freeze-in-place spell I'd performed on Priti was wearing off. She moved her foot forward, relief flashing across her face. When I reached her, she scowled at me, the hurt expression on her face breaking my heart.

"I'm sorry. I know you meant well, but I had a feeling direct confrontation wouldn't work on him. And I knew you couldn't flirt with him to get the information we needed."

Some of the pain drained from her face and she nodded. "Okay, true, I wouldn't have flirted with him. I'm no good at it. Did he spill what she was up to?"

I nodded. Looping my arm through hers, I whispered the incantation to release the spell completely, then pulled her away before Owen saw us together.

Dropping my glamour when we hit the lobby, I filled Priti in on what he'd told me.

"We need to figure out what that spell is."

"I need to get her out of the spirit house before I go in. If she has to be in proximity to say a spell, getting her out would prevent that. But I also need to avoid the cursed objects if possible."

Priti frowned. "It annoys me that she's going to ruin Ostara for you."

"Don't be annoyed yet. I'm going to head to the library

to get some books on the festival. We can meet in our room to go over them."

Priti nodded. "Okay, sounds like the start of a plan."

Priti raced up the stairs to the second floor, while I continued down the corridor to the library. With luck, we would figure out which objects she planned on cursing, I would avoid being tied to a Maypole, and my first Ostara would be fun.

The day before the spring festival, most students were planning which stalls they would visit. Almost no one was thinking about studying or classes. A map of the vendors' stalls arrived out of thin air that morning before classes started. Some events were mandatory for all, like the ceremony through the spirit house. Other things were optional. I planned on checking out the henna tattoo tent, the sweets stall, and the weapons.

The library was quiet. Again the help desk was empty and I wondered if anyone ever worked the desk. Had I hallucinated the few times I'd seen someone there?

Quickly checking the card catalog, I found the information for which row the books about the festival would be in. I walked down the aisle and stopped short when the first reading nook came into view.

I quickly backed up. Tess, Hailey, and Renato sat in the overstuffed chairs surrounding a small table, holding steaming cups of coffee. Throwing up the glamour of Sarita, I continued down the row, found the books, and contemplated trying to listen to what they were saying. Maybe they would mention the plan.

I inched back to where I could observe them, casually pulling books off the shelf to inspect. Then putting them back.

Out of the corner of my eye, I spotted Hailey lean

closer to Renato. He leaned into her. Their legs touched. She rested her hand on his knee. He rubbed her thigh.

Acid burned my stomach. Heat flushed my face. I put my covert book back and pulled out the spell book I always kept in my pocket.

"*Amicus vel inimicus.*"

A red aura surrounded all three of them. How was I going to break it to Priti?

Saturday morning, I woke to the sounds of Priti going through her closet. The clang of hangers and her grumbling made me smile. At least I didn't have that worry. With only a few outfits to choose from, it was easy to figure out what to wear on the rare occasions we didn't have to don our school uniforms.

I sat up in bed, rubbed my eyes, and yawned. A few more minutes, maybe even an hour, more of sleep would have been preferable, but I could feel her excitement from across the room. Next year, I might be just as excited, especially if we managed to foil Tess's plan.

The thought of Tess's intent to embarrass me upset my stomach. Avoidance wasn't an option, not just because the ceremony through the spirit house was mandatory, but because if I flaked out on such an important celebration, the bully won. I could not let that happen.

Priti bounced over to her bed. "Aren't you excited?" Tossing the clothes she'd picked at the foot of her bed, she took a seat in the middle, crossing her legs under herself.

"Sure. I'd be more excited if I knew for sure the plan would work. I don't relish being tied to the Maypole against my will. Who knows what else she has planned."

Priti nodded toward my desk. Books from the library,

strewn all over the surface, lay open from the research we'd done last night. On top of some of the books were pages of notes. Others had Post-it notes marking various important passages.

I ran the ideas we'd come up with in my head a few times. The wording was a little clunky, but I hoped it did the job. Due to the candles, we had to get creative. An elemental spell, one that called on one or all of the four elements, wasn't feasible. Wind rushing through the spirit house would snuff out all the candles students lit before the spell was cast. I didn't want to ruin their Ostara.

"We're halfway there with coming up with a spell. We'll figure out the rest. It will work. She's not going to do anything to you. I refuse to let her ruin your first celebration of spring."

I put my legs over the side of my bed and stretched. The effects of sleep lingered, leaving me with still blurry eyes and an urge to snuggle under the covers again. A slight fog refused to be dispelled. I shook it off and stood.

A trip to my closet proved faster than Priti's. I picked the cleanest, most modern top I had, pairing it with my newest pair of jeans.

We'd worked halfway into the night, coming up with the part of the spell we had to get Tess out of the spirit house before I went in. But thinking about them now, I knew we couldn't use them.

"We vetoed wind because it would kill the candles, but we can't use fire either. Water is out too. And earth won't help us get her out unless we cause some sort of shifting of the foundation. But again, that won't work because we'd destroy the house. So we're back to our basic get her out of the house."

Priti frowned. "You're right. Then what can we do?"

I tossed my clothes on the bed and sat in the middle of

the mattress. Unlike Priti, I let my legs stretch out in front of me. Like a lightning bolt, it hit me. "What about smell?"

"Smell?" She wrinkled her nose.

"Yes." I jumped off the bed and ran to my desk. I flipped through pages of my grandmother's spell book on top of the pile. She had some of the most unusual spells I imagined ever existed. "We make smell emanate from her somehow. She won't be able to get away from it, even when she leaves the house."

The more I thought about a cloud of putrid odors following her everywhere, the more I liked it. The question was, how did we accomplish such a task?

I handed the book to Priti. She flipped the page back and forth, her eyes widening.

"Your grandmother was a badass."

I smiled. "She was. I wish I had more time with her. To think they kept this huge secret from me still hurts." How much closer might we have been if I'd known the family secret?

Priti handed the book back to me and I went through the spell. It wouldn't be easy. We'd need both of our magic to make it work. And we would have to get close to her, or close enough to get something personal from her that we could enchant.

The less I saw her today, the better, but I would make the sacrifice if I had to.

"We need something of Tess's," Priti said.

She was dressed now. Fresh and ready to go.

I nodded. "That might be a little difficult. She hates me. There's no way I'm getting near her."

"What about Renato? He hasn't had any run-ins with her."

The image of him and Hailey crashed into my brain. My heart hurt for Priti. There was a reason he was impartial on the outside. Why we never saw him near Tess or her friends. A spy in our midst.

"No. We can handle it. How about Nia?"

I pulled my tablet out of my backpack that sat at the foot of my bed. Sending her a quick text, I took a deep breath. The entire plan hinged on us being able to get something personal of Tess's. If that failed, I would have to go through the spirit house and inadvertently cast the spell on myself.

A few seconds later, my tablet pinged with a text.

On it.

Meet me on the festival grounds.

N

"Nia's on it."

I tossed the tablet on the bed. Without the spell, I didn't want to step foot on the festival grounds. I padded over to the window to look outside. The back of the castle grounds had been transformed into a Renaissance-type festival look. Stalls of all kinds surrounded a center court. Weapons, flowers, a henna tattoo tent. Hastily constructed buildings dotted the outside of the circle, where students and staff could take shelter from the cold and wind. Despite a clear blue sky and bright sun, the temperature wasn't expected to go higher than ten degrees Celsius. We would need jackets. Past the grounds, inside the forest, was the spirit house. Overnight, with magic, the house had been built or called into existence. From what I'd read of the festival, the house was always there, shielded from everyone until Ostara. After the celebration, it would be cloaked in magic again.

That explained one of the reasons we weren't supposed to venture into the forest. We might walk straight into it, hurting ourselves.

"Are we waiting for Nia?"

As much as I wanted to have the object in hand before venturing out, I shook my head. "She's going to meet us on the festival grounds."

My stomach lurched. Hands shook as I donned my clothes. At the last second, I hurried to the closet and grabbed my jacket.

"Ready?" Priti hoisted her backpack over her shoulder.

Taking a deep breath, I grabbed the books I thought we'd need for the spell and put everything in my backpack, balancing the tablet on top.

"I guess."

"It will be fine, you'll see."

The halls were already empty. The usual chatter from Saturday morning early risers long gone. Even the students who liked to sleep in were already out on the festival grounds.

We walked through the courtyard, through the back gate, and onto the grounds. The atmosphere was completely different from school. In one of the buildings on the perimeter of the grounds, Miss Carmina performed magic that we hadn't learned yet as freshmen. A glimpse into what our futures would be like, what our magic would be able to do after four years of study.

In another building, Damien demonstrated various advanced self-defense moves.

"Where do you want to go first?" Priti asked.

My stomach grumbled. "Hunger wins."

She nodded to a stall close to the gate. "We can get some French fries there."

I was reminded of a Renaissance fair I had been to ages

ago. Not into the scene at all, my foster family at the time didn't care, bundling us all into a car and forcing frivolity on us. They played a knight and a maiden during some of the plays at the festival and couldn't leave us at home. Shortly after, because of a runaway attempt on my part, I was shipped off to the Brennans. Older, wiser, I saw now how much fun I could have had if I'd kept an open mind. Back then all I wanted was what I liked. I didn't have room for new things in my life.

Bellies full, washed down with a magical drink that tasted vaguely of peach iced tea, we meandered through the stalls, checking out the various offerings. Clothes could wait until I had time to get another job, save some money. But other stalls were free.

Priti stopped in front of the henna tattoo place. "I've always wanted one."

I shrugged. "Sure."

Nia was still absent. Maybe it had been harder than she thought to get close to Tess. It didn't surprise me. Tess deemed her a traitor now that Nia spent her lunches and the rest of her downtime with us. But maybe Nia still held a little sway with the blond beauty.

Inside the tent, candles flickered on tables at the back and sides. In the center of the enclosure, a petite woman with long dark hair sat at a round table. Sketchbooks of all sizes littered the surface, some open to tattoo designs, others closed, waiting for someone to peruse them.

Priti picked up a book, flipped through the pages, then placed it gently back on the table.

"Nothing to your liking?" The woman's voice was soft, quiet.

"I have something specific in mind," Priti said.

That was news to me. She'd never mentioned wanting a tattoo before, let alone what she wanted it to be.

The woman waved her hand toward the chair on the opposite side of the table. "Sit, sit. Tell me what you want and I will oblige."

Priti sat, shifting in the chair until she was comfortable. She dropped her backpack on the ground. "I want a symbol of old magic. A triquatra flanked by two crescent moons."

Eyes wide, horror flashed on her face, and the woman leaned back, shaking her head. "That is very powerful. I cannot mark your body with such a symbol. But I can do something similar."

Priti nodded.

"Excellent. Where would you like the tattoo?"

Priti shrugged out of her jacket, rolled up her sleeve on her left arm, and shifted in her seat to give the woman easier access.

I smiled. The same spot where my mark was, except Priti's wouldn't be invisible.

While the woman worked on Priti, I flipped through the books and took notes on how we could get a spell to work. It all hinged on Nia getting a personal item from Tess. The spell could be over before it started if we didn't have that piece of the puzzle.

Twenty minutes later, the woman sprayed the henna tattoo on Priti's arm with something to seal it.

"That will last fourteen days."

Priti beamed. "Thanks. It's perfect."

The object on her arm was remarkably similar to mine, but it wouldn't glow if she was angry or scared. It probably wouldn't hold in any power either. It was a nice symbol of magic and our friendship.

Priti stood and grabbed her backpack. "Ready to find Nia?"

I nodded. "I hope she was able to complete her mission."

"Mission." Priti grinned. "It all sounds so cloak and dagger."

Exiting the tent, I took a deep breath of the fresh air. It was cooler out there too, the candles inside causing the temperature in the tent to rise.

Across the field, I spotted Nia. She looked up and saw us. Checking her surroundings, she dashed through the field, a huge smile on her face.

"Glad I found you guys. I got it." She held up a hair tie. "I don't know how long until she misses it."

Making sure no one saw us, we crept behind the tent. I pulled out the spell book. We formed a small circle, with the hair tie on the ground in the middle. I reached into the backpack and pulled out magical lilac dust.

"*Flos odorem vertit foetorem.*"

A brief flash turned the hair tie a sickly green, then it turned back to its usual black. I picked it up and handed it to Nia.

"That's it?" Nia looked at the tie, which didn't appear any different.

I shrugged. "Once she puts it in her hair, it should release the stench of the death flower."

Priti and I stayed behind the tent, peering around it as Nia walked across the field toward Tess. How good was Nia at sleight of hand and subterfuge? Nia bumped into Tess, knocking her slightly, and dropped the tie into her purse.

I let out a breath.

"You're up," I said to Priti.

Because she'd grown up knowing she was a witch, she could already manipulate the elements to a degree. Right now we didn't need much, no more than a sudden gust of wind.

Priti rattled off a few words in Latin I had no idea what they meant, pointing her finger at Tess.

Tess's hair blew off her shoulders, whipping into her face in a blond tornado. Tess huffed, blowing the hair away from her cheeks. When that didn't work, she dug into her purse, pulled out the hair tie, and gathered her hair in a ponytail. With a few quick moves, she secured her locks with the tie.

I let out another breath. "Phase three complete. I don't know how long it will take the spell on the tie to activate."

Tess wandered through the grounds, checking out stalls until I thought she would never go to the spirit house.

Her nose wrinkled, but she kept walking toward the house. Finally, she went inside and I spotted Hailey and Owen go with her. Checking my tablet, I noted the time, ticking off the seconds in my head. How long would it take for the accumulation of the scent in closed quarters to force her out?

After five minutes, Tess and her entourage ran out of the house, waving hands in front of their noses. Tess's face was crinkled with revulsion. Hailey coughed so long and hard I thought she might snap a rib.

"It worked!" I looped my arm through Priti's and we sauntered to the house.

Nia waited for us outside. The grin on her face was infectious. "You were too far away to hear the shrieks."

I laughed. "She shrieked?"

"Did she ever. Barely finished the ritual. Actually, she might not have completely finished."

A twinge of guilt tickled in the pit of my stomach. "If she didn't complete the ceremony, what does that mean for her?"

Nia shrugged. "I'm not sure. She'll have the opportunity to do it again later if she wants to."

As long as Tess was far away from the house when I went through it, I didn't care about her ritual at the moment. A tightness settled in my chest and acid churned in my stomach.

Nia held the creaky, weathered wooden door for me and I stepped through.

Inside the house, the rooms were bathed in candlelight. No artificial light lit our way. With large windows free of coverings, sunlight streamed into the exterior rooms of the house. Interior rooms glowed thanks to the dozens of candles already lit.

Along the entrance hallway, a garland of flowers tacked up on the wall guided us to the first room of the ritual. We shuffled into the room. A smiling sophomore handed me a coin.

I smiled back, and without her noticing, I put the coin back on the table and grabbed another one from the back of the rows of coins. Behind me, Nia and Priti received their coins.

We continued into the next room. This one sported a fountain in the center of the space. Water flowed over the delicate marble into the pool at the bottom. We murmured our thanks to the goddess and tossed our coins in.

Whispers behind me, in front of me, urged me on. I could swear one of them was my mother. It had been so long since I'd heard her voice, but I still recognized it.

Encouraged, I followed the trail of flowers to the next room. Here, a junior handed me a candle. Not sure who Tess had recruited for her little stunt, I was taking no chances. While Nia and Priti occupied the guy's attention, I swapped my candle for another one. This time one from the far right, middle row.

As the ceremony dictated, we took our candles to the next room. A table, pushed against the wall, held all the candles from the people who had gone through the house before us. We used one of the lit candles to light ours and placed them in the front row.

So far so good. I held my breath for a moment, then let it out. There was one more part to the ceremony and then I was free.

The next room was sponsored by a senior. A curvaceous girl worked a table with saplings. She smiled as we entered. She handed me a sapling first. As with the other rooms, Nia and Priti kept her busy while I swapped mine out for a different one.

For good measure, I planted the sapling in a different pot than the one indicated in the planting room. Rows of already planted saplings lined the floor against the wall. By the time all students traversed the house, there would barely be a path for the teachers to walk through. From my readings about Ostara, I knew the young trees would be taken to the greenhouse and later planted at the other edge of the forest when the weather was right.

With the last task complete, I waited for Nia and Priti to finish, then we walked through the last door before the exit. There, a garland of flowers floated down from the ceiling, gently circling our necks. Resting on my shoulders, the scent of jasmine teased my nose.

Nothing seemed out of the ordinary, but I waited for something else magical to happen. The dreaded pull through the exit toward the Maypole. Nothing happened.

I took a deep breath and pushed through the exit, tilting my head to the sun.

Tess, still wrinkling her nose from the smell of her hair tie, stomped her feet. "No!"

I smiled. "Did anyone ever tell you skunk is not a good scent for you?"

Behind me, Nia and Priti giggled.

Tess shot daggers at me. Hailey snickered but quickly stopped herself. Owen let out a boom of laughter. Tess's face flushed red. If looks could kill, I would have been toast.

I looped arms with my friends, and we went off in search of Saad. I hadn't seen him all morning. He'd gone through the house earlier than us, having no need to perform a spell first.

For the first time in a long time, I was happy. Tess had been foiled. Our Ostara rituals were a success. And we had the feast to look forward to later this evening.

Until the feast was served, we had the rest of the day to roam the grounds. Careful not to fill up on the sweets from the vendors, we hit the weapons tent instead. I wanted another dagger. I cherished the one Damien had given me, but two were better than one.

***

Tired after a day of wandering through the grounds, eating more sweets than intended and taking part in the self-defense demonstration Damien put on, Priti returned to our room. I told her I had the business of returning books to the library to attend to. Not that it had to be done now, but I was still restless, waiting for the other shoe to drop. If anything did happen to me, I wanted to be far away from my friends.

With Priti safely back in our room, I went in search of her boyfriend. The image of him and Hailey plagued me every time I saw either of them. They played the part of not knowing each other well, but what I saw could not be denied. Priti deserved so much better than him.

After checking the festival grounds, I found him beside the sweets tent. Thankfully, he was alone. Tess and Hailey wouldn't risk being seen with him if they still needed him to spy for them.

"We need to talk."

He sneered at me. "I don't think so."

I pulled him behind the henna tattoo tent with more force than I had intended. He stumbled, righting himself before he hit the ground.

"Hey!"

"You'll listen to me if you know what's good for you."

"Fine."

"Did you ever have feelings for Priti?"

Eyes widening, he took a step back. "Of course I have feelings for her."

"It was you who sent that message about study group being moved to the greenhouse, wasn't it?"

I wanted to smack the sheepish grin off his face.

"You'll never prove it. Especially not to her."

I took a step closer to him. "You will break up with Priti. You will do it right. Make it all your fault. She deserves better than you."

"I don't think so." A smirk turned the corners of his lips up.

"I do. Or else."

"Or else what?" He crossed his arms over his chest.

Anger flooded through me. Heat rushed to my face. My fingers tingled. I pointed a single finger at him and he went flying three feet through the air. I marched over to him again.

"I've been holding back all this time. I'm fucking founding magic, asshole. You think I couldn't squish you like a bug? Or make the rest of your stay here miserable? Make Hailey's stay here miserable?"

Beads of sweat popped up on his forehead. He dropped his arms to his sides. "Fine."

"Properly. Let her down as easily as you can. And do not tell her about seeing another girl. Neither you nor she would like the consequences very much if you spilled those beans."

He blinked. "I promise."

Without a backward glance, I stalked away from him, taking the chance he might attack me. I doubted he would, not with people still lingering for the festival.

I stalked back to my room. What would I find there? The best way for him to dump Priti was in person, but I didn't want that. In person, she may be able to convince him not to, or worse, wheedle it out of him why he wanted to break up in the first place. He needed to cut off ties fast, with as little contact as possible.

Inside the room, Priti sat on her bed, tears streaming down her face. They dropped in fat splashes against her tablet. She looked up at me as I entered. Red-rimmed eyes pleaded with me, clutching at my heart. More tears dripped down when she blinked.

I rushed to her bed, sitting beside her. "What's wrong?"

She handed me the tablet. The text from Renato was still on the screen. "He broke up with me."

I put my arm around her shoulders and squeezed. "I'm so sorry, sweetie."

Sobs wracked her body. She clutched the tablet to her chest. "What did I do wrong?"

I tensed. "Don't think that way. You didn't do anything wrong. He did something wrong by not seeing what he had."

She read the text again. Fresh sobs bounced against the walls. "I thought we were happy."

I gave her a side hug. "There is someone so much better for you out there. You'll see."

Priti shook her head. She collapsed back onto the bed, dropping the tablet by her side. "But what if I don't?"

"What if you do? Why don't we order some junk food? We can go to the media room and watch movies. Have popcorn?"

Priti sniffled and sighed. "What if he's there?"

"He won't be. I'll reserve it for the night for just us."

Priti gave a little nod. "Okay."

I hoped I didn't sabotage her final exams. By then I hoped she'd be over the breakup and ready to kick some ass. Having the spy out of our camp was for the best.

Chapter Seventeen

Sunday morning, mind still reeling with the events from the Ostara, I was still in bed, staring at the ceiling. Besides the festival and the feast, my mind wandered to finals. They'd be happening in a little less than a month. My stomach twisted at the thought of going back to Toronto after that. Once the school year ended, I had nowhere to go. But I would worry about that later. The most immediate problem to solve was passing finals.

Priti groaned from her bed as she sat up. "I'm still full."

"Me too." I grinned. The feast offered more food at one time than I'd ever seen before. Clearly spring was a huge deal and I never realized how much until now.

Before I had a chance to shake the fogginess from my head, my tablet pinged with a text.

So much for sleeping in and taking it easy today.

I got out of bed and padded over to my desk where I'd left my tablet, books, and the remnants of the spell we'd performed yesterday.

A text glowed green on the screen. It was legitimately from the person who claimed to have sent it.

I rubbed my eyes to see who it was from. The dean.

Knots squeezed my stomach. "This isn't good."

Priti was up and beside me, looking over my shoulder. "What?" I showed her the screen. "Oh."

The text was short.

My office. Now.

Dean Garrick

Hurriedly, I dressed in the only thing I had clean. An old T-shirt that was probably ready for the trash heap. But it was comfy, fit just right, and one of the few items I cherished. And my older pair of jeans.

"Wish me luck."

"Good luck." Priti twisted her hair over her shoulder and wrinkled her brow.

By now I was familiar with the castle, so it took less time than I wanted to get to the dean's office. Dawdling wasn't an option.

I knocked on the door, pushing it open when his booming "Come in," answered.

Inside his office, he sat behind his huge wood desk, hands clenched on top of some papers. On one side of him stood Mrs. Sapienti, shaking her head. On the other, Miss Carmina let out a heavy sigh.

Tiny birds took flight in my stomach, roiling the contents until I thought I would throw up. Nerves. That's all it was. I had never seen the dean look so annoyed and disappointed at the same time.

"Sit." He waved to the chair in front of his desk.

I sank into the soft leather, wishing it could swallow me and deposit me back in my room.

"Do you know why you're here?" He folded his hands on his desk.

"No." I had an inkling, of course, but I couldn't be sure. And how could Tess be the reason I was here? No one involved in the spell would spill the beans about it.

A niggling worry crept into the back of my mind that I had rid our group of one spy while leaving another. But Nia had done nothing to make me question her loyalty, and she'd even been instrumental in getting the necessary ingredient to our spell.

"You chose Ostara to make a fool of someone. Any other day I might have overlooked your behavior, chalking it up to school hijinks. But Tess is still in her room. Hailey is bunking with someone else right now until we can get the smell out of the room and off of Tess." He leaned back in his chair, shaking his head. "Tell us what you did and how to counter it."

"I was only defending myself. Tess was going to have me tied to the Maypole."

The dean raised an eyebrow. "I highly doubt that. No student would participate in such shenanigans on Ostara. Especially not one who grew up with magic."

I bristled. Heat rose to my cheeks. "So you're throwing that in my face. It's not my fault I'm an orphan and don't know the customs. You had me put in an ordpops foster home."

Dean Garrick's nostrils flared. "No, I am not throwing that in your face. You've been here for almost seven months now, learning about magic and the history of magic. The importance of the festival was covered in arcane history." He pulled out a file from his desk. Flipping it open, he scrawled something on the page with a quill he'd dipped in ink. "I love the feel of ink on paper." He fastened a stare on me. "I am putting a note in your permanent record for a stunt that could have ruined the celebration for everyone if it had gone wrong."

"It didn't go wrong. And she got what she deserved. Everyone knew what she was planning for me in the spirit house."

Had this been her plan all along? Float rumors of what she was going to do so I would counterattack with something that would get me into trouble and leave her looking innocent?

Had her boyfriend been playing me all along? He couldn't have known it was me. I glamoured into a junior I didn't even know, except in passing in the hallway.

"What did you do, Alex? Tess can't leave her room because of the smell. She's wearing a mask to block as much of the scent as she can."

I crossed my arms over my chest. "I'm not saying."

Miss Carmina clasped her hands in front of her. "She's rubbed her arms and upper body raw trying to get the smell out."

I covered a growing smirk with a cough. I couldn't tell them what we did, reveal that I had help. Priti and Nia didn't deserve to get into trouble. There was no way I could reveal the spell I'd used either because I wasn't supposed to have my grandmother's spell book. It was part of the library archives for a reason. I'd get into even more trouble if they knew I had that.

"There is no way to break the spell. But she can get rid of the thing that is releasing the stench. Her hair tie."

"Her hair tie?" the dean asked.

I nodded. "That's what I cursed. If she gets rid of it, and really, I recommend burning it, the smell will dissipate."

The dean nodded to Mrs. Sapienti, who hurried out of the room. No doubt racing to Tess's room to let her know.

It was small comfort that the tie was her favorite one and she'd have to burn it.

"You're dismissed. I think it's best if you stay in your room today."

I shoved the chair back and left his office. I wouldn't have needed the spell if I had more magic. My magic still wasn't completely unbound. Maybe Mrs. Sapienti failed, on purpose, both times she'd done the spell to unbind it. That didn't matter right now. If I wanted to pass finals and stop Tess from trying something else closer to exams, I would have to unbind my magic myself.

I stalked back to my room to find Priti gone. It was just as well. I didn't want her around just in case I failed. The message on the blackboard behind the door told me she'd gone to the common area to hang with Saad, Kisha, and Conrad.

I flipped through my grandmother's book to find a spell I'd noticed before. When I first found it, I was ready to try the spell. I didn't have enough magic to make it work, never mind having no idea about spells at the time. Going through the list of items I needed, I ticked them off in my head as stuff Priti had in the room. I grabbed everything I needed, including matches and a pewter bowl, and went in search of an empty training room.

Since the basement was out considering the last time I'd ventured down there, I sat in an often used trashining room beside the change room in the gym. The memory of the magical spiders in the dank basement pulled a shiver through me. I shook it off. There was no time for regrets. I needed to finish the unbinding, or at least unbind another layer of magic if I wanted to pass. And if I wanted to outwit Tess at whatever her next game would be.

On Sunday, this part of the castle was usually empty. Students ventured this way as far as the dining hall but rarely came to the gym. Unless they wanted extra training. But after the Ostara celebration, most residents of the castle were taking it easy. When the spell was finished, I would catch up with my friends and fill them in on my reprimand. Priti would jump to confess her part, but I would refuse. There was no point in anyone else getting in trouble.

I created a circle on the floor with powdered sand I found in Priti's bottom drawer. Inside the circle, I carefully placed five candles at key spots. I laid out the rest of the ingredients from my backpack. Sitting in the circle, I placed my dagger within reach. Lights flickered overhead, but I chalked it up to an aging castle and faulty wiring.

What if I somehow conjured a demon? Suddenly unsure, I flipped to the spell, reading every line three times to make sure there would be no surprises. A plain unlocking spell that had notes in the margin from my mother.

After I laid out the pewter bowl, I dropped in the herbs the spell called for. I picked up the dagger and pressed the sharp tip to my finger until a drop of blood pooled there. Positioning it over the bowl, I squeezed until the drop splashed into the herbs. Taking a deep breath, I counted to ten to stop my racing heart. Every noise, every creak, pulled my concentration away. No one should be here today, not today.

Satisfied the gym was still empty, that I wouldn't be interrupted, I lit a match, lit the candles, then dropped the flame into the bowl. Matches were crude, but I hadn't mastered elemental magic to start a fire myself. Hopefully, that would come before I graduated as a senior.

I grabbed the spell book and started the incantation.

"Hecate, *ceangail an draíocht seo. An veil a ardú.*" I repeated the order to unbind my magic three times, then tucked the spell book back into my jeans pocket.

The flame burned red, then blue. Pain seared my arm where my mark was. The tattoo there glowed brighter than before.

A noise from the gym snagged my attention. I turned to watch the door, waiting for it to open, holding my breath. Nothing happened.

The pain burned deeper in my arm, like fire working its way down through the limb. After seven months of magic school, I recognized it was the metaphysical burning of the binding, but Mrs. Sapienti's spell hadn't caused this much pain. Or any pain. Something had gone wrong.

The mark glowed brighter and burst into blue flame, searing the sleeve of my T-shirt. I yelped.

Frantically, my gaze flitted around the room, looking for anything I could use to put out the fire. Springing to my feet, air passed in a rush over my arm, causing the fire to burn brighter.

I rummaged through every cupboard I could find, looking for something to help me. A blanket, a towel, anything to wrap around my arm to stop the burning.

Now white-hot, the pain seared through the rest of my arm. Tears streamed down my face. Heart racing, I sucked in breaths of air in an attempt to calm down. Panicking would get me nowhere.

I burst out of the training room. Cried out again in pain. Fell to the floor when it got to be too much. My knees hitting the hardwood brought more tears to my eyes.

Damien's office door flew open. Through a haze of pain and tears, I watched him race over to me.

Blue fire licked up my sleeve, leaving charred fabric in its wake. If it wasn't put out soon, it would reach my shoulder, then my neck, and jump to my hair.

With a calm that shouldn't have surprised me, Damien clamped a hand over the flame. "*Exstinguetur ignis.*"

Smoke rose from between his fingers. The scent of burned flesh and fabric wrinkled my nose.

"I knew you would try something after your meeting with the dean. But what exactly were you trying to do?"

"How did you know?"

"You're just like your mother."

With the fire out, a new sensation washed over me. Power. A little more power than I had before, but not as much as I knew was still bound.

"My mother set herself on fire?"

Damien lifted his hand and frowned. "No, but she was always trying things she shouldn't. This is a nasty burn."

"It hurts like crazy."

He walked over to the training room and peeked inside. "What exactly were you trying to do? Dr. Dotair will ask when I bring you to the infirmary."

I shook my head. Although I knew I wouldn't be getting out of going to see the doctor, I couldn't tell him what I was doing exactly.

"You're going to the infirmary."

"I know." I winced at the pain in my arm. "I was trying to create a flaming dagger." I pointed at the dagger still on the floor. In my haste to find something to put out the fire, I'd kicked the candles and dagger out of the circle. Sand, once a perfect arc around where I had sat, now looked like someone had dumped part of a beach on the floor.

"Don't do that anymore. It's a senior thing. Freshmen

shouldn't be playing with fire spells." He let me gather my things, even the candles, before he escorted me to the infirmary.

Bright lights in the infirmary forced me to squint at Dr. Dotair. Smoke still rose from my arm as Damien ushered me to a bed. I hopped up on it while he talked to the doctor. Pain throbbed in my arm under the developing blisters.

"She was doing something with magical fire and got burned."

The doctor tsked at me as she peered at my arm. "Severe burn. From the looks of it, second degree." She held her hand over the burn. "Heat emanating from the wound. What color was the fire?"

"It started red and changed to blue. Light blue." I pulled in a breath and held it, suddenly wishing I had jumped into the pool to cool off my arm.

"Hmmm. Interesting." The doctor walked over to a medical cabinet and pulled out a small bottle.

"Can you heal it, Doc?"

"Because magic created it, magic can cure it." She focused on me. "Once it's healed, you should still take it easy for a week at least."

I nodded. The only strenuous thing I planned on doing was eating ice cream. I could make it through defense class using only my right hand, especially with Damien in on why I shouldn't exert myself.

She sprinkled a soft, yellow pastel powder over my burn. "*Sana adusta cute.*"

Pain drained away from my burn, down my arm, until it dripped out the tips of my fingers. The blisters shriveled.

As I watched, the skin knitted together again. The ugly red and yellow of the burn faded, turning a healthy pink until it matched the rest of my arm.

I flexed my left hand and lifted my arm perpendicular to my body. "That's amazing."

"Yes, well, don't go thinking you're indestructible. Magic healing only works for wounds caused by magic. That does not include demons, unless they use a magical weapon."

"She'll be okay?" Damien asked.

"She'll be fine. I want her to stay here overnight to make sure the healing is complete. After that, she can resume her normal activities. Take it easy on her in defense class for the next week."

Damien looked at me. "Get some rest. I'll let Priti know where you are."

The doctor helped me get settled in the bed, insisting on removing my shoes and covering me with a thin blanket. When the door swished shut, the doctor's face changed. Suspicion twisted her features.

"I know what you were up to. I don't know how you managed it, what spell, but there are safer ways."

Feigning ignorance, I said, "Safer ways to get a flaming dagger?"

"The aura of your magic leaks out of your arm, through your tattoo. The aura goes deeper today than it did before. You shouldn't try to unbind your magic again on your own. Mrs. Sapienti is the only person who should unbind more of your magic."

"Then you know I'm tethered. No one else is." I leaned back against the pillow in a huff.

"It is not up to us to question your mother's wishes. She and Mrs. Sapienti did this. Do not attempt it again."

Three guys burst through the doors. Two large sopho- mores, and in between them, Nathan.

The doctor pointed to the bed beside mine. "Over there." She pulled a curtain out of nowhere to block me from seeing anything.

"What happened?"

"Dude was trying to levitate," one of the guys said.

"It didn't last very long," the other guy said.

"I'll take it from here. You two carry on with your day."

She snapped the curtain aside and marched over to the medicine cabinet again. She pulled out some pills. Then went to another taller cabinet and retrieved large trian- gular pieces of fabric.

On her way back to attend to Nathan, she paused by my bed. "Looks like you'll have some company for the night. Try not to stay up chatting too long."

Great. I'd be stuck next to Nathan all night. "No worries there. I plan on ignoring him."

Chapter Eighteen

Three weeks later, the day before the last day of finals, I sat in the dining hall with Priti, Saad, Kisha, and Nia, pushing food around on my plate. During exams, the menu had been specifically designed to help us study and do well. With plenty of fish, berries, and vegetables, I was looking forward to finals being over and indulging in fried anything and chocolate cake. The bright and sunny day called for a long walk around the grounds. Fresh air would do us all good, but cramming for our last final would serve us better. At least it would for me.

Stomach in knots, I took a deep breath and tried to shove my exam scores out of my mind. None of the tests had been particularly difficult, similar to semi-finals. But I still lacked the confidence of other students, who had grown up with magic. I had to go with the belief that I had passed all my other tests.

Something crackled. I jumped in my chair. "What the hell is that?"

Priti laughed. "They hardly ever use it." She pointed to small dots in the ceiling. "The PA system."

"Tomorrow is the last day of finals. All students are reminded that the day after finals, buses will arrive to take you back to Toronto. If you are traveling farther than Toronto, arrangements will have been made already for you."

My stomach knotted. I'd forgotten I wasn't able to stay here year-round. I still had no idea where I would go once the school year ended. My foster family wouldn't welcome me back with open arms. And there was the lack of a job situation.

"Start your day off right tomorrow with some healthy proteins and a banana. The dining hall will be open late tonight for snacks and studying. Get lots of rest. We'll see you at finals."

The dean's voice faded away and the shriek of the microphone made me flinch. Then the sound stopped.

Chatter picked up again in the hall. One more day.

Pings, all at the same time, echoed through the room as texts arrived on our tablets. I turned mine over beside my plate.

Attend the media room at two o'clock for a refresher lecture.

Dean Garrick

"They didn't have refresher lectures for our other exams." I turned my tablet face down again. The food on my plate looked like a congealed mess, so I pushed it away.

Saad nodded. "The final is like nothing we've done before apparently."

We finished our lunch, grabbed our books and backpacks, and headed to the media room. Memories of sitting in the middle row with Nathan and Nia brought a smile to my lips. I thought that would be the worse Christmas of my life with all my friends gone, but those two made it enjoyable. And Nia was proving to be a great friend.

We took seats at the back, the only ones left by the time we got there. Turned out the rest of the school deemed it too important to finish whatever they were doing at the time the text came in.

Mouth dry, stomach flip-flopping, I shifted in my seat. Mr. Keen entered the room from a door I hadn't noticed before, near the large screen. He walked across the raised stage and stopped in the middle. A microphone rose from the floor and stopped at the perfect height for him. When he cleared his throat, all conversation stopped.

"Welcome to your refresher lecture. For some of you, this will be the fourth time you've heard this. Even that is not enough. Once you go out into the world to hunt demons, you won't have the protections of the school. Malum is immortal and evil incarnate. He is the source of all evil and all demons. The demons, his minions, are also immortal in the sense that when you kill them, they go back to hell. But they can claw their way out of hell if they become powerful enough again. Or are summoned by someone foolish enough to think they can control a demon."

He paused to make sure everyone was listening. The lecture went on for another hour about the various kinds of demons. Something we'd gone over the third week of class. He finished with a wish of luck for our finals.

"And now, the dean will say a few words."

He walked off stage and the dean took his place in front of the microphone. He pointed a finger and the microphone rose a centimeter to make it easier for him to speak.

"You've all passed all of your finals up to this point or you wouldn't be here for this refresher. Get some rest. The demonology final tomorrow is the one that determines if you pass or fail your year. Freshmen, this will be new for you. The rest of the school knows the demonology final is the most important exam you will take."

He paused, glancing over the faces in the room, stopping at the freshmen to make sure we understood.

"Is he serious?" I leaned over to Conrad.

"Yep. As an accountant at tax time."

"If you fail, you have one chance to redo the exam the following day. If you fail that, you cannot continue your studies at Hell's Watch."

Panic chased fear through my body. "Has anyone ever failed it twice?"

Conrad nodded. "There have only been five students to flunk out of the school in the 155 years it's been operating."

Any odds that weren't 100 percent in my favor were not good odds at this point. I had to get more power. Everyone else grew up with theirs, was better at controlling it, had all of their magic at their fingertips. Mine was still bound. How much was bound I had no way of knowing, but I needed access to more.

My arm tingled at the reminder of the fire the last time I'd tried to unbind my own power. My mistake had been trying to do it myself.

"Enjoy some of the day, then study like your life depended on it. Good luck tomorrow."

The dean walked off the stage. Some students stood. Others remained seated like they were waiting for the extra scene after the credits of a movie.

"Catch up with you guys in the common area?" I asked. "I have to talk to Mrs. Sapienti for a few minutes."

Priti raised an eyebrow at me but nodded. "Sure. I'll bring snacks."

The hallway outside the media room was a traffic jam of students and teachers. Everyone loitered like there was nothing better to do. I craned my neck back and forth but didn't spot Mrs. Sapienti amongst the crowd.

I raced down the corridors until I stopped at her door. Dragging in a deep breath, I tried to slow my heart rate.

A soft but firm "Come in" floated into the hallway.

I opened the door to find her sitting behind her desk. She looked up without a trace of surprise at my appearance in her office.

"What can I do for you, Miss Kavanagh?"

Even though she hadn't indicated the chair in front of her desk, I sat anyway. "What do you know about my mom and my power?"

Giving a solid nod, she leaned back in her chair. "I know she wanted your power bound for good reason. She feared demons would come after you because of it and she was right. I've done what I can for you. You should get to studying. The final exam is not an easy one."

"How do you know all this stuff about my family? Do you know how much it hurts that I don't know anything about my family except what I learned in textbooks this year? There's so much more I want to know."

"I knew your parents when they went here. Not growing up with them was hard on you, I know that. But I've got your best interests at heart."

I slumped my shoulders. "Do you know how hard it is being a foster kid and not know any of this? If I flunk out of school, I don't know what I'm going to do. I won't be able to come back here. There is no permanent home for me to return to. And I might flunk because I don't have access to all of my power."

Her eyebrows knitted together. "So that's what this is about."

"Only you can unbind it more." As much as I wanted to pass, I did not want a repeat of what happened when I tried to unbind my power.

She folded her hands on top of her desk. The stare she gave me tightened the knots in my stomach. "You would have an unfair advantage over the rest of the students if I gave you full access to all of your power. When the time is right, you'll be able to unbind it, but right now this is as much as I can give you."

I frowned. The ominous way she said it sent a chill up my spine. "So you're saying with what little power I have, I'll be able to pass the final?"

She sighed and leaned forward in her chair. She gazed at the Baroque ceiling, seeming to get lost in the intricate pattern. When she finally looked at me again, she smiled.

"Even when your power was completely bound as a child, your defensive magic saved you and Nathan from the demon sent to capture you."

"But...wait a minute. Capture?"

All this time, I thought the demon had been there to kill me. Nathan's parents died because a demon was trying to capture me? What sick purpose would a demon have for a child? Visions of torture, hard labor, burning fires of hell swam into my mind.

"Yes."

"I thought they wanted to kill me."

She shook her head. "Trust me. They wanted to capture you. Now go. Get some rest. Tomorrow is a big day."

I left her office with no more magical power than I had going in, but more knowledge than I had before. And knowledge is power.

The next day, I woke up well-rested but nervous. Before going to sleep, I'd volleyed back and forth between believing Mrs. Sapienti and not. But there was no choice really. I couldn't unbind more of my powers myself, and she refused to do it. If the dean could help, he would have been the one to unbind them at the beginning of the school year.

"Ready for today?" Priti sat up in bed, looking refreshed.

We'd stayed up until the wee hours of the morning, testing each other. After each snippet of fact, we would then practice hand-to-hand combat. I wished I knew what the final exam would entail. But none of the other classes would reveal anything about it.

Our tablets pinged as one. Priti grabbed hers first.

"It says after lunch, at two p.m. sharp, report to the basement. Bring the ingredients for a simple spell, a small pewter bowl, potion bottle, and your weapon of choice."

The memory of spider legs whispering across my skin made me shiver. Were the spiders there to prevent us from finding out more about what or who was in the dungeon? With all of us going down there, I assumed the creepy crawlies would be deactivated, but it didn't make the memory of them any less horrible. Goosebumps rose on my arms and another involuntary shiver shook my frame.

"That's so far away." The uncertainty would last almost all day.

After a hurried morning ritual, we met Saad, Nia, and Kisha in the dining hall. Too nervous to eat, I pushed my food back and forth again while around me, the hall was abuzz with nervous chatter.

Seniors, currently taking their final exam, trickled in as they completed the test. By the looks on their faces, it was a hard exam. I couldn't tell how many of them passed or failed. The horror was reflected in all of their pale faces and shaking limbs.

We pulled out our books to quiz each other while we waited for our turn.

Saad nodded at a senior with an angry red claw mark down his arm. "I heard this one is the hardest of all."

Kisha nodded. "Some of the seniors didn't get past the gatekeeper. At least that's what I heard."

A forkful of fluffy scrambled eggs paused in mid-air. I pinned Kisha with a stare. "There's a gatekeeper?"

Saad shrugged. "The actual test is hush-hush, but there are rumors that we have to fight a demon. They couldn't make it that easy for us, though. We have to pass some sort of test to get to the test."

"Great." I eyed my backpack, which sat on the floor by my feet.

My grandmother's spell book was still in there. I didn't go anywhere without it even though I was sure the library would miss it soon. Before I left the school, I would have to copy it all down. During the summer, assuming I passed this final exam, I would need to practice what I'd learned here so I wasn't rusty when the new school year started.

Despite my promise to Mrs. Sapienti, I wanted to look into unbinding more of my power. That didn't mean I would actually perform a spell again. But there was no harm in researching it, was there?

We stayed in the dining hall, quizzing each other, going over demons and their physiology, hand-to-hand combat tips, until it was our turn for the exam.

Over the course of the day, the juniors, then sopho-mores wandered in, wild-eyed, limping, famished. They dove into food as soon as they sat down. The seniors had all left once the sophomores began to arrive.

Unlike the rest of the year, the path to the basement

was prominently marked with stand-up signs along the corridors. The door to the basement was similarly marked. Turning the handle this time brought trepidation instead of the excitement of discovery.

The stairs, already crowded, creaked under the weight of us all. Students pooled at the bottom, causing a backlog of us waiting to continue our descent.

From the golden glow below, a teacher's voice drifted up the stairs. "Please move fully into the basement, along the walls, and find a nook. We'll begin when everyone is present."

The line moved again as the students at the bottom dispersed.

When we got to the bottom, the basement appeared cleaner than when I'd been there before. The nooks were all dust-free. Sconces flickered. Overhead lights that I hadn't noticed before glowed with a calming yellow light. Every three meters, a name appeared on the wall. Student names.

Priti and I settled into the nook area I'd used before. Saad, Nia, and Kisha continued to the next nook.

Once we were all settled, the dean arrived. He cleared his throat and all conversation stopped. This was it.

My insides knotted. Hands trembling, suddenly freezing, I shoved them under my thighs to warm them up.

"When your name is called, your exam begins. Four students at a time will be going through their exam. The first part of your test is to find the door to your exam. Next, you will have to get past the gatekeeper and open the next door that will lead you into a mini theater. Once inside, you need to slay the demon."

Acid bubbled up my throat and the cold from my hands seeped into my jeans. He made it sound simple. In truth, it would be one of the most difficult things I'd done.

I recognized that before anyone's name was called. By remembering the faces of the students who trickled into the dining hall today after their tests.

"Good luck. Teachers will be in the observation lounge marking your performance."

Professors walked around the corner to the left to a flight of stairs I hadn't noticed before. I looked up. Based on the number of stairs it took to reach the basement, the ceiling should be higher up. But I guess that was the observation area.

"Willow Abbott, you're one of our first four. Take your spot in front of your name."

The student sprang off the hard stone bench in the nook three over. Three more students were called. It made sense they were doing them in alphabetical order, but that meant I would be finished long before Priti had her shot. At least I hoped I would be finished, triumphantly, by then.

Priti reached over and squeezed my shoulder. "You'll do great."

"Thanks. You will too. We can celebrate later."

As I watched Willow struggle with the first part of the exam, my confidence dropped. The door to her test still remained concealed. Surely, for this the guard spiders would not interfere. So the spell I'd used before that inadvertently revealed the door might work again.

I rummaged through my backpack and withdrew the spell book. Flipping through the pages, I skimmed the spells until I found the one I needed. I showed it to Priti.

"This might help."

"Thanks."

We went over the spell over and over again, memorizing every word.

Finally, Willow revealed the door and she stepped

inside. As soon as she was over the threshold, the door clanged shut again.

Less than ten minutes later, bruised, bloodied, and burned out, she emerged from the same door. A smile on her face screamed victory.

The others had varying degrees of success. One failure. Minutes after revealing their door and going through, he emerged again. Either he was super fast, or the demon beat him. At least the creatures weren't allowed to kill us. But from the scratches I'd seen before and the limp he had, the demons could inflict some harm.

Finally, my nerves almost hair-thin, the dean called my name.

"Ms. Kavanagh, you're up. Good luck."

Priti nodded. I took a huge gulp of air and stood. Trembling legs ferried me toward the wall that now had my name and no trace of a door.

Everyone else so far had created a potion for the door, throwing it against the wall. It seeped into the crevices of the door to reveal it with a warm orange glow.

Spell or potion? With little time to make a decision, I searched my memory for the ingredients for the potion. If everyone so far had gone that route, I would too. Risking the return of the spiders wasn't worth the faster option of the spell.

I pulled what I needed from my backpack and quickly mixed the potion, poured it into a bottle, and shook it. Taking a deep breath, I tossed the bottle at the wall. If I'd remembered correctly, I would be inside the dungeon soon. If I had to start over, I only had so many tries to get it right. Though the pockets of our uniforms were deep and seemingly never-ending, our backpacks were not. I only had the ingredients for three more tries.

The bottle broke, and the potion reached out to all the

crevices. A light orange glow surrounded the door and the latch appeared. I opened the door and stepped inside.

Frozen in my tracks, eyes wide, hands trembling, I stared down a huge beast guarding a door on the other side. Arms crossed, with snarling fangs, it glared at me in the dim light. A ring of keys on his hip jingled as he stomped his feet left and right. Behind me, the door clanged shut.

Diminished light made it hard to see the beast's movements. I took a step forward, darted to the right, and rushed him. He flung out a large arm. I barreled into it and hit the ground, hard. Jumping up, I tried again. This time he grabbed me by the shoulder and shoved me so hard I hit the wall behind me, the door I'd come through no longer visible. Shaking my head to clear it, my mind raced for another solution.

The longer it took to defeat the gatekeeper, the less time I had with my actual demon. If I didn't pass...

No, not passing wasn't an option. I'd come too far this year to let some gatekeeper best me. Freshmen went through this test every year. All of them last year must have passed because the sophomore class had fifty students. There was a way. I had to calm down and think it through.

I inched closer to him, getting within arm's reach. When he picked me up, I snaked out a hand and grabbed the keys on his hip.

He tossed me aside, but I was ready this time. I rolled with it, jumping to my feet again.

"*Caligo et nebula.*"

The beast grunted, arms flailing in front of him, trying to dispel the mist.

"*Improbi* Alex." I pointed to the wall beside the beast.

With a growl, he moved toward the image of me in the mist.

Before he could realize it wasn't me, I dashed to the door, inserted the key, and turned it. The lock clicked. The door swung open to reveal a small area-type theater with the demon who tried to kill me in Toronto chained to the back wall. He grinned at me and gestured me forward with both clawed hands.

Chapter Nineteen

Gasping, my mind reeled with memories of the last time I'd encountered this demon. Leg muscles tightened. I couldn't move from my spot. I flinched when the door clicked shut behind me. No escape. I had to fight or fail.

The last time hadn't gone so well. At least this time, the demon was chained to the wall six meters away from me, out of reach. I assumed the chains were made of iron. Nothing else would be able to hold him.

Shaking, I glanced around the arena, then looked up. Professors stood at a railing, looking down on us. My demonology professor in the middle, ready to mark me on my progress. Damien stood close by, also prepared to mark me on my combat skills.

I suddenly wished I'd paid more attention in all of my classes. Fought harder during hand-to-hand. Perfected my weapons training.

The dean stood beside Mr. Keen. "This is your final exam. Defeat your demon and pass."

My demon. In so many ways he was my demon. The

thing that introduced me to the idea of magic and evil and creatures that weren't human.

The demon snarled. "Malum wants to sway you to his side, but I plan on killing you. How revered will I be once I kill you?"

I grinned, despite my fear, and glanced up. "Pretty sure they won't let you out of here if you kill me. That would be a one-way ticket to hell if you do that. Plus, I don't think they're in the habit of letting demons kill their students."

At least I hoped they weren't. That would be an evil thing to do. Not something a school claiming to train demon hunters would do. Right? All the classes this year were full, so no one had failed in the past four years. The existence of the make-up exam, if you failed it once, calmed my nerves a little. Failing the first time didn't mean dying. And it didn't mean failure if you could pass it the second time.

The demon strained against the chains. Grunts and growls intimidated me, but I held my ground. As long as he was chained, he couldn't get to me.

He scoffed. "There's always a way out. Malum has his little minions working behind the scenes, keeping tabs on you, waiting until you venture beyond the school again."

I glanced around and up at the observation lounge. *But, note to self, obey the school rules and don't venture out again unescorted.*

He laughed. "You'll never know. Not that it matters because I'm going to kill you. Before you have a chance to decide to fight for good."

It was my turn to laugh. "Newsflash, buddy. I already decided. I'm here learning about magic and how to kill things like you."

That set him off. He growled again. Pulled at the chains, straining against them so hard his body shook.

"Just being here doesn't mean you've decided. People can be swayed. And with the darkness running through your veins, evil has a pull on you."

What the hell was he talking about? The texts in arcane history didn't mention anything about evil and my family. Everything mentioned about the Kavanaghs was good and light and founding magic.

"You're wrong."

The rumors that my father was bad, somehow corrupted, came back to me. The textbooks rarely mentioned him. Only my mother and grandmother.

I thought back to events in my life. Had I ever done anything purely out of spite? Just to be mean? I couldn't think of anything except wanting Tess to see her boyfriend kissing another woman. And that wasn't evil. It was come-uppance.

"We won't have a chance to find out. You'll be dead."

Squaring my shoulders, heat rising within me, my mark glowed softly. "I'm determined to pass my final, so I'll have to put a wrench in your plans."

The chains holding the demon back fell away. As soon as they left his skin, he charged forward, nostrils flaring, claws ready.

Still developing my fight plan, I dove when he neared, rolling behind him. He stopped, grunting. Turned around.

"You'll tire quicker than I will."

No doubt that he was right, I continued to move, dance away from him every time he approached. I needed some-thing throwable that I could lose for the moment. I had to hold onto my dagger. If I lost that, I would have no weapons at all. I remembered the last time I nicked him with the dagger. The anger in his eyes. Damien's words came back to me.

"Don't piss him off."

I reached into my pocket and pulled out the dagger. Brandishing it like it was a sword, I danced away from him. The demon's lips curled into a smile that sent a shiver down my back.

He lunged forward, a huge arm arching wide, and knocked the dagger out of my hand. I stumbled backward. Glanced around. There was nowhere to hide. Nowhere to dart behind. At least at the coffee shop, I'd had furniture to shield myself. And Damien watching, ready to jump in if needed.

This was where he'd sent the demon after I couldn't even get in a good shot. Here, to be my final exam.

The demon swung his arm again. I jumped back, out of reach of the claws.

Close enough to get in a few punches, I pummeled the demon's stomach. He didn't even flinch. He flicked me away like I was no more substantial than a fly. Dust kicked up, teasing my nose when I landed.

My dagger lay on the ground, almost completely covered by the dirt the floor was made of. He stood between me and my weapon. There was no way for me to get past those claws.

My mind searched for the spell to call for my weapon. *"Arma ad me."*

Instead of the dagger coming to me, throwing stars zinged through the air from the observation area. A few screams of surprise followed. Professors ducked. Damien nodded, making a note on the tablet he was looking at.

My mind went back to the first time I'd been down here. Revealing the door had activated the spiders. They'd scared the shit out of me and I dropped the box of my throwing stars.

They landed gently in my hand. I had four shots to throw him off guard enough.

I threw the first one. Watched it clip him in the shoulder. He grunted, but it was more from annoyance than pain. But he moved a few inches to avoid the next one I threw. I threw the last two, backing him up enough to grab my dagger again.

Hand-to-hand combat would not win me a pass. With ten times more strength than me, a punch wouldn't knock him out unless I had the power of a god behind me. In time, with more practice, our strength might be enough to faze them so a quick spell could finish them off. Right now, the dagger was my only hope.

I moved close enough to annoy him with a high kick to the face. Three in quick succession pushed him back against the wall.

Massive arms came around me. Squeezed. I couldn't breathe.

The smell of his rotting breath choked me. My lungs burned from lack of air. He squeezed so tight I couldn't expand my lungs.

Squirming, shaking from side to side, I kept him focused on squeezing instead of using his claws or his teeth. Black eyes gleamed with triumph at me.

I raised my arm and jabbed the dagger into his back. He howled. Anguish dripped from that howl. Pain clouded his eyes. The grin faltered.

I had never killed anything before. Though I had no choice, I hesitated. But it was him or me.

His grip tightened. The grin changed into a scowl. His eyes brightened.

As sure as I was the school wouldn't let him kill me, I wasn't positive. And I refused to fail. Not again.

Squirming, wriggling to free myself, panic set in. Barely able to take in even a short breath, heat rushed to my face. Instead of fear, white-hot anger seized me.

His eyes widened in surprise.

I plunged the dagger deeper.

In a haze of heat, I could breathe again. The demon's arms dropped away from me. Before I hit the floor, I pushed my hands out in front of me. My defensive magic shoved him away at the same time he exploded out of existence.

The force threw me across the theater. Everything went dark before I slid down the wall to the ground.

A pounding headache pulled me out of a dreamless sleep. Brain fogged with exertion, not enough sleep, and hitting a wall, I shook my head to clear it but groaned at the fresh pain exploding down my body.

Taking inventory of myself, I moved my arms. Searing pain crawled up my arm. I flexed my feet, moved my legs. Muscles in my thighs ached from exertion, but not injury. A tingling in my arm replaced the unbearable pain.

Cracking an eye, I squinted as bright light pierced my retina. I half opened my other eye and took in my surroundings. The infirmary.

"She's awake." Relief dripped from Priti's voice.

As my eyes became accustomed to the lights, I opened them wider. Surrounding my bed, in various stages of dishevelment, Saad, Nia, Nathan, Mrs. Sapienti, and Damien peered down at me. I wasn't imagining Priti's voice, it was clear as day.

I craned my neck around and saw her in the bed beside mine. She looked better off than I felt with a small gash on her arm and a bruise blooming on her cheek.

Trying to sit up, I groaned at the various jabs of pain that protested the movement. Saad picked up a control panel lying beside my leg and pressed a button. The bed tilted up so I could see everyone better.

"How did everyone do?"

Priti, sitting up on her own, smiled brightly. "We all passed. We were worried about you. You've been out for five hours."

"I'm worried about you."

Priti shrugged. "Zigged when I should have zagged. Got him, though."

Nathan moved to the top of the bed so he stood beside me, blocking my view of Priti. "Glad you're not dead. We'll both be sophomores next year." A pink tinge covered his cheeks for a brief moment. I thought I imagined it.

One issue taken care of. I would have a place to stay for eight months once school started. But for the rest of the year, I still had no idea what I was going to do.

"Joy. But glad you passed."

"Thanks."

Saad nudged Nathan away so he could take his place. "You did have us worried."

"I'm fine. Give me a few more hours and I'll be out of this bed and running circles around you guys."

Dr. Dotair ambled over and shooed them all to the other side of my bed so she could take my vitals. She listened to my heart, checked my pupil response, and took my blood pressure.

"You'll be doing no such thing. An overnight stay is mandatory after the knockout you took. Not to mention the poison."

"Poison?" My heart raced at the mention of poison.

"The demon's claws were poison-tipped. He didn't get the cuts deep enough for the poison to immediately be absorbed into your system, but even a surface exposure is not good. Don't worry, we had antidote serum."

When the doctor walked away, Priti smiled at me. "You can see now why we were so worried."

On the bed, spread out on the blanket, were her mother's pâté and a sampling of crackers. She loaded up a paper plate and handed it to me, floating it across the gap between our beds.

Munching on the treat, calm washed over me. The tingle in my arm lessened. My head pounded a little less. All I needed was comforting hot chocolate and it would be perfect.

Damien walked up from the foot of my bed and smiled. "Congratulations for passing. I worried for a minute it would be like the coffee shop, but I wasn't allowed to help you this time."

I remembered the howl of pain the demon let out when I plunged the dagger in. And the exploding out of existence with the second stab. "Does the dagger kill all demons or just that demon?"

"Not all demons. Most. Some are more powerful than even the dagger."

"So it's special. Blessed somehow?"

"It was your mother's. And yes, it was blessed by the founders themselves and passed down through the generations."

Panic bubbled in my chest. "What happened to it?"

"It's fine. It's safe back in your room with your things."

I breathed a little easier knowing it was okay. Knowing its importance now, I wanted to keep it on me at all times.

The doctor cleared her throat to get everyone's attention. "Time for everyone to leave so my patients can get some rest."

My friends and Damien muttered acquiescence and shuffled out of the room. Mrs. Sapienti smiled at me from the foot of the bed.

"I'm glad you're okay. See, the magic is fine. There is no need to unbind your power again."

Later I would figure out why she refused to unbind the rest of my power. Now that the binding had been nicked, messed with, a little more power leaked out every day. Not so much that it was obvious, but in some areas, I felt more powerful. As long as I continued to pass my classes, I would have three more years to figure out how to unbind the rest, and why she was afraid to do it.

"Okay." It was easier to agree than fight at the moment. And if she thought I wasn't determined to release the magic, she might let her guard down.

She patted my foot, smiled, and left the infirmary.

"Time for some rest, you two." Dr. Dotair smiled. "*Obscuro lumine.*"

The bright lights dimmed. The doctor retreated to her office, leaving Priti and me alone.

Too wired now to sleep, we continued eating pâté and chatting into the night. Finally, exhaustion forced us to close our eyes and we fell asleep.

Chapter Twenty

Two days after the final, the scratch marks were almost faded, my headache was gone, and I had most of my strength back. A little brain fog lingered, but the doctor promised to check in with me weekly during the summer to go through cognitive exercises.

Priti and I only spent one night in the infirmary. It gave us the day before move-out day to chill with our friends, compare final exams, and prepare ourselves for getting back to the real world.

Everyone, except me, was more than ready to go back home.

In our room for the last time, Priti paused in the middle of packing her stuff, plopped onto the edge of her bed, and released a long sigh. We'd dressed in our street clothes that morning before breakfast.

"I can't believe it's over."

"I know. Me neither." I tossed my uniforms into my trunk. I didn't worry about wrinkles or folding them. With a magic utterance, the wrinkles would melt away when I pulled them out again in the fall.

The school gave us three hours to pack up our stuff. A bus was leaving at 11:00 a.m. sharp. Priti had been packing since we left the infirmary. With so few of my own belongings to worry about, I started an hour ago. But I did have more than when I arrived. The school uniforms, the book of shadows, the throwing stars. The stars were in my room after I got out of the infirmary. Damien revealed they were a present from him. Other students had a variety of weapons to choose from. They came from magical families, some of whom had their own blacksmith. The throwing stars did not belong to my mother.

I picked up the dagger. Knowing its importance now made me cradle it like it was porcelain. She fought with this dagger. Killed dozens of demons with it, but ultimately it couldn't save her.

"It's going to be weird sharing a room with my sister again." Priti launched herself off the bed and continued packing items in her trunk. "I'm going to miss you."

Warmth settled over me. "I'm going to miss you, too."

"We'll be back here before you know it." She closed the lid on her trunk and took a last glance around the room.

"Can't be soon enough for me."

I made sure I had everything, which didn't take long, and closed my trunk. It was too bad we couldn't take the tablets with us, but they were the property of the school. Once we graduated, we had the option of buying the one we'd been using. I was already taking something that I shouldn't have. All the spells from my grandmother's spell book. Before breakfast, I had returned the original to its place in the library, still loathe to give it up. On the off chance there was some sort of alarm enabled so books from the academy couldn't leave the grounds, I parted with it.

My handwritten copy would have to be enough for now.

We left the room and made our way to the lobby and then outside to the waiting buses. There were two remaining. Juniors and seniors had left already.

When Damien saw us, he gestured to the first bus.

Leaving our trunks by the baggage compartment, we boarded the bus. Saad, Nia, and Kisha sat halfway down on the bus in the booth-style seats facing each other. I slipped in beside Saad and Nia. Priti sat beside Kisha.

Behind them, Nathan and Conrad sat chatting about sports.

A quick glance at the back of the bus revealed Tess and Hailey huddled together whispering. I hadn't asked if Tess passed. I didn't really care. But I suspected she did. The look on her face would have been much more sour had she failed.

Damien settled in at the front of the bus. After doing a head count to make sure all freshmen were present, the driver closed the door and the bus eased into motion.

Peckish, our last meal had been at eight that morning, I pulled out an apple from my purse. It felt odd carrying the thing again after eight months of leaving it in my room. The uniform and its never-ending pockets made a purse unnecessary.

"Good idea," Priti said. She pulled out a snack card. "*Pomum.*"

I took a bite out of my apple, savoring the tartness.

Priti bit into hers, finished chewing, and swallowed. "Should we quiz each other?"

Everyone in the immediate vicinity groaned.

"Let's relax for a bit," Saad said.

Priti nodded. "Okay. I guess there's all summer to study."

Groans rang out all around again. But I smiled. I was with Priti on this. I didn't want to get rusty over the summer.

An hour and thirty minutes later, we pulled into Union Station. Students grabbed their purses, sweaters, backpacks and disembarked.

Family members rushed over to hug Priti. Saad's parents hurried over to embrace him. The rest of the students had various family members dashing to embrace them and help with baggage.

Even if my foster family knew where I'd been, when I'd be back, no one would have come to greet me. I didn't care. I wasn't expecting them to. It still kind of made me feel like an outsider.

"Keep up the studies, Alex. Can't wait to see what we get up to sophomore year." Priti leaned over and wrapped her arms around me in a comforting hug.

I squeezed back. "Can't wait."

After I'd hugged Saad and Nia, Nathan stepped up for one. "Really?" I raised an eyebrow at him.

He pouted.

"Fine." I gave him a brief hug and pulled away.

"Have a nice summer, Red."

"You too."

Damien, my trunk trailing behind him, sidled up and smiled. "Ready to go back to your life?"

"Not really. There's not much there. But I guess I've got no choice."

"You might be surprised."

I followed him to his car.

Quiet since we left Union Station, looking out the window, I turned my attention to Damien, whose slight smirk intrigued me.

"Where are we going?"

While sure he would be bringing me back to my foster family, this neighborhood wasn't the one I lived in. After months of no contact with me, I didn't think there was anything I could say that would convince them to let me back in. I'd taken all of my stuff when I left. They probably had a new foster kid by now. Mrs. Brennan did like the paycheck that came with "looking after" another kid.

"You'll see."

He continued to drive, the smirk changing to a grin.

I leaned back in the seat and continued to check the windows. As he drove, the realization of where we were headed hit me.

Confirming my suspicion a few minutes later, he pulled into the parking lot of the coffee shop I used to work at. Used to being the operative words.

I shook my head. "Seriously, what's going on?"

"Follow me."

The driver's side door creaked when he opened it. He got out, fetched my belongings from the trunk, and walked to the door. When I didn't follow, he sighed.

"When are you going to trust me?"

I got out of the car and jogged to the door. "I do trust you."

"Good." He held the door and I preceded him through.

When the bell above the door jingled, Lacey looked up. Her shoulders dropped and she sighed. "Good! Finally! You're almost late. Mr. Archer will have your head if you're late again."

I took a step back. "But he fired me. What is going on?"

I stared at Lacey, then at Damien.

"Cute. You can't get out of work that way."

Pointing my thumb at Lacey, I looked at Damien. "What is she talking about?"

A wide grin curled up Damien's lips. His eyes sparkled with mischief. "All that is fixed. It took a combination of a forgetting spell, some amnesia dust, and some power of persuasion."

I sank into a chair near the door. "So I'm not fired?"

"No, you're not. And you're living with Lacey now."

I wanted to dance, burst into song. I hugged him. "Thank you."

Damien shrugged. "It was nothing."

Lacey wiped a few tables on her way to the front of the shop. "How was school?"

Panicked, I looked at Damien. He smiled, then leaned in to whisper in my ear, "University. She thinks you're majoring in creative writing with a minor in history."

"It was great." What else could I say? I hoped she didn't ask for specifics. Over the summer I would have to research creative writing courses just in case.

"Tell me all about it during our break. Right now you should get ready for work. Put that in the back for now." She pointed at the trunk.

I turned to Damien again. A lump formed in my throat. "Thank you so much."

He smiled. "You're welcome. See you in September." He walked out of the shop.

I grabbed the extended handle of my trunk and pulled it to the back room. When the bell over the door jingled again, I rushed out to see if Damien had returned. Or a demon had come to finish me off. But it was a regular customer. A lovely, gray-haired old lady who came in every week for a coffee with her book club.

I returned to the back to change into my coffee shop uniform. The combination on my locker still worked. Inside, my uniform was still there, my name tag firmly secured on the left just under the collar.

Malum thought I hadn't chosen my path, but I had. There was no way I would choose evil, the darkness, over good magic when it was dark magic and demons that killed my parents.

I still had to figure out what my demon meant about the darkness already inside me. But I wouldn't let that stop me. It would not get in the way of me being good. I would be the best damn demon hunter they had ever seen.

And when Mrs. Sapienti was ready, I would have access to all of my magic.

Dear Reader,

Thank you for reading my book!

Please consider signing up for my mailing list to get emails about more books in the series, new series, cover reveals, cat talk, maybe a few recipes: http://www.cindycarroll. com/ffml. I'm planning for a few books next year, one of them being the first book in a new series starring Alex! You'll be able to see what's happened to her since magic school.

Happy Reading,

Cindy

Thank You!

A huge thank you to all of my Kickstarter backers for helping to make this book a success before it even hit retailers.

Special thanks to Nikki Morton, Patricia Martino, Heidi Franz, Christy Bormann, Jamie Davis, Sarah Biglow, Patrick B, Chris Pakes, Robin Polakoff, Jeffrey.Tristan.Thyme, maileguy, Kate Baray, Gerald P. McDaniel, Deborah Hedges, Terri McMillan, Rob Steinberger, Kit Daven, Ro Raviv

About the Author

Cindy is a member of Sisters in Crime and a graduate of Hal Croasmun's screenwriting ProSeries. She writes screenplays, thrillers, horror, urban fantasy, science fiction and paranormals, occasionally exploring an erotic twist. A background in banking and IT doesn't allow much in the way of excitement so she turns to writing stories that are a little dark and usually have a dead body. She lives in Ontario, Canada with her husband and two cats. When she's not writing you can usually find her painting land-scapes in oil, playing video games (Sims 3 and Sims 4 are favourites), or watching her favourite television shows marathon style.

Check out Cindy's website:
https://www.cindycarroll.com
Check out Cindy's other books:
https://books2read.com/cindycarroll